LIE

———

BETROTHED #8

PENELOPE SKY

Hartwick Publishing

Lie

Copyright © 2020 by Penelope Sky

All rights reserved.

CONTENTS

ONE

HEATH

It was late at night in the bar, the very bar where I'd ambushed Damien the night I'd intended to execute his old man. I had a scotch on the rocks, not my usual choice, but they were out of vodka.

Balto stared at me with a rigid expression, his large size blocking out a portion of my view because he had burly shoulders and his body was a thick mass. Whenever he grabbed his drink, he always used his left hand, and on his ring finger was the skull diamond identical to my own. "How's Vox behaving?"

"I thought you didn't care about that shit anymore?" When Balto handed over the reins, he'd washed his hands clean and wanted nothing to do with his former business. He never asked questions, never got involved, said he was a retired man.

"I care about the men staging a coup against my brother."

"Not gonna happen." I had eyes and ears everywhere, spies against spies. Vox wasn't silent about his distaste for the new leadership, obviously finding Balto's decision incredibly biased. Vox was a brutal man, a soldier who had the cruelty that was required in leadership. He probably would've made a good leader.

But too bad, because it was me.

"Don't be arrogant. Never be arrogant."

"You're the most arrogant man I know," I said with a laugh.

"I'm retired. I can afford to be headstrong." He lifted his hand and pointed at me. "You can't."

Not too many rulers could get advice from their predecessors like I could. Former Skull Kings usually handed over their titles when they died. Balto's retirement was unconventional. But now, I always had an experienced mind to give me advice, not that I needed it much.

"And Damien?"

That man was a goddamn joke. He'd pissed me off when he pretended to be too good to submit, but then he got my brother mixed up in the bullshit and that just made me angrier. Then he had the audacity to threaten me, *again*, when I was the one who let his sister go.

In his defense, he had no idea about Catalina. "He's a pain in the fucking ass."

"Still?" Balto eyed me incredulously, mirroring my reactions because of his identical features. "How can the man still be a problem? Your job is to eliminate problems. Why is this guy still walking around and breathing?"

"You were the one who saved his ass." I took a drink, the ice cubes sliding and tapping against my lips. I let the booze wash down my throat and into my stomach, the usual burn absent because I'd been drinking hard for so many years.

"I owed him. What kind of man would I be if I didn't honor

my debts?" His arms rested on the table, and his shirt was tight on his muscular arms. He wasn't the leader of an underground army anymore, but he kept his remarkable fitness at the same level as if he was still in charge.

"You never told me how he saved your life."

"Doesn't matter. Deal's over."

My brother wasn't much of a talker. I was definitely more of a conversationalist. "How's the wife?"

He gave me a glare.

"What? I'm not asking because she's hot." I loved to get under my brother's skin, push his buttons, and talking about his brunette woman sitting at home was the best way to accomplish that.

His blue eyes darkened noticeably as his fingertips rested on the rim of his glass. He stared me down like he wanted to slam my face into the surface of the table. But, of course, he never did anything, because I was his flesh and blood. "She's fine."

"Shouldn't your wife be more than fine?"

"Shut the fuck up, Heath."

I leaned forward. "Maybe I could teach you some moves. Maybe you've gotten a little rusty—"

He slammed his glass down. "I will break this into shards and shove them into your eyes."

I raised both hands in a form of a mocking surrender and leaned back. "Alright...just trying to help."

A babe in a short dress came to our table, her eyes on Balto first. "Hey, I'm Tess."

My brother became a committed and monogamous man when

he met Cassini, which was fascinating because he used to be deep between a woman's thighs every night of the week. He was either at the whorehouse or at the bar, picking up a new woman for entertainment. But ever since he settled down, he didn't look, didn't even glance, at someone other than his wife. That was exactly what he did now as he rejected her. "I'm married." He brought his glass to his lips and took a drink, his eyes still on me.

Tess looked at me next. "Please don't tell me you're married too."

I patted my thigh. "Nope. Come on down, sweetheart."

She smiled as she moved into my lap, her arm circling my neck. "I prefer the tattoos anyway..."

I pulled up my sleeve to my shoulder and revealed my flexed bicep. "Then check it out." I pointed out the different images in black ink, knowing women got a kick out of all the demented stuff I put on my skin. She touched me every chance she got, leaning closer into me like she was already prepared to sweat on my sheets.

Balto kept drinking, staring at his glass so he wouldn't have to watch me get frisky with Tess.

She drank my entire glass before she pouted her lips. "All gone." She got off my lap and stood near the table. "How about I get us a few more rounds?"

I relaxed into the wooden chair. "Good idea, sweetheart."

She turned around and headed to the bar.

I looked at my brother again. "Jealous?"

His eyes smoldered in annoyance. "That bitch has nothing on Cassini."

I shrugged. "Maybe. But she's easy."

"You're easy."

"Is that an insult?" My eyes went to the bar to watch my piece of ass fetch us drinks, but then I noticed somebody else who looked familiar. With long brown hair, an athletic and petite figure, and rocking heels that were so high they seemed impossible to walk in, she looked just like my former prisoner.

She was with a group of other women, all similar builds, all wearing short dresses with the intention of having a good time this evening. She ordered a shot right away, downed it, and then threw her arms in the air to release a shout. "Yaaasssss!"

Shit, it was her.

Balto noticed my sudden change in mood. "What?"

"There's a woman over there that I think I know." I continued to watch her hang out with her crew, hog the bar, and commander the bartender's complete focus. The woman I'd had on my lap minutes ago was standing at the bar, being ignored because she couldn't compete with that group of women.

A few guys stood at one of the tables, dressed in suits like they'd just finished their jobs at the office before coming to the bar to wind down. One guy in particular was staring at Catalina.

She ordered a vodka cranberry and did a little dance between her girlfriends, shaking her hips from left to right like she was ready to salsa.

One of the guys approached her, a playful grin on his face, and walked right behind her. He was a decent-looking guy, but I knew Catalina could do much better. He was about to get rejected, buy her a drink that would never turn into sex.

But then he did something I didn't expect.

He squeezed her ass.

Both of my eyebrows rose at the very stupid thing he'd just done. "He just fucked with the wrong woman…"

Balto turned in his seat to see what I was talking about.

Just as I expected, Catalina turned around and didn't shrink down at the size of her assailant. Her eyes were filled with the flames of hell as she slowly walked forward, sizing up her opponent. He was nearly a foot taller than her.

Did she care? Nope.

One hand was on her hip, and her short blue dress was constructed of straps across her body and in various other places, leaving lots of beautiful skin to be viewed. With her long hair, bright eyes, and legs for days, she was definitely the most beautiful woman in that bar. She cleaned up pretty damn good. "Do you want to die, motherfucker?"

Stupidly, he smiled because he didn't see her as a threat whatsoever. "I was just trying to get your attention, sweetheart."

"Congratulations." With the same unparalleled speed she'd shown me behind the theater, her hand moved to his crotch and she gripped one side of his sac through his slacks. "You have my full attention, asshole." Then she squeezed.

The guy tried to cover his scream, but he couldn't. It was unmistakable, even over the music playing from the speakers. He tried to push her wrist away to free his balls, but when he tried to push down, her fingers inched closer together. She was like a crab—the more you tried to get free, the harder she squeezed.

"I'm sorry, does this hurt?" she asked loudly so everyone could hear.

He whimpered, breathing hard through the excruciating pain. He gave a quick nod.

"My bad." She squeezed his entire sac with all her fingers. "Did I just humiliate you in front of your friends?" Her voice was filled with sarcasm, and she destroyed his dignity right in front of everyone in the bar. "You want me to let you go and leave you alone?" She tilted her head and started to talk in a baby voice.

He nodded, seething.

"Then don't try that shit again." She released his balls and stepped back.

He fell backward into his two friends then kneeled over as he breathed through the pain. "Get me some fucking ice."

I watched the episode unfold, thoroughly entertained.

Balto turned back to me, slightly impressed. "Is that her?"

I nodded.

He grabbed his glass and finished it off. "I like her."

BALTO TOOK OFF, and then it was just Tess and me. But I was more distracted by the magnetic brunette who'd stolen everyone's attention inside the bar. She didn't pay for a single drink because rounds were constantly purchased by her admirers. And she was so free, moving with a self-assurance I'd never seen on a woman before. She wasn't conceited about her appearance, and she didn't have an inflated ego either. It was hard to describe. She was just confident, plain and simple. She collected a few phone numbers throughout the evening and stuffed them down the front of her top.

She was owning the night.

It'd been about four weeks since the last time I'd seen her. I'd dropped her off at her apartment, and I didn't think about her again. She was just an obnoxious memory I chose not to dwell on. Never had I ever had a prisoner who was so much work.

It would be easy for me to slip out of the bar without her even noticing I was there. We didn't have anything to talk about anyway, and I didn't exactly look forward to a conversation about the past. But I found her so interesting, I couldn't stop staring.

Tess noticed I was distracted. "Do you want to get out of here?"

My eyes stayed on Catalina. "Yeah. I just need to talk to someone first." I got out of the chair and walked across the bar until I reached her. She was still surrounded by her girls, talking to a handsome guy, a drink in her hand and her cheeks flushed because of the booze in her system. "Call me." She handed her drink to a friend and pulled out a permanent marker. "Are you left-handed or right-handed?"

The guy held up his right hand.

Catalina wrote her digits in big numbers across his palm. "That way, you'll think of me next time...you know." She winked.

He smiled before he turned away. "Oh, I definitely will."

She gave a playful wave before she took her drink back from her friend. This woman was the winner of the room, owned every guy in sight so there was no one left for anyone else. It wasn't just her dark hair, tanned skin, and tight body; it was this infectious spirit that filled the bar with so much energy.

I almost walked away, but now I was more intrigued than before. I walked up to her and stared.

She sipped her drink as she stared at me, taking a few seconds to process my features until she finally recognized me. "Oh my god, the Skull King?"

And just like that, I remembered why I hated this woman.

"What are you doing here?" She broke apart from her group and came closer to me, not nearly as afraid as she should have been, considering I'd kidnapped her four weeks ago. Since we were in public, she probably assumed she was invincible.

No one was invincible...from me. "It's a bar. I'm doing the same thing you are." I glanced at the guy she'd just given a permanent hard-on to. "Just not quite as well."

"What's that supposed to mean?"

"You have better game than I do."

She gave me a suspicious look and tipped her glass to take another drink. "I thought you said I would never see you again."

"That was the plan. But, you know, shit happens."

"This shit could've been avoided if you'd just walked out." She wasn't the fun, outgoing woman I'd been watching all night. Her memory must have caught up with her, reminded her that I took away her freedom and threatened to kill her. Now her guard was up, and so was her attitude. She looked nothing like she had in my cage, when her skin was caked in my blood and her dress was ruined.

"My curiosity got the best of me."

"And what are you so curious about?" She'd been drinking all night, but she didn't slur her words or slow down her firing ammo. She was witty and quick, far more intelligent than the average person. She seemed to have inherited the smart gene, and Damien didn't.

"Why didn't you tell him?" The question was another reason I hadn't left. I could've taken Tess home and I would be fucking her right now, but I was too curious about Catalina's silence. She could've told Damien what I did, but she chose to keep her secret.

Once the question was in the air, she lowered her glass and turned stern. "What makes you think I didn't?"

"Because one of us would be dead right now." When I'd confronted him at his office and collected my money, he was angry about my part in Liam's plan, but he didn't mention his sister at all. He was impulsive and emotional, so if he'd known that I threw his sister in a cage and intended to kill her, that night would've gone very differently.

She crossed her arms over her chest and ignored the drink resting between her fingers. "Why did you let me go?"

I'd expected an answer, not a question. My eyes narrowed in annoyance. "What does it matter? You're free and clearly enjoying it."

Her attitude flared. "Again, what's that supposed to mean?"

I'd been privy to her most personal thoughts when I listened to her pray, when I listened to her confess her sins and ask to be blessed. It seemed wrong to subtly mention it because it was none of my business in the first place. "Just answer me."

"I don't owe you anything."

"I let you go, so I disagree." My anger started to rise just as it had in the basement. She was so difficult, so resistant; it was impossible to accomplish anything. I'd never met a woman so combative all my life, physically and emotionally.

"Oh, so I owe you now?" Her voice rose an octave, her rage coming out.

"Damn right. And you wouldn't want me to take you again, right?"

Now both of her eyes were wide as if she couldn't believe I had the balls to say that to her. She turned to her friend and tapped her on the shoulder. "Hold my drink." She walked up to me and reached her hand down like she was going to grab me by the balls, just like she had with that other guy.

I backed up instantly. "Alright, alright."

She flicked her hair dramatically. "That's what I thought, bitch."

I'd come to her looking for an answer, but instead, I'd turned her into a raging bull. She bowed her head and pointed her horns at me, ready to stab me in the gut. My intention never landed with this woman because her intense reactions always took the conversation in a different direction. "You were much more pleasant last time I saw you."

"Because you were being a dick."

I could walk away at any time, but I continued to stay there, continued to look at her beautiful face, her unblemished skin that was free of scars, unlike mine. When her makeup was done like that, she had the look of an actress or a model. When coupled with her fiery attitude, she could be anything she wanted to be. I'd never encountered a woman like her, who would fight with everything she had, didn't shy away from a man twice her size, and stood up for herself when people disrespected her...including me.

Tess came to my side and slipped her arm through mine. She couldn't look more different from Catalina. With short blond hair and fair skin, she was the exact opposite. Tess was pretty, but she didn't have the brilliance Catalina possessed. "Babe, let's go." She claimed me like she was trying to get rid of Catalina. She rose on her tiptoes and kissed me on the neck, as if that would entice me to ignore the woman I was speaking to.

Catalina didn't look at Tess. "Enjoy your night." She sheathed her anger once someone else was in our presence and turned away.

"Cat?" I remembered what she'd said when she got out of my truck, what her friends called her.

It was enough to make her look back at me.

"This conversation isn't over." I had wondered why Catalina didn't sell me out to her brother, but it hadn't consumed me like it did now. After seeing her in the flesh again, I felt my curiosity turn into obsession. I needed this answer, and the more she resisted me, the more I needed to know.

She raised both eyebrows, one hand on her hip as she slightly turned back to me. Whether she realized it or not, she posed. Her hourglass frame was obvious in that skintight dress. Her breasts were small, but they were big for her petite size. Her legs were so lean and toned, runway material. The blue color of her dress went well with the rest of her features, making her impossible to resist. "Yes, it is."

TWO

CATALINA

When I woke up that morning, my date was still there.

He took up most of the bed, manspreading in the most obnoxious way. On top of that, he snored.

I had taken me forever to get to sleep.

I woke up and set a fake alarm so he would wake up and get the hell out of my apartment. I'd brought him home because he was hot and confident, but he ended up being selfish in bed. He got off quickly, didn't care about me, and then went to sleep.

It sucked.

When the alarm went off, the noise made him stir right away.

"Look at the time," I said sarcastically. "Time to go…" I got out of bed and pulled on my sweatpants. I did my business in the bathroom then walked into the kitchen to make a pot of coffee.

He took his sweet-ass time leaving.

When he was finally dressed and had his wallet and keys in his pocket, he walked into the kitchen, his eyes still tired. He was a beautiful man with brown eyes and a shadow over his jawline, but it was all fake advertising. He had the kind of lips that would be perfect between my thighs, but of course, he did as little as possible to please me.

He'd totally used me.

In a deep voice, he said, "Good morning."

Good was debatable. "Morning." I walked to the front door and opened it promptly.

He stilled at the way I hurried him out, but then complied with my body language. He stopped in front of the door then looked down like he was going to kiss me. "Do you want to go out to dinner tomorrow night?"

I didn't want to lead him on, and I didn't want to waste my time either. "This was a one-time thing for me..."

"If you're just looking for sex, that's fine with me too."

I was just looking for sex—but *good* sex. "I'm married." It was the best way to get rid of a guy I didn't like without hurting his feelings. I probably should tell him off for being such a shitty lover, but that seemed a bit harsh.

As if my husband would appear from the closet, he looked around like he was afraid to get caught. "Oh...gotcha." He walked out the door and into the hallway. "Well, if anything changes..."

"Bye." I shut the door in his face and locked it.

I SAT at my vanity backstage and powdered my face.

Tracy looked at me in the reflection, wearing her leotard and skirt. "How'd it go with that guy last night?"

"Yuck." I grabbed the eyeliner next and started to trace the bottom of my lid. "Terrible."

Her blond hair was pulled into a tight bun, and she stood with one hand on her hip. "What happened? He was hot."

"Let's just say he's one of those guys who doesn't give a damn about you getting off, just about him getting off. It lasted, like, two minutes? And then he snored all night and slobbered on my pillow."

Tracy cringed. "Gross..."

"So, I told him I was married to get rid of him."

"Oldest trick in the book. Well, sorry it didn't work out."

I shrugged and stopped doing my makeup. "I wish guys came with a thirty-second trailer, so we would know what we're getting into. Save us some time, you know?"

She took the seat beside me and crossed her legs. "What about the guy you were talking to at the bar last weekend?"

"What guy?" I asked. "I talked to a lot of guys." I grabbed my brush and ran it through my hair so I could pull it into a perfect bun. It would be so tight I would have a small headache by the end of the night.

"I don't know his name. He had really bright blue eyes, he was super tall, you were talking to him when you asked me to hold your drink."

The Skull King? "Oh, him? No...he's not my type."

"What are you talking about? He's, like, the sexiest guy I've ever seen."

I was probably immune to his charms because of our history. The guy tried to assault me in the middle of the night and then threw me in a cage like I was an animal. Our conversations were always painful because we didn't get along—at all. "I can tell he's bad in bed. Not gonna bother."

"Why do you say that?"

"Because he's a dick."

"I thought you said the assholes are always the best?"

"Oh yeah..." I forgot I'd said that. Unfortunately, that rule always seemed to apply, and I had a feeling it would definitely apply to him. "Well, not this guy. I can tell you that much..."

AFTER THE CURTAINS closed and the performance was finished, I sat at my vanity and ripped that band out of my hair and let the tight bun come loose. "Oh sweet Jesus..." I ran my fingers across my scalp and massaged the area, finding instant relief once those strands were free. I closed my eyes and moaned, noticing the headache disappear instantly. I loved my job, but keeping my hair back was the one thing I despised.

Tracy appeared in my reflection again, her hair already loose and her outfit changed. "Girl." Her eyes were wide like she had a juicy story to tell.

"Girl what?"

She glanced over her shoulder, looking for something, and then turned back to me. "I don't know what the odds of this are, but the guy we were just talking about it is here...and he's asking for you."

"What guy?"

"The hot one. Blue eyes."

"Hold my drink guy?"

She nodded.

I'd thought I would never see him again after our awkward run-in. "What does he want?"

"Don't know. Didn't ask. Do you want me to tell him to come back here?"

"Hell no." He said our conversation wasn't over, but I'd hoped that was an idle threat. I thought he would be gone forever when he dropped me off at my apartment, but I guess not.

"Then, what do I say?"

"Tell him I'll meet him in the auditorium when I'm done."

"Okay...so you are going to meet him?"

I shook my head. "No. He's just going to *think* that. I'm gonna head to my car and get the hell out of here."

I WALKED to my car with my keys in hand. There was no one else out there but me, so I knew he hadn't followed me. Maybe I would have to get my brother involved in this, tell him what was going on. I didn't like running to someone else for help, but if I couldn't shake this guy, I didn't know what else to do.

I could kill him...I guess.

When I got closer to my car, the shadows in the darkness weren't as sharp, so I could make out details that were impossible to see when I was farther away.

What I thought was a shadow covering my car was actually a grown-ass man.

I stopped and sighed. "You've got to be kidding me..."

He leaned against the car with his arms over his chest, his skin covered in black ink. A slight smile moved to his lips, and his eyes had a slight twinkle. "You have no idea how many times I've said that."

I opened my purse and pulled out my knife. "You really wanna do this again?"

He didn't flinch at the sight of my blade. "I thought you would learn from your mistakes."

"Excuse me?"

He pushed off the car and straightened, his six-foot-three frame full of muscle and power. He was masculine and strong below the collarbone, his hands were big enough to crush my skull, but his face was beautiful, with fair skin, blue eyes, and a clean jawline. I preferred facial hair and a bit of chest hair, really masculine traits. He didn't have that, but he was definitely built far more solidly than any other guy I'd seen. He was like a tank, and he could probably grow a beard in a couple days if he wanted to. "You're decent with a knife, but you should be packing a gun. One squeeze of the trigger and your opponent is gone."

"You didn't bring a gun."

His smile faded away, and he turned deadly serious. "Because I don't need one."

I lowered my knife, exhausted by the idea of fighting him again. Last time it was a shitshow anyway. "So, what do you want? If you're here to abduct me, it's going to be worse than last time. I'm gonna stab you so hard I'm going to hit an artery."

He tried to keep a serious expression, but there was a slight quiver of his lips, like he wanted to smile. "If that was my plan, would I have told you I was here?"

"I told you I would meet you in the theater. So why are you out here?"

"Because I know you." He came closer to me and slid his hands into his pockets. Now that we weren't physically engaged in battle, I could really size him up, see the definition in his shoulders and forearms. Whenever he spoke, he had the baritone of a beast, a bear. "When you didn't meet me right away, I knew you'd run."

"So, you don't take rejection well."

He shrugged. "I don't take anything well." He looked at the knife still in my hand. "Put your pocketknife away, and let's go."

"This is a seven-inch blade." I held it up again. "If I'd gotten another crack on you, you probably would've died."

"I doubt it."

"Why?" I asked incredulously. "Do you think you're invincible?"

He shook his head slightly. "Immortal." He walked to the passenger side of the car and tapped his knuckles against the window. "Let's go."

"I'm driving?"

"Yeah."

"Where am I driving us to?" I sheathed my knife and returned it to my purse because he didn't seem to be a danger if he was allowing me to drive. He also didn't seem to be armed. Last time, he didn't have a gun, and he didn't have one now either.

"Dinner."

I walked around to the driver's side of the car and pressed the button to unlock the doors. "Are you crazy?"

"You just danced for two hours. Figured you'd be hungry."

"Well...I'm always hungry. That doesn't mean I want to get dinner with you."

He rested his arms on top of the car and faced me, his shoulders wider than the entire door. "And you wanna keep talking here? Would you rather eat bread and enjoy your glass of wine? Plus, it's a free meal. Consider it reparations for throwing you in my cage."

I opened the door. "I prefer a gift card, but whatever." It didn't seem like this guy was going to go away until he had my attention, so I got behind the wheel and started the car.

When he sat in his seat, the car dipped noticeably under his weight. "Where do you want to go?"

"Oh, I get to choose?"

He looked out the windshield with one arm resting on the center console, taking up all the free space in the car. "I always let the lady choose."

I rolled my eyes and hit the gas.

THE WAITER CAME to our table. "Can I interest you in a bottle of wine—"

The answer came out so fast, he was slightly stunned. "Yes. A cab from Barsetti Vineyards."

The Skull King didn't seem offended by my need for alcohol.

"She can have the bottle. I'll take a scotch on the rocks. Let's do an appetizer too, whatever you recommend." He ordered without taking his eyes off me, having the confidence to run the conversation without eye contact.

"Very well." The waiter walked away.

I couldn't believe I was sitting across from this guy, the very guy who'd had me in a locked cage. My arms crossed over my chest, I stared at him incredulously. I even shook my head slightly because I couldn't even convince myself this was real.

We were silent until the waiter returned and poured my glass of wine and served him a scotch.

I grabbed the glass and downed the entire contents with a single go. The waiter barely had time to place bruschetta on the table before he picked up the bottle and refilled my glass. "I'll give you a few minutes…" He disappeared.

I grabbed a few pieces of the bruschetta and placed it on my plate. No amount of discomfort could chase away my appetite. I danced my heart out every night, pushed my feet to the brink, gave it my all. And now, I was starving.

He took a few sips of his drink as he stared at me, relaxed, like there was nothing odd about this dinner. He was in a gray V-neck and black jeans, his muscular size undeniable. The cut of his t-shirt showed he had ink to his collarbone, and there seemed to be a hint of hair underneath too.

"Well?"

"Well, what?" He didn't take the bread from the center of the table, letting me have all of it.

"What do you want with me?"

"I told you our conversation wasn't over." He held the glass to his lips for a moment as he stared at me before he took a sip. "Do you want to answer my question?"

I took a few bites of the appetizer, my stomach rumbling with gratitude. "Why is it important to you?"

"Curious. When I dropped you off, I was sure that decision would bite me in the ass. I was surprised when it never did."

When I went to Damien's and rushed into his arms, I'd intended to tell him everything. But once I was there, looking into his eyes, I'd suddenly changed my mind. "I was going to..."

His blue eyes were an odd color for his features, because they were so soft when the rest of him was hard. He always had a dark expression, always had a formidable air to him, but then he had the most beautiful eyes I'd ever seen. "What changed your mind?"

The only reason I was there with him was because I believed I wasn't in danger. If he intended to do me harm, he would've done it already. He wouldn't let me sit behind the wheel. He wouldn't invite me to a public place. He was proving he was no threat to me. "Because you let me go."

"I never gave you conditions for your freedom. I never asked for your silence."

"I know. But it seemed like you spared me because you wanted to, and I thought keeping it a secret was a good way to repay your kindness." When he'd first taken me, he'd seemed much more callous than he did when he released me, as if something changed, as if he didn't wanna do it anymore. Maybe that assumption was wrong...I might never know. "I answered your question. Now answer mine."

Both of his hands cupped his glass, which was half empty now. "Why do you assume letting you go was my decision?"

"I really don't know. Am I wrong?"

He dragged his feet, holding his silence because he didn't want to give me the answer. His eyes wandered around the room as he cradled his booze in his fingertips. When he finally made peace with his answer, he looked at me again. "No. You aren't wrong."

I still didn't like him because he'd taken me in the first place, but any hesitation I felt around him was now gone. If he were truly evil, why would he change his mind? "If you hate my brother so much, why the change of heart?"

"Because you aren't your brother."

The waiter returned to take our order.

I was so absorbed in the conversation I hadn't even glanced at the menu, but I was so hungry, I'd eat anything with a smile on my face. "I'll take the ravioli, extra cheese." I placed the menu on the edge of the table.

"Caesar salad is fine." He placed the menu on top of mine. "Add chicken."

The waiter walked away.

I continued to drink from my glass, but I knew I had to pace myself. Getting belligerently drunk was never a good idea when I was around a stranger.

After our questions were answered, there wasn't much more to say. But he continued to stare at me, as if he'd just asked a question and still hadn't received an answer.

"So, you and my brother are still enemies?"

He nodded. "Unfortunately."

"You can always change that if you want to."

He gave his answer by shaking his head. "No, I don't think so. Our hatred runs too deep now."

"If that's true, the last thing I should be doing is sitting here right now." I came from a family that believed strongly in loyalty and commitment, and if this guy was really an enemy to my brother, then he was an enemy of mine.

"Probably."

"So, can I leave?"

He took another sip and licked his lips. "You aren't the kind of woman to ask for permission."

"No. But based on our history, I haven't had a lot of freedom..."

"Yes." His low voice was deep, like a hole that went all the way to the center of the earth. "You can do whatever you want."

But I continued to stay...for inexplicable reasons. I told myself it was the food, but that wasn't true.

He stared at me in a way no one else ever had before. He wasn't afraid to give me his full attention, stare at me with such focus that I felt like the only woman in the room. I got a lot of male admiration, but this was such a concentrated and potent amount, it rivaled the attention of every other man in the world. His blue eyes were pretty, but also deadly. "I was hoping you'd stay."

"I'm not going to abandon those ravioli."

He looked at me like he didn't believe my excuse, but he didn't call me out on it. "How long have you been a dancer?"

Was this the same man who locked me in a cage and fed me a bagel for breakfast? The same one who choked me out and tried to put me under so he could take me? Now, he was asking me questions like we were on a date or something. "All my life."

"And how long has that life lasted?"

"Twenty-five years."

"You're wise beyond your years."

It was an odd observation to make, so I raised an eyebrow. "You don't know me."

"I know you well enough. Most people don't think on their feet clearly like you do. They become overwhelmed and lose focus. You always look for a way out, even attacked me with a plunger, which really wasn't the worst idea. And I watched you at the bar all night. When a guy, regardless of his size, treats you like garbage, you don't put up with it. You stand up for yourself. You get big and loud. You act like a woman in her fifties rather than her twenties in that regard."

My eyebrows slowly relaxed as I listened, and then I pulled my glass closer to myself because I needed a drink. "Did you just give me a compliment?"

"I simply observed your behavior." He took a drink from his glass until it was empty. "It's positive by nature, not by description."

"Whatever. It sounds like a compliment. A lot of guys get annoyed with me because I am... How do they say it? Difficult. Opinionated. Annoying."

"They just don't like it when a woman calls them out on their shit." He set the empty glass at the edge of the table so the waiter would know he needed another.

I swirled my wine before I took a drink. "I called you out on your shit."

"And I liked it."

My fingers stopped caressing my glass, and I stared at him for a moment of silence. I suddenly felt tense, like the nature of the conversation had shifted in a whole new direction. "You aren't my type."

He didn't react whatsoever. And he also didn't try to pretend his words meant something else. "What's your type?"

"Tall, muscular, stubble along his jawline..."

"Alright, check all the boxes."

I pointed at my chin. "You've got nothing going on here."

"Give me a few days. Problem solved." When the waiter didn't come, he took matters into his own hands. He raised his hand slightly then snapped his fingers.

The waiter ran over like a hungry dog. "Let me refill this for you." He returned to the bar, grabbed a fresh glass, and made it a double for making him wait. He dropped it off before disappearing once more.

"I've never had a thing for tattoos...and you have a lot of them."

"Ever been with a man with ink?"

I shook my head.

"Then you'll change your mind." He grabbed his new glass and tilted it back so the amber liquid flooded his tongue and then his throat.

"I like it when a man has a little hair on his chest. Not a lot, just some."

"You got it." He went along with everything I said, as if his interest in me had been sexual since he saw me in the bar.

"You could be everything I want, and you'll never be good enough." It was a harsh thing to say, but this man locked me in a cage, could've killed me if he hadn't changed his mind. He was also my brother's enemy, which made him my enemy. "I would never be with a man who had a vendetta against my family. You want to hurt my brother, the best guy I've ever known, and I don't accept that. Even if my brother was wrong, even if he's the one who did you wrong, my loyalty lies with him."

He shook his scotch gently, his eyes guarded. "I'm not asking you to be my wife."

"Then what are you asking?"

He never answered. Instead, he stared me down like he was a predator and I was the prey.

"I'm never gonna fuck the guy who put me in a cage."

"Then who would you rather fuck? All those dipshits at the bar?" He leaned forward slightly until his glass was in his shadow. "The guys you pick up may be good-looking, but they have no idea how to fuck a woman. More times than not, you take a guy home and he disappoints you."

How the fuck did he know that?

"And the men who actually know what the fuck they're doing never call you back. Why? Because men like that always have a new woman on their hook—there's always something better waiting. You're just the next one in line."

"How would you know any of that?" I didn't admit that he was right, just challenged his statement.

He brought his hands together and held them under his chin, keeping his voice low so no one else could overhear our conversation. "Because I'm the guy who never calls back." After he made his point, he sank back in his chair and pulled the glass toward him.

He may be totally right, but it still wasn't enough to entice me. "I'd rather be alone than be with you."

He flinched at my words, like they cut deep into his skin. "You say that now, but you'll change your mind."

A sarcastic laugh escaped my throat. "Trust me, I won't."

The waiter brought our food a moment later and set it down in front of us. My appetite had dwindled somewhat, but once I saw the melted cheese, my stomach growled. I grabbed my fork and started to eat. I could storm out now, but I may as well get a free meal out of it.

He ate like he hadn't just asked to fuck me. He stabbed his fork into his food and took big bites, his jaw working hard to crunch the croutons. He didn't need to watch his hands to keep track of what he was doing. His eyes remained on me, scooping random pieces of his salad into his mouth.

"I don't know anything about you." He'd told me he was the Skull King, but that didn't mean anything to me. He must have a real name, but he never told me what it was. All I knew was he tried to imprison me to get back at Damien, and now we were eating together like we were friends.

"What do you want to know?"

I took a bite of my ravioli. They were stuffed with an assortment of cheeses and slathered in homemade marinara sauce. "First of all…" I placed a ravioli into my mouth and chewed quickly, ready to continue my questions. But then I said something else and went in a completely different direction. "Jesus…this is good." I took another bite. "Damn." I never finished my question because I had to get a few more bites in my salivating mouth.

He stopped eating, his fork between his fingers as he watched me make love to my food. His blue eyes were steady on mine, wide-open and unblinking. He was so focused, it was like he was watching a TV screen.

"Sorry, I just haven't had pasta in...forever. And holy shit, that is good." I continued to demolish my meal with a couple more bites, unable to control the hunger pangs in my stomach. I was always on the edge of being hungry, restricting my calories so I never gained weight. But when something so delicious was placed in front of me, I lost my self-control.

He started to eat again. "Why is that?"

"I'm a ballerina. I have to keep my figure."

While his eyes were focused, the rest of his expression was blank. "I don't see why you can't accomplish that and eat."

"I can eat. Just not whatever I want."

He'd finished half his salad a minute later, eating a light meal for a man so large.

"It looks like you watch your weight too."

"No. I eat thousands of calories every day. I'm just selective." After a few more bites, his dinner was completely gone. With his arms resting on the table, he watched me finish my food.

"So, do you have a name?"

His eyes watched my movements, focusing on the way the food entered my mouth. Then he watched my mouth, as if he was fascinated by the way I moved my lips.

I grew uncomfortable by his stare. "You've never seen someone eat before?"

"Not like you."

"Tell me your name. Because I'm not gonna call you the Skull King. People really call you that?" I couldn't imagine someone taking the time to say three words every single time they addressed him. Instead of it being a sign of respect, it just seemed stupid.

"If you visited my world, you would understand why people call me that. And yes, everyone calls me that." He spoke with a quiet and stern tone, his voice low so no one else would hear his words. He possessed deep confidence, immune to the way I mocked his title. "But my real name is Heath."

"Really?" I asked in surprise. "Like Heathcliff?"

He seemed irritated by the comparison to old romantic literature. "As in Heath."

"You just don't look like a Heath."

"Then what do I look like?"

I shrugged. "I don't know...never met anyone like you."

"And you never will."

I could feel the power that radiated from his presence. The longer I was around him, the more potent he became. If I'd known his strength before he captured me, I probably would've been much more afraid. "I'm glad I don't have to call you by that other name now."

"You're one of the few."

I knew I shouldn't eat everything on my plate, but the food was too good and I was starving. I ate every single ravioli then dunked the extra bread into the sauce before I devoured that too.

He seemed to be entertained watching me.

"Don't judge me."

He smiled slightly. "I'm not the judgmental type."

When dinner was finished, the waiter brought the tab.

Heath grabbed it right away and threw some cash on top.

I grabbed my wallet and unzipped it.

"What are you doing?" The anger in his voice showed his disapproval of my actions.

I pulled out a bill. "Paying for my half. This isn't a date, you know."

Without turning around, he raised the bill so the waiter would run over and take it. "Whatever it is, you aren't buying." The waiter took it out of his hand and walked away.

I rolled my eyes. "I hate that macho bullshit."

"It's not macho. And it's not bullshit."

"If you're trying to get me to sleep with you by paying for my meal, that's not gonna work either. Takes a lot more to impress me."

He returned his arms to the table and leaned forward slightly. "From what I can see, it doesn't take much."

My eyes narrowed on his face, and the adrenaline spiked in my blood. If steam could've erupted out of my ears, it would. "That better not mean what I think it means." I liked to enjoy my youth by spending time with handsome men. I wasn't afraid to put myself out there, enjoy myself until it was time to find something real. "How are we any different? You can sleep around with whoever you want, and it doesn't matter. But when I live my life that way, it's degrading."

"That's not what I said at all."

"You've implied it three times now."

He was quiet for a while, his hands coming together on the

table now that the food was gone. The bill had been paid so we could leave whenever we wanted, but we continued to sit there. "I'm implying that you barely learn a guy's name before you bring him home, but you won't even give me a chance and I'm a million times better than any other guy you've been with."

I shook my head because I was frustrated. "None of those guys have ever put me in a cage."

"None of those guys would have freed you if they had."

I cocked an eyebrow. "Do you think you can spin that and make it sound good? You're delusional. You say people call you the Skull King because you're in a gang or something, and you admitted that my brother is your enemy. You have no chance."

"But you willingly had dinner with me. I haven't kept you here. You chose to be here. You drove me here."

This man was infuriating. He'd manipulated me to this point, and he knew it. "Then I guess walking out will make my feelings perfectly clear." I grabbed my purse and rose from the chair. "Thanks for dinner, asshole." I left and walked outside. He didn't seem to follow me, so I slowed down as I headed out to my car at the curb. Hopefully that was the last time I would see him, that he would accept my rejection and move on.

Then his voice sounded behind me. "Catalina."

I gave a quick jump because I hadn't even noticed he was there. I turned around and saw a massive man behind me, but I hadn't heard a single sound as he approached. "Jesus, you scared the shit out of me."

"You should've assumed I would follow you."

"Well, I chose to assume you could take rejection." I pulled my keys out of my purse and turned around to head to the door.

He grabbed me by the elbow and steered me back.

I quickly twisted out of his hold. "Don't touch me again."

His expression was blank, not apologetic at all. He slid his hand into the front pocket of his jeans, like he was trying to prove he was no threat. "Just give me a chance."

"I don't owe you anything, despite what you think." He'd let me out of that cage, and now I had to kiss the ground he walked on? "Was that why you let me go? Because you wanted to sleep with me?"

He looked down at me because he was so much taller when I wasn't in heels. "After I dropped you off, I didn't think about you again. So, no."

"Then forget about me again. I've already forgotten about you." He was a handsome man with a ripped physique and the prettiest eyes I'd ever seen. Maybe if it were a different scenario, I'd say yes. But the line had been drawn between us, and I was so loyal that I would never betray anyone I cared about.

His gaze was still cold, impossible to read, unlike other men I met. He could be stoic as a statue whenever he felt like it. He was a master at hiding his thoughts, or maybe he just didn't have them at all.

"I know you probably never get rejected so you don't know what it feels like, but I'm not interested." I turned to walk away.

"What makes you think I don't get rejected?"

I turned back to him. "Come on, you know why."

He tilted his head slightly. "So, you do think I'm hot."

I released a loud laugh, brushing off the embarrassment I felt at his observation. "I do not think you're hot. I understand why other people might think that, but I certainly don't. I'm not attracted to a man who locks up a woman in a cage."

He still showed the same bored expression. "Then why did you have dinner with me?"

"Because I was hungry. Obviously."

"You know that's not why." He shook his head slightly. "I can respect your loyalty to your brother, but I don't appreciate the bald-faced lie you're telling. You say you're not attracted to me, but I know that's bullshit. So, just admit it."

"It's not gonna change anything. It's not gonna change my decision."

He stared me down like he thought otherwise. "You think I'm sexy." Victory was in his gaze.

I rolled my eyes then turned back to my car. "Good night, Heath."

His eyes burned into my back, the heat of his gaze so potent it burned me to the skin. "Because I think you're the sexiest woman I've ever seen."

I should just get in the car and drive away, but something made me turn back to him, made me face the man who didn't deserve any of my attention. "You also said I'm the most annoying woman you've ever met."

"And I stand by that." His eyes remained hard and hot, but a slight smile moved onto his lips. "You feel that?"

I crossed my arms over my chest in defiance.

He remained on the sidewalk, his hands in his pockets. Tall, muscular, and with a persona so dark, he cast the entire street in shadow. "That chemistry...it's unbelievable. I bet we fuck just the way we fight."

I couldn't believe he'd said that out loud, even though no one was around.

"You need a man who can keep up with you, who's turned on by your bossiness rather than bothered by it, who likes watching you tell him off because it's cute to see you try. You flirt with guys at the bar in the hope they'll be something special. But you aren't gonna find anything more special than me."

I almost let his words sink into me, almost let them affect me. His confidence was unparalleled, and that was something I found really attractive in a man. And unlike the others, he didn't seem intimidated by my bluntness. "I'm not interested in anything serious—with anyone. I'm just looking for a good time."

"I can give you the best time of your life."

If we'd met under any other circumstance, I wouldn't have hesitated. He was hot. He was also smart and quick, confident and sarcastic. But he could be fucking perfect, and it wouldn't change anything. "The answer is no. It will always be no. No."

THREE
HEATH

I sat at the table with a pint of beer in front of me. My men were scattered around the bar at our headquarters, talking quietly to one another while some of the topless servers humored them. It'd been days since Catalina made her feelings for me perfectly clear.

She wanted nothing to do with me.

I could move on with somebody else quickly. I could either pay a whore to make me forget about her, or I could do it the old-fashioned way and pick up a woman at the bar. Tess was always a rebound option too. She'd love to see me again.

But I kept thinking about Catalina anyway. When she tasted those ravioli, her eyes rolled into the back of her head, and she moaned like she was having the best sex of her life. Her full lips pressed tightly together, like she was gonna bite down on her lower lip. It was a hint of what she could be in the sheets, her passion and loud personality coming to the forefront.

It only made me want her more.

When we first met, I couldn't stand her. But listening to a strong woman ask God for help, not even for herself, changed everything; it changed me. It was such a short moment in comparison to my lifespan, but it was enough to change a part of who I was.

When I saw her again, I was smitten. I loved the way she owned the room, the way she handled herself like she didn't need a man at all. She was the most unique, interesting, fascinating woman I'd ever come across. Sometimes her confidence was her weakness because she assumed she could handle anything on her own. Sometimes she was too sensitive to criticism that she even gave herself. Sometimes she was frustrating when she teased me. And her stubbornness was always maddening.

I didn't see how one night together would be a betrayal to her brother. It was just physical, a man and a woman pleasuring each other. It was nothing more than that. We'd fuck, be satisfied, and then move on.

Steel sat in the chair beside me. We brewed our own beer here now, so that was what we usually drank. He set his glass down and leaned back in his chair. "The guys just told me he showed up at the parking garage."

"Good." I took a drink of my beer.

Steel was my right-hand man, one of the guys in my inner circle. If I had bloody business to take care of, he was usually the one I brought along. "What's with the attitude? It's worse than usual." He was also one of the few people who could be straight with me, who had the luxury to speak his mind without getting his skull destroyed.

I stared straight ahead and waited for my guest to arrive. "I don't have an attitude."

He stared at the side of my face hard, his silence being his rebuttal.

I took a drink and licked my lips. "Long story short, there's a woman…" I knew Steel would continue to ask me questions until he got to the truth, and since we had time to kill, it would be the subject on the table.

"What kind of woman?"

"The kind I want to fuck."

"Is she too expensive?"

My life would be easier if that were the case. "Too stubborn."

"What are you gonna do?" There was a large fire burning in the rear wall, a hearth big enough to fit a car. It illuminated the room with a gentle glow, which we preferred over fluorescent lights. Since we were underground, it was cold, even in the summer.

"Nothing." I'd put my offer on the table, and she didn't take it. There wasn't much else I could do. I knew I would be waking up next to her every morning if Damien weren't such a problem, and that made me hate him more.

"Nothing?" he asked in surprise. "I've never seen you give up on anything."

"This is different. I have beef with her brother. It's a conflict of interest, basically."

"Gotcha." He took a long sip of his beer and wiped the foam from his upper lip. "Not much talking during sex, so I don't see you discussing your conflict of interest much, but you know how women are. They overthink."

She didn't overthink. She was loyal, and I respected that.

"You could always do something to change her mind."

"Believe me, I've already tried." I'd thought a simple conversation over dinner would change her mood. There was a combustive chemistry between us, and it was there the night we met, I just didn't recognize it. But now, anytime we were together, there was a raging fire between us, a powerful energy that filled the room.

"You can always make her trust you."

I turned to him. "What are you talking about? I locked her in a cage a couple weeks ago and threatened to kill her. It's not gonna happen. Don't blame her."

"But you let her go, right?"

"Yes." But I didn't grant her freedom because of the way I felt.

"You could just set something up, you know, damsel-in-distress type of thing. Have a couple guys steal her from a restaurant or something. You come in and save the day. Her attitude will change real quick." He snapped his fingers.

It might work, especially if she was truly scared. She would look at me with new eyes, like I was her savior rather than her captor. She probably wouldn't care about my problems with her brother. But that was manipulative and deceptive, and that wasn't the type of man I was...at least not to a woman. I wanted a woman if I earned it, if I was the man she chose. I wanted her to get what she saw, to know I wouldn't lie or play games. I wanted her to trust me, to know I was an honest man, just not a good one. "No."

He shrugged. "You got a better idea?"

I shook my head. "No, unfortunately. I don't think it's gonna happen."

"And you just accept that?"

I liked Steel's determination because he got shit done. There was no obstacle that could defeat him; if there was a will, then there was a way. When it came to work, that kind of attitude was essential. But for something like this, it was inappropriate. "Yes."

The men turned to the stairs when an outsider entered our lair. Tall, with dark hair and dark eyes, the guy had the audacity to grin when he stepped inside. "You've got a nice setup down here." He glanced at a topless server as she passed with a tray then gave her a slight look of approval. "And nice tits." He moved to the chair beside me and took a seat.

I knew his casual attitude was a poor attempt to deflect his fear. When any man was summoned to the Skull Kings, his heart beat a little faster, his adrenaline ran a little higher. I didn't buy his relaxed demeanor.

He waved down a waitress. "What do you recommend, sweetheart?"

She knew he wasn't one of us, so she wasn't so kind. "Beer."

"What kind?"

Her attitude was the same. "Beer."

I interceded. "He'll have what I'm having, Janet."

She walked off, tits up.

He turned back to me, his hard features unmistakable. He looked at Steel before he looked at me again. "You called?"

I leaned forward and placed my hands on the table, getting close to him and making subtle threats with my proximity. "You can expect me to call whenever the fuck I please." I could feel the men turn toward me once they heard my tone change. Only Janet was unafraid and delivered the beer like I asked.

He finally dropped the act.

"Ash, this is how it's gonna work." I didn't give him the opportunity to speak because he would just be a smartass. "You're going to give me a twenty-percent cut of your business every month. Don't skim off the top because I'll know. I always know. Don't fight me because I'll win. And I get special treatment with your girls."

Ash wore a leather jacket with a dark pair of jeans. He had fair skin and a deep shadow along his jawline. His resemblance to his brother was unmistakable. He definitely had Lombardi blood. "Now I understand why Damien's annoyed..."

"And he'll be the first to tell you that annoyance was a mistake." He'd almost lost his father, his sister, and his own balls. "In return, I offer services you can't get anywhere else. Immunity against any enemies you could possibly have."

He pulled his beer closer to him. "Enemies? I'm a pimp. Don't have any enemies. I have the hottest chicks in the city who will do whatever you want for the right price. Trust me, I don't have any enemies." He lifted the mug and took a drink, and once he set it down, he gave his stamp of approval. "I'm not a beer guy, but that's pretty good."

"My girls brew it."

"Damn, wish my girls did that..." He took another drink and returned the glass to the table when it was half empty.

"Are we gonna have any problems?"

He crossed his arms over his chest and dropped his gaze for a moment. "No. I've got more important things to do than fight you. But I can't give you special treatment with my girls. Who they fuck is their decision, not mine."

His business was unique because the women were employees, not slaves. They got an equal cut of the profits and simply used him for protection. "Fine." I expected him to resist based on his relationship with his brother, but Hades had never been stupid like Damien, so I guessed it wasn't that surprising.

"That applies to both locations." I held up two fingers, indicating his two residences. He started off in Rome, and when that was a success, he moved to Florence.

He shrugged. "Fine. Does that mean I can come in for a beer?"

"Are you one of the Skull Kings?"

"No. Can I apply? Is there a little form to fill out?" He looked around the room, half smiling like his mockery would go unpunished.

I was out of my chair so fast, he didn't have time to react. If he thought I would take his disrespect with no retaliation, then he was dumber than Damien. I yanked on the chair so he fell out of it and crashed to the floor.

Ash landed with the loud thud against the concrete, his hands spreading to catch his fall. "Bad joke, alright. Sorry—"

"Too fucking late." I slammed the wooden chair down on his back, hitting him so hard the wood shattered into several pieces. His body collapsed under the force, and he gave a suppressed moan at impact, unable to hide his reaction to the pain, but then he passed out seconds later, his body giving out

I tossed what was left of the chair aside. "I reject your application. Asshole."

IT'D BEEN two weeks since I'd seen Catalina.

A guy like me should've forgotten about her after two days. I was a busy man with a packed schedule, could have any woman I wanted, and I had better things to do with my time than chase down a woman who didn't want me.

But I hadn't forgotten her.

Her spirit was still fresh in my mind, like standing next to a fire that gave off waves of never-ending heat. She didn't smile much when she was with me, but sometimes a sarcastic expression would come on to her face, and that was beautiful to me. She was so quick and witty, and I actually missed our debates. It was like having a friend you hadn't talked to in a while. And she had such a nice body in those tight dresses that I was anxious to see what was underneath.

I could show up at her apartment, and she would probably attack me with a frying pan—or, better yet, a plunger. That night wouldn't end with me getting laid. I could show up at one of the bars she frequented on the weekends, but I really didn't want to see her get hit on by some guy then go home with him.

Not when she should go home with me.

But my desire never waned, and if anything, it only rose. I knew she had a performance tonight, and against my better judgment, I bought a sport coat just to have something nice to wear so I could attend the theater.

A man like me didn't own a suit. Because I didn't fucking need one. I was just as powerful in jeans and a shirt, even more powerful naked. Only pussies like Damien wore suits, because they needed a false sense of success to feel secure, needing to trick people into believing they had power based on their attire.

I didn't need that shit.

I went to the theater and took a seat in the front row, dead center. The first time I'd come here was to ambush Damien. When his father was in the bathroom, I intimidated him, but when he gave me that lip, I made him bleed inside.

But this time, I was there for Catalina. I opened the program they handed out and searched for her name. She had one of the biggest roles because she was one of the lead dancers. Not only was she talented, she was easy on the eyes, and that made everyone adore her. I stared at her name on the page.

I'd beaten Damien.

I'd taken her father from his bed and intended to shoot him in the back of the head, regardless of if Damien cooperated or not.

I'd helped Liam take Anna from the hospital after he shot her and aided in her kidnapping.

I'd threatened Damien more times than I could count, and I humiliated him every time I went to his office to collect my cash.

And then I'd stolen Catalina and put her in a cage like an animal.

I had no fucking chance. She was absolutely right not to want me, to want to steer clear of me and never see me again. Why would she want the man who had done all those terrible things? I suspected she didn't know every single truth, because if she knew what I tried to do to her father, she would have already told Damien about me. I should just walk away and leave her alone.

But I stayed.

The lights were turned down, and the stage came to life. The curtains rose, and there she was, right in the center, holding an elegant pose with her chin tilted to the floor. She had the athleticism to hold her body is such rigid positions without flinching. She was so elegantly trained, you didn't even see her breathe. She was so confident that she had her own glow on that stage. She got lost in her element, her art, and forgot about the audience altogether.

The music began and she danced.

I wasn't a man with sophisticated tastes. I didn't read Shake-speare, I didn't go to the opera, I didn't have a single piece of art on my walls—unless my designer picked it out. I didn't care about flowers in spring, the sound of the violin over dinner. I had no class at all.

But I was mesmerized by her performance anyway. Fasci-nated, I watched her spin so her skirt rose around her hips. I watched her leap and jump, always pointing her toes and creating perfect lines with her body. I watched her focused expression, watched her dominate the stage and outshine everyone else around her.

I rubbed my palms together slightly because it was hard for me to sit still, to absorb the poetic feelings she inspired inside me. Her performance affected me, made me feel something, made me want that same passion but in a different location.

I wanted this woman beneath me, dancing, concentrating, fighting. I wanted her fire, her disobedience, her sass. My jeans were a little snugger because I pictured exactly how it would be if we were together, our bodies covered in sweat, wrapped in mutual passion and hatred.

The music stopped suddenly, and she paused, becoming still on the stage. She faced the center of the auditorium, and by chance, she looked right at me. Her green eyes gave away her reaction, her surprise, and then her unease. But like the profes-sional she was, she quickly adopted her stern expression and carried on.

As if she hadn't seen me at all.

ANOTHER WEEK PASSED, and I assumed she'd leave my

thoughts after seeing her reaction during the performance. I didn't show up at her car or try to visit backstage. I decided to leave because I shouldn't have come in the first place.

But now I was back to where I started.

I wanted to see her.

She had performances several times a week, and those seemed to be the evenings that she went out with her friends. It wasn't my finest moment, but I sat in my truck and watched her walk to her car from a safe distance. She was already in her dress and heels, so my assumption was correct.

I followed her.

After she walked into the bar with her girlfriends, I waited half an hour before I walked inside, to make it less obvious I'd followed her. She was too smart not to figure out I was stalking her, but there might be a seed of doubt, maybe a small chance she'd think it was a coincidence. We had run into each other before.

When I walked inside, she was already talking to someone. He was tall and on the lean side, handsome enough but not exactly eye candy, and certainly nowhere near her league. They enjoyed their drinks standing at a high-top table, exchanging a few laughs and smiles. I moved to the bar and got my drink before I watched them, waiting for my opportunity.

Just when I thought their interaction was going well, something good happened.

She slapped him across the face and shoved him in the chest.

Yes.

Everyone turned to look at the commotion, and I was about to take a sip from my glass when I realized something serious was about to happen. I watched the fire in her eyes, the resilience of an unconquerable woman. I wondered what he'd said to provoke her hostility.

He started to argue back, inaudibly, and she threw her drink in his face.

That was when he lost his cool and grabbed her by the wrist. He raised his voice. "Bitch, knock it off." It was obvious he was grabbing her hard by the indentation in her skin where his fingers squeezed. "Fucking whore."

She socked him in the stomach. "What did you just call me?"

He bent over and heaved as he choked on air, and when he stood upright, he looked insanely pissed off.

I downed my glass and left it behind before I intervened. I suspected this wasn't going to end well. While the guy would be stupid to assault a woman in public, men were usually dogs. I placed myself in front of her and faced him, using my body as a shield to protect the tiny woman behind me. "Time for you to leave."

My intervention pissed him off more, but he didn't do shit because he had absolutely no chance against me. He didn't even try to talk shit to me or her. "Fuck this." He slammed his glass on the table before he walked off, pushing past people who stared at his departure.

Her heated voice came from behind me. "You know, if I were a little taller and weighed a few more pounds, I would totally kick your ass."

And just like that, she brought me back to life, reminded me why I was there in the first place. The corner of my mouth rose in a smile because it was a ridiculous comment for her to make, but she somehow made it cute. I turned around and faced her. "You mean, if you were a foot taller and weighed an additional 120 pounds?"

She did the quick math in her head. "You weigh 230 pounds?" she asked incredulously.

"It's the muscle."

"Alright...never mind." She put one hand on her hip with her other arm resting on the table, and the flames in her eyes that had decreased to flickers rose quickly once more. "Either way, I don't need you to fight my battles. And secondly, what the fuck are you doing here?"

"What was firstly?"

"What?" she asked blankly.

"You said secondly, but you never said firstly."

"Not fighting my battles, obviously. I don't need to say first. It's implied."

I'd successfully distracted her. "You want another drink? You know, because yours is on some guy's shirt?"

"No. Who knows what you'll put in it."

I gave her a blank stare. "Yes, I released you from a cage, caught you off guard at your car, took you to dinner, watched you in the theater, just to lead to this moment to drop a pill into your drink. How did you figure it out?"

She rolled her eyes at my sarcasm. "You're an asshole, you know that?"

"I do. But not because I came over here and fixed your problem."

"He was *not* a problem," she argued. "I was handling it."

I shook my head. "You need to be careful. Not all guys will put up with a woman grabbing their balls. They might do something terrible to you, might hurt you. You can walk away. You don't always have to fight."

"In case you haven't noticed..." She came closer to me, bringing her face up next to mine. "I'm not the kind of bitch to walk away." She was in a purple dress, backless, and a beautiful color for her dark hair and perfect complexion. Her long hair was straight down her chest, and she wore a diamond necklace around her throat. "If you disrespect me, there will be consequences. I don't put up with bullshit. I don't put up with misogynistic assholes who think women are inferior to them."

I never cared about women's issues because I had bigger fish to fry, but hearing her talk like that aroused me. I was the kind of man who didn't put up with shit from anybody. If they had a problem with that, they could enjoy a beating with a chair. I was in charge, I was a leader, I was fearless. It was the first time I'd met a woman exactly like that. She wasn't the leader of an underground cult, but she was a leader of her own life. It was hot. "What did he do?"

She rolled her eyes. "Doesn't matter. Already forgotten about that jerk." She waved down the waitress so she could order another drink. "I'll take a cosmo." She turned to me. "Do you want anything?"

Guess she didn't hate me that much if she wanted me to order. "Moscow Mule."

The waitress walked away.

She wore gold earrings and a matching gold bracelet around her wrist. Her eye shadow was darker than usual, sultry and smoky. Instead of wearing red lipstick, she wore purple, which was unusual but so sexy on her. "You're a vodka man?"

"Yes." I was impressed she knew the contents of my drink. Whenever I saw her drinking, she was always enjoying something different, whether it was wine, beer, or an assortment of cocktails. She didn't have a specific drink. "It's probably in your best interest to tell me what he said to you."

"We're still on that?"

"I'll kill him for you if you want." She probably thought I was joking because she had no idea how honest I was, that I killed people all the time, that I took my job very seriously. She didn't want me, but maybe if she knew what I could do for her, she would feel differently.

"He deserved to be kicked in the stomach, but death is a little harsh." When the waitress returned with the drinks, Catalina immediately brought it to her lips and smeared her purple lipstick on the glass. "But thanks for the offer...I guess."

I watched her take another drink. "You think I'm joking."

"God, I hope so." She grabbed my glass and took a drink, testing it out. "That drink's never really been my thing. It's just too... I don't know." She pushed the glass back toward me. "Anyway, I guess you should get going."

Now that I'd absorbed her energy, I didn't want to go anywhere. It was addictive, infectious. I wanted to keep talking, keep thinking about that purple lipstick smeared on my neck when I looked in the mirror tomorrow morning. I'd always thought black was a sexy color, but she somehow made purple irresistible. "We're just getting started."

She ran her fingers through her hair and gave me an exasperated expression. "You don't quit, do you?"

I shook my head. "Never."

"Well, I don't change my mind either. Looks like we're at a stalemate."

"That's fine with me." I tapped my glass against hers. "Cheers."

She rolled her eyes but took a drink anyway.

I stared at her as I drank half the contents in a single swallow. The more I was around her, the more attractive she became. Initially, I found her unremarkable. But now, every time I saw her, she got sexier and sexier. It wasn't just her looks, but her bold attitude. "You were beautiful the other night."

Instead of firing off with a comeback, she actually took the compliment to heart. There was a slight softness to her, a calmness that came over her features. She blinked more often, let out a gentle breath rather than an annoyed sigh. "Thank you..." Her heart and soul were dedicated to ballet. She gave it her all every night, and even when she wasn't dancing, she still personified a professional ballerina with her poise and elegance. It was clearly her passion, her drive, her reason to be alive. "I knew that was you."

"I sat in the front row for a reason."

"I was surprised you weren't at my car later."

"All I wanted was to see the show. Nothing more." My arm rested on the table, and I focused on the woman in front of me. My eyes didn't wander to the rest of the options in the room. Every time I walked into a bar, I quickly scanned the area to see who was worth my time. But now, I never looked because there was only one target that required my aim.

"And why are you here? I know it's not a coincidence."

I didn't deny it. "Wanted to buy you a drink."

"I can buy myself as many drinks as I want."

I knew she didn't make a high income as a dancer. Judging from her car and apartment, she didn't have much, but she was so pretty I doubted she ever bought herself a single drink in her life. "You wanna buy me a drink, then?"

Her eyes turned back to me, surprised by what I'd said. "If I were trying to get you into bed, maybe."

"I'm ready to go now if you are."

She laughed off my comment as if it was absurd. "I can't believe you're still on that."

"The heart wants what it wants."

She laughed again. "You mean your dick wants what it wants."

I shrugged. "Trying to be a gentleman about it."

"You want to be a gentleman?" Both of her eyebrows rose. "Start by not throwing me in a cage."

"No regrets. We wouldn't be here now if I hadn't."

She laughed again, this time darkly. "You know—"

I changed the subject before she could tell me off. "How long do you intend to keep dancing?" I knew dancers had an early retirement like athletes. Sometimes careers ended even sooner because of an injury. I hoped that never happened to her because she loved her work so much.

She answered my question, probably because this was a topic she was quite interested in. "Until I turn thirty."

"That seems young to retire."

She held her glass with her slender fingertips and took a sip. "It is. But I have to have my kids by then."

So, she did want something serious. "I thought you said you just wanted to have fun."

"I do, for the next five years. I'm not interested in a relationship. I'm not even trying to look for the right guy. I'm looking for all the wrong guys, actually."

"Well, I'm the definition of a wrong guy."

"Trust me, I know. And if you hadn't crossed my brother, you would probably be another notch on my bedpost by now. But you made your choice, and that's it." She took another drink. "I'm just trying to enjoy my youth right now. My girlfriends get into relationships so young and not even with the right guy. I've never wanted to waste my time. I wanted to learn and grow. Have fun." She watched my expression over her glass. "You can think I'm a slut all you want. I don't care."

"I don't think that."

"Sure..."

"I just think it's unfair that I can't enjoy you. Being with me isn't a betrayal. You would use me just as I would use you. I would be nothing to you. It's not like you love me. It's not like you even care about me. It means nothing. So, what's the harm?"

She considered my words for a long time, holding her glass close to her face. Her eyes slightly shifted back and forth, and she eventually lowered the glass and straightened. Seemed like my words actually got to her, impacted her. Maybe she realized she was overthinking everything, that we didn't have to mean anything. "I told you my answer wouldn't change." She finished the rest of her glass before she set it down. "Let it go, Heath." Her voice wasn't full of fire, and her eyes weren't full of attitude. She was actually somber, like she hated giving that answer. "Goodbye." She turned away.

I grabbed her by the arm and pulled her back. With one gentle move, I pulled her into me, her chest against mine, and placed my kiss on her lips.

I closed my eyes at the connection, finally feeling those full lips that I had stared at so many times. My hand slid from her arm and down her back, coming into contact with her bare skin for the first time. My outstretched fingers planted across the expanse of her back, and I drew her into me, invigorated by this sexy woman.

She didn't pull away.

She didn't fight, kick, or bite.

She surrendered.

She was still at first, taking seconds to process what I'd just done. Last time I grabbed her, she spun out of my grasp so fast, it was clear that my touch was the last thing she wanted. Now, she submitted, completely gave in to me when she felt my mouth on hers.

Fuck, it was nice.

She pulled away, taking her lips off mine so she could stare at me. A dazed expression was on her face, as if she couldn't believe what had happened. My hand was still on her back, but she didn't push it away. She didn't grab a drink and throw it in my face. She could easily knee me in the balls right now. That didn't happen either.

She cupped my face and pulled my mouth back to hers, kissing me hard, kissing me aggressively like that had been all she wanted to do since she'd laid eyes on me. Her lips were hungry as she kissed me, and she breathed into my lungs and took my oxygen away. "Asshole..." She moved closer, her tits right in my chest. Her fingers moved into my short hair, and she moaned into my mouth as she kissed me.

Damn.

I matched her desire with my own hunger, falling into the best kiss of my life. I could feel how much she hated me, but I could also feel how much she enjoyed me. Somehow that made the experience even better, feeling her battle both emotions. She knew how to kiss a man, how to give her tongue in the sexiest way. She knew how to breathe, how to pace, how to kiss without tapping her teeth against mine. Her hand slid down my neck to my chest, and she tugged on my shirt like she wanted to take it off. My hand slid up her back and moved into her hair, coming into contact with one of her softest features.

She quickly pulled away, that fire back in her gaze. Now she looked at me like she really did hate me, but she hated me more because that kiss was so damn good.

She slapped me across the face—not hard, but not soft either. Her palm struck my cheek with purpose.

I didn't turn with the hit. Part of me expected it to happen even though she'd kissed me, because her emotions were always erupting at unpredictable intervals. I wasn't angry.

In fact, I kinda liked it.

Then she grabbed my arm and yanked me into her again, kissing me with the same intensity.

Fuck.

I smiled against her lips and cupped the back of her head, my fingertips sliding into the fall of her hair. I fell harder into this woman than I ever had with anyone else, suffocated by our volatile chemistry. I never knew what was gonna happen, and that made me so fucking addicted. She might hate me one moment, then need me the next.

She pushed me away again. Self-loathing was written all over her face, her eyes skeptical as if she couldn't believe what she'd just done. She released a big breath, packed with so much irritation she didn't know what to do with it. "This is over." She turned around and walked off, her nectarine ass so fucking plump.

I wipe my thumb over my lips, tracing the areas where her lipstick was now on my face. There was no reason to chase her because I had everything I needed. She wanted me, felt exactly what I felt with that kiss. She would come back for more.

It was only a matter of time.

I GAVE her a few days to process what happened. She loved that kiss; she loved my lips. She hit me because she was angry by how much she liked it, not because of my actions. The memory of our embrace would make her hot whenever she thought about it, and maybe my distance would make her want it more.

She was worth the wait, so I could be patient.

I decided to go to her show again, but this time, I didn't sit in the front row. I enjoyed her in the back, watching her move across the stage without her having any idea I was there. Now that I'd kissed her, I desired her even more. Watching her move her body in the most elegant ways was so sexy.

Fuck, how did she move in bed?

When the performance was over, I leaned against her car and waited for her to show up. I didn't feel guilty catching her off guard because she knew I would show my face eventually. There was no way she thought I would lose interest after that kiss.

Or kisses, I should say.

She walked down the path to her car, her bag over her shoulder. She walked at a quick pace, as if she had somewhere to be. Maybe she had plans tonight. She'd changed into a blue dress and flats, her hair free from her bun.

When she was close enough to make out my body, she stopped. She was fifty feet away, but her sigh was loud enough to reach me. She put both hands on her hips before she sighed again and kept walking. "You better be gone by the time I get there!"

With my arms crossed over my chest, I continued to lean against the car. "Or what? Are you gonna kiss me again? Slap me? Because you know I like those things."

"Argh!" She threw her arms down and came closer to me, her gait quick and purposeful. When she reached me, she dropped her purse on the ground like she expected to fight me. "I said this was over."

"Strange. I don't remember that. Did you say it when you were kissing me?" I was gonna throw it in her face every chance I had, to remind her she wanted my dick as much as I wanted to give it to her.

She stomped her foot like a child. "I said this was over. I mean it. I had way too much to drink at the bar. I don't know what happened, alright? And you're the one who kissed me."

"And then you kissed me back."

She stood in front of me and stared me down, like she didn't know how to fix this problem. Her hands moved to her hips, and she looked around, as if searching for a tool that would help her get rid of me. When there was nothing at her disposal, she crossed her arms over her chest and looked at the ground. "Look, maybe I do think you're hot. Maybe we do have great chemistry. Doesn't mean I wanna be with you."

Now that I knew she wanted me, I was gonna be a total dick till I got what I wanted. I angled my head slightly as I looked at her, seeing the sexiest lady try to worm her way out of the situation. It was hot watching her deal with her conflicting feelings, kissing me because she liked it, and then pushing me away when she remembered I'd locked her in the cage. But one look at my handsome face made her forget that, and then it started all over again. "It does mean you want to be with me."

"You've never seen a hot chick but didn't wanna fuck her?"

That was the dumbest question I'd ever heard. "No." I cocked an eyebrow.

"Okay..." She shifted her weight and looked down the sidewalk. "Bad example." She sighed and looked at me again, her eyes ferocious. "I just meant it doesn't mean anything. I told you I'd been drinking."

She'd only been at the bar for thirty minutes, so I didn't buy that excuse. "Have you been drinking tonight?"

Her attitude flared, her nostrils expanding like a bull that had just spotted a red cape. "I've been dancing for two hours. What do you think?"

I couldn't suppress the smile wanting to form on my lips. I dropped my arms to my sides and straightened, ready to take what was mine, ready to prove my point. "Just answer the question." I moved closer to her and stopped when we were just inches apart, my neck bent down so I could look into her beautiful face and vicious eyes.

She wanted to fight me and remain silent; it was obvious by her deep hostility, by the way she stayed defiant until the bitter end. She answered. "No..."

My hand grabbed the front of her neck, my fingers wrapping nearly all the way around the slender column, my fingertips feeling her racing pulse. She didn't flinch at my touch, didn't shudder at the intimacy, didn't shiver at the pure sexuality of it, but she inhaled a deep breath when she realized what was about to happen. I leaned in and kissed her.

She didn't push me off.

My mouth had a gentle landing, lightly bouncing against her full, soft lips. My tongue gave a gentle lick to the corner of her mouth before I kissed the other corner. I knocked softly at her door, asked to come inside.

She opened her mouth wider, her tongue ready to feel mine, her lips ready for my kiss.

I kissed her harder, my head tilting to the other side so I could kiss her mouth in a different way. Every kiss was slow, purposeful, but filled with so much intention that it made us both breathe hard instantly. Just having my hand on her neck made me hard, knowing I could control the angle of her face, kiss her how I wanted.

And the fact that she allowed me to grab her like that, like I owned her, like she was mine...fuck.

Her arms had been by her sides the entire time, but when she fell into my kiss, her hands moved to my arms, one hand on my bicep, the other on my forearm. She tilted her neck back so she could accept my kiss, her tongue a landing strip. She was a damn good kisser, moving her tongue in subtle but powerful ways, breathing into my mouth with suppressed moans.

I turned her around and gently guided her backward to the car so I could pin her down and really enjoy her. She allowed me to steer her, her eyes closed and her mouth focused on mine like she trusted me, or better yet, she didn't give a damn what I was up to.

With her back pressed into the car, I continued to kiss her, our bodies intertwined, her tits against my chest. It was dark, and there wasn't a streetlamp nearby, so we had privacy until somebody decided to take a late-night stroll. She and I kissed each other like we were alone in the world, didn't even need a bed to have the best sex of our lives.

She didn't stop me or push me away. This time, she couldn't resist. This time, she was addicted. Her hands started to explore my body, gliding over my hard chest before she felt the strong the muscles in my back. Her lips started to move faster; she breathed harder. She moaned into my mouth like my fat dick was inside her.

I undid the top of my jeans and let them sink down just a little before I grabbed her leg and hiked it over my hip. Her short dress rose to her hips, her panties visible if anyone was looking. If I could get a peek, I would, but I was too busy kissing this delicious mouth.

Now, I pressed my body into hers again, this time pressing the outline of my dick in my boxers right against her pussy. I wanted her to know exactly what I had to offer, what I could give her if she took me home right now. I ground against her, thick fat shaft hitting her right in the clit.

Her nails clawed at my chest, and she moaned loudly into my mouth. "Oh wow…" She opened her eyes for a moment to look into mine, her lips still kissing me. Her gaze was filled with so much desire, it looked like she couldn't think straight, couldn't think about what she was doing. She just enjoyed it. I continued to grind into her with slow and even strokes, showing her how I would fuck her if she dropped her panties for me. My hand moved into her hair, and I supported her head as I continued to kiss her, enjoy her, prove I was the man for her.

She spoke between her kisses. "Damn…that dick." She sucked my bottom lip into her mouth and gave me a gentle bite. She drew a little blood, and I could taste it on my own tongue.

I didn't flinch because I liked it.

She whispered against my lips. "Babe…you're gonna make me come."

Did she just call me babe?

I smiled against her lips before I continued to kiss her. I rubbed my dick harder and harder against her clit, kissing her and allowing her to breathe against my mouth because she was nearly out of breath.

Her nails dug deeper, and she even grabbed my ass and tugged me into her, not afraid to show me how she wanted me to move against her. She stopped kissing me altogether, her head tilted back, her lips parted, her eyes on mine.

I halted.

Her eyes turned wild, and she pulled on my ass, like I was a machine that had just stopped working on her.

"Take me home." I wasn't going to give her the goods until she gave me what I wanted first. Knowing her, she would take that orgasm to-go and walk off. I wanted more, to be inside her and fuck her all night. I'd already proved I could be the man who wouldn't disappoint her, so now I had my terms.

Her eyes turned to fire. "You asshole."

"Come on, baby. If I can make you feel this good against a car, imagine what I can do in bed."

Now, she pushed me off, pulling down her dress like she hadn't just ground against my dick until her panties were soaked. "I don't want to see you again. I mean it."

I zipped up my jeans and smiled at the soaked stain on my boxers. "Why? Are you drunk right now?" I asked the question like a smartass, unable to hold back my sarcasm.

She picked up her purse where she'd dropped it on the ground. "Oh, fuck off." She walked around the car to the driver's door and flipped me off as she went.

I moved around the other way, meeting her before she could get inside. I placed my palm against the door so she couldn't open it. "You just soaked my boxers and called me babe. Cut the shit, and let's go. You're the tease here."

"I am?" she has incredulously. "Am I the one showing up everywhere, trying to seduce you?"

"I wish you were. I suspect you'd be good at it."

She raised her palm and slapped me.

I could've stopped the hit, but I didn't want to. "You know I like it when you do that, right?"

She growled and tried to yank the door open.

My palm remained flat against the door so she couldn't move it at all.

She let out a quiet scream and threw her arms down. "Just let me go."

"So you can go home and finish yourself off while thinking about me?" If she was gonna think about me and come, then I was gonna watch it happen, watch her and come myself.

"What I do at home with my vibrator is none of your business."

"It is my business when you should be using my dick instead."

She was affronted by what I said, unable to believe I spoke to her like that. "I'm tired of playing this game. I told you I don't want to see you, and I stand by that decision. You manipulate me to get the answer you want, make me do something I don't want to do—"

A deep chuckle escaped my throat. "I'm definitely not making you do anything you don't wanna do."

"You know exactly what you're doing." She shoved her fore-finger into my chest. "You're playing on my emotions and seducing me into bed, but I want to be loyal to my brother. That's the kind of person I want to be. Yes, we are so fucking hot together, and I'd rather bounce on your dick tonight than be alone, but I know where my allegiance lies. Don't make me be the person I despise."

The emotion in her voice actually got under my skin a little bit. "Fucking me doesn't make you any less loyal."

"I disagree. Now take your ape-size hand off the fucking door and let me go."

I kept my palm there, too determined to let her walk away. All I had to do was stroll into a bar and find somebody to replace her, but I didn't want to do that. I wanted this woman more than any other woman on this planet. Maybe it was just because I couldn't have her. Maybe it was a subconscious dig at Damien. Or maybe it was because I truly, deeply wanted this one woman.

"If I see you again, I'll tell Damien. Everything." Confidence was in her gaze, as if it wasn't an idle threat, just a final warning. She was a spontaneous and emotional person, so she ignited when she had my mouth on hers, but once that physical embrace was gone, she was cold like a warlord. She was prepared to destroy me like she had no other choice.

"Do you think I'm scared of him?" Fucker was under my thumb, my little bitch. I collected my money on a regular basis, taking his hard-earned cash his men risked their lives for. I made him suffer for so many reasons, just because I was petty.

"If he knew you were coming after me, then yes. You should be fucking scared." She pulled on the door again, and this time, it opened because I backed off. She threw her purse into the passenger seat and gave me one final stare. "Thanks for the dick." She grabbed the front of my shirt and pulled me into her, planting one final hot kiss on my lips. Then she pressed her palm into my chest and forced me off before she got into the car and drove away.

After I watched her taillights disappear, I closed my eyes and ran my fingers through my hair. I actually felt devastated at the loss, like I'd lost something really special. The shit that came out of her mouth turned me on like crazy. She took what she wanted like she couldn't live without it, and then threw it away a moment later like it meant nothing. So hot. "Fuck."

FOUR

CATALINA

"How are things with you guys?" I sat across from Anna at the café. We'd just finished our salads and soups, and now we enjoyed our Americanos and biscotti. I probably shouldn't eat something so sweet, but I hadn't been in the mood to really care about being meticulous with my calories lately, so I placed it into my mouth and took a big bite.

Damn, that was good.

Anna had a noticeable glow to her, an infectious smile that showed how happy she was now that the worst was over. She was in a strappy summer dress with a jean jacket, her brown hair hanging down her chest. "So good. We're happy."

"You've been living together for a while, and you still like him?" I dunked the biscotti into the coffee before I took another bite. Coated in espresso, it was even better, the mixture of coffee and sugar.

"Oh, I love him." Her eyes were filled with emotional sincerity, and she glanced down to stir her coffee with her biscotti, a slight smile on her lips. "At first, I was going to move back to my apartment, but he asked me to stay. I didn't want to rush things, overstay my welcome, but I love being there with him. I love waking up to him, going to sleep with beside me."

It was a little weird to hear her describe my brother in that way, but she was my friend before my future sister-in-law, so I didn't gag or make a disgusted face. "I'm happy for you guys. After all the shit you went through with Liam, you deserve this."

"Thank you. And I'm glad you approve of me for your brother."

"Of course. You're awesome. I mean, I think you might be too good for my brother."

She laughed as if I'd made a joke. "I know you don't mean that, but thanks anyway."

I thought the world of my brother, but I never admitted it. I stirred my coffee and had the last of my biscotti. "Girl, this shit is so good. I can't wait until I retire so I can get as fat as I want. Just have to find a husband that'll fuck me the same at my bigger size." I tried not to think about *him*, but of course, he got into my mind because that sounded exactly like something he would do. If I had a fatter ass, he would just love having more to squeeze. If my tits were bigger, he'd probably like it. He was such a big guy that I could be any size and he would still be much bigger than me.

"Are you seeing anybody?"

It was a harmless question, but it felt like an interrogation because I had something to hide. My neck felt a little warm at the same time as I could feel the color draining from my cheeks. I cleared my throat and sipped my coffee. "Not really." It was the truth. I hadn't met anyone because he'd been bombarding me every place I went. And then we ground against my car last week, and I was still masturbating to the memory.

"Really?" she asked. "I feel like you've always got a guy on your hook."

I had a very big guy on my hook right now. "Just been busy at work…" When I'd threatened to tell Damien, I meant it, and he must've believed me because he hadn't bothered me since I'd driven off. Not seeing him gave me clarity, because getting involved with him really was a mistake. Whenever we were in the same room together, all the hormones, lust, and chemistry fucked up my brain, and I couldn't think straight. Everything was calm, sensible, and…a little boring.

After we paid the bill, we walked back to her place. We'd just eaten, but Patricia had homemade muffins right out of the oven, so we grabbed a few and went to her suite upstairs. I shouldn't eat this, but whatever. I scarfed it down so fast.

We went through the bedroom and sat on the patio. "The place looks the same."

She chuckled. "You should see his closet."

I laughed. "What about his dressers?"

"Took over those too. And his bathroom."

I nodded in approval. "That's how it's done." I walked back inside and helped myself to their liquor cabinet. I pulled out a bottle of wine and had just uncorked it when Damien walked inside, wearing jeans and a shirt as if he'd had a casual day at the office. "Do you want a glass?"

"Why are you in my bedroom?" He tossed his keys onto the table as he headed closer.

"Alright, no wine for you…" I poured two glasses then turned around and took a sip.

Damien's gaze focused out the window, staring at the woman who looked over his balcony. It was a simple look, didn't last more than a few seconds, but it showed the depth of his feelings, the way he was enamored of that five-foot, petite brunette.

I covered my smile by drinking my wine. "How was your day?"

He turned his gaze back to me and approached me. "Do you really care?" He grabbed the bottle and poured himself a glass.

"You know me. I wouldn't ask if I didn't."

He shrugged. "It was fine." He swirled the wine and took a drink.

I glanced at Anna then turned back to him. "She told me how happy she is with you." I tipped the glass and let the wine slide down my throat as I watched his reaction.

He tried to keep a straight face, but that smile was impossible to control, especially when it entered his eyes. "Yeah?"

"Yep."

"Say anything else?"

I shrugged. "More of the same. Likes going to sleep with you, waking up next to you, taking all the space in your closet..."

The warmth in his eyes was indescribable. "Giving her my closet was a small sacrifice."

A year ago, I wouldn't have been able to imagine my brother with anyone, but now I couldn't imagine him without Anna. They were cut from the same cloth, two peas in a pod, Romeo and Juliet. "When are you gonna ask her to marry you?" I glanced out the patio window and saw her scrolling through her phone, oblivious to the fact that Damien was home and talking about her.

He was about to take another drink, but he stilled and stared at me with narrowed eyes, like he imagined I said something completely different. "I'm surprised you just asked me that."

"Why? It's not like I asked when you lost your virginity or something." I rolled my eyes and turned back to the wine in my grasp. Damien and I didn't really talk about that stuff, but since we were spending more time together, I thought it was time we started. Instead of teasing each other, we could choose to be friends. Our dad wouldn't be around forever, and all we would have was each other.

He chuckled slightly then looked down into his class. "Cassandra Davies."

I turned back to him, eyebrows raised. "What?"

"Remember her? I think I was a freshman in high school at the time."

I made a disgusted face. "Gross. Damien, I wasn't actually asking. I was just making a point."

"To answer your first question, I don't know." He drank from his glass as he looked at her on the patio. "I'd ask her now if I knew she'd say yes."

"Oh, she'll say yes." A woman didn't talk about a man like that unless she wanted him forever.

"We talked about it several weeks ago, and she said it was too soon. Not too soon for us, just too soon for her to get married again."

"Well, I don't think she feels that way anymore." The last person on her mind was that jackass Liam.

He shrugged. "She'll tell me when she's ready."

"What kind of fantasy is that? A woman doesn't want to *tell* a guy she's ready. She wants him to *know*." I set my glass down and refilled it, because I usually blew through wine like it was water. "I'll feel her out for you."

"I don't need you to do that."

"I'll just nudge her. Come on, we're friends."

"Fine." He grabbed the extra glass of wine. "Don't make it obvious." He went to the patio and set the wine down in front of her.

When she looked up from her phone, she realized he was there, and she quickly tossed her phone onto the table as she rose to her feet, her eyes brighter than the sun. Her arms wrapped around his neck, and she leaned into him hard to kiss him.

His arms circled her waist he tugged her body, kissing her like he hadn't just seen her when they woke up that morning.

I wished I could find a love like that, but that simply wasn't in the cards for me.

THE THREE OF us had dinner together on the patio, Damien and Anna sitting close together with their hands intertwined on the armrest of the chair. Their fingers stayed locked together and they occasionally exchanged glances, like they were thinking about what they wanted to do once I was gone.

I felt like a third wheel and tried to leave, but they made me stay, made me watch them be madly in love.

I took a bite of the tiramisu, knowing I was eating way too many calories, fat calories, but I chose not to give a damn.

Anna kissed him on the cheek before she excused herself to the bathroom.

My brother was a perv, so he turned to stare at her ass as she walked away.

"Ah-hem."

Damien turned back to me, a boyish grin on his face. "What?"

"Don't be gross." I sliced my spoon into the layers of dessert before scooping it into my mouth.

"That's my girlfriend. Not gross."

"It's gross when your sister is watching."

"Then don't watch."

I took a few bites as I stared at him. "Next time I come over, I'll bring a blindfold."

"Bring some duct tape too." He smiled.

I rolled my eyes dramatically, but picturing the tools used to kidnap somebody made me think of Heath. He didn't try to do any of those things when he grabbed me. He probably would've had a much easier time if he had, but he'd completely underestimated me. "What's the Skull King?"

Damien's smile quickly vanished at the perverse question. His entire body stilled, and he looked at me like I'd said something incredibly offensive. His elbow rested on the armrest, his fingers brushing over his chin. "Where did you hear that name?"

"Anna." It was the truth; she had mentioned him a few times when we were together, talking about her time with Liam and his relationship to the Skull King.

He continued to give me a dark look, like he was so angered with the question he couldn't answer it. "Why are you asking?"

"I mean, people actually call him that? Is he an actual king of the city? The title seems ridiculous. I just don't get it."

"Not an actual king, more like a ruler." Even though he was his enemy, Damien didn't mock him or drag his name through the mud. He didn't deny his credibility or pretend he was a minor enemy.

That was a little frightening.

He continued to speak. "He basically runs the country, keeps competing businesses distinct and separate so there's no monopoly on any specific product, like drugs, weapons, women, etc. He collects a fee for his work, and he keeps the peace...basically."

I was stunned when I heard that answer. "Really?"

He nodded. "That's why I haven't killed him. How do you kill someone who has everyone in his pocket? I know the smart thing to do is just let it go, but after what happened with Anna, I don't think I can. I need to kill the Skull King."

I guess people actually did call him that. He actually terrified people...including my brother. "I think you should let it go."

His eyes narrowed on me.

"You and Anna are happy together. Liam kept his word. Just be happy." I wasn't sure why I gave Damien advice about his feud. Being around Heath made me realize he really was powerful, even though I couldn't directly attest to his abilities. The best thing for both of them was just to move on. Maybe I had my own reasons for influencing Damien, because if there was no feud, there could be no betrayal.

He looked down at his hands and shook his head slightly. "I can't. I just can't."

"But do you think you can even kill him?"

He considered the question in silence. "Yes. But it's going to take a lot of planning. That man has wronged me so many times, continues to collect my money when it doesn't belong to him. I can let that go, but the fact that he took Anna from her hospital bed, which could've killed her, makes it impossible for me to just move on. I could've lost her forever because of him."

When I saw the determination in those green eyes, I knew my brother would never feel differently about the situation. If he knew I was sneaking around with Heath, it would be a personal attack, a betrayal. This was a battle that would never go away, and until Damien was the victor, the war would continue.

"She's everything to me...and he crossed the line."

WHEN ANOTHER WEEK passed and I didn't hear from Heath, I realized he'd actually listened to me. He seemed like a guy who wouldn't care about my wishes, who would keep trying after he got his dick wet against my panties, but he'd finally backed off.

I'd be lying if I said a part of me wasn't disappointed. When I'd first looked at him, I didn't see anything remarkable, but then again, I was thrown into a cage and treated like a dog. Once he let me go, I started to look at him differently. Then I noticed how beautiful his eyes were, how chiseled his arms were, how deep his voice was. He was tall, big, masculine...all the things I liked in a man. He was confident and not the least bit turned off by my attitude. And most importantly, he knew how to kiss a woman.

And that dick...damn.

I really felt like I was missing out on something good. When he pinned me to the car and rubbed up against me, it was so hot.

Feeling his hard dick pressed against my clit like an On button felt so good, especially with his tongue in my mouth. I knew he could've made me come then and there, but he held my pleasure hostage to get me to cooperate.

I hadn't found a better man. I still went out to the bars with my friends and met guys, got a few phone numbers, but nothing ever happened. I went home alone because I didn't want to risk being disappointed...again.

I knew where he lived, so I could stop by if I wanted to, but I knew that would be a mistake. I just needed more time to stop thinking about him, to move on and get back to my regular life. I wanted to be like my brother, loyal and strong, and sleeping with Heath would make me feel so dirty. I made the right decision. I knew I did.

So I told myself to move on.

After a performance, I went to the bar with a few friends. It was a good time with good music and good drinks, making it a night like the rest. I met a few guys, got a few numbers, and then excused myself to the restroom.

There was a long line for the bathroom, even though most of the girls probably just wanted to fix their hair and touch up their makeup, but that could take longer than a piss.

So I went to the men's room instead.

What? I didn't care.

I walked past the urinals with my hand covering one side of my face. "Don't worry, not looking." I headed to the stall and locked the door behind me.

The guy standing at the urinal finished and flushed. "You're welcome to take a peek, sweetheart." His accent was distinctly Russian, distinctly creepy.

I sat on the tissue paper that lined the toilet and released my bladder, the sound of my urine filling the bowl while we spoke. I stuck my finger into my throat like I was gagging even though he couldn't see me. "Thanks, but I'm good."

He turned on the faucet and washed his hands.

I finished my business and flushed before I stepped out of the stall and headed to the sink.

The guy was still there, leaning against the wall, his knee bent with his foot propped against the tile. His hands were in the pockets of his jeans, and he stared at me with a menacing expression, as if he owned me when he didn't even know my name. It wasn't the focused intensity Heath displayed—or maybe it was exactly the same, but that man was actually sexy. This guy was sleazy-looking.

I washed my hands and glanced at him in the mirror. "Do you mind?"

"You're the one who came in here."

"To piss. I come in peace."

"Well, I'm not breaking any rules by staying in the men's room. If you can look at my dick, why can't I look at you?"

I grabbed a few paper towels and dried my hands. "Look all you want. Just don't touch." I tossed the moist towels into the garbage then turned around to leave.

But he blocked my way.

He had bushy eyebrows, a crooked nose, and brown eyes that almost looked black. He was in a long-sleeved shirt even though it was way too hot to wear something like that. His hands were no longer in his pockets, but instead by his sides, as if he expected to fight me. "What's your name?"

Now this was getting weird. "None of your business." I moved around him then headed to the door.

He took a few steps back then turned the lock so it bolted the door shut.

Now, I was scared, but mostly pissed. "All I have to do is scream."

"And then what? By the time they get here, I'll be finished."

Both of my hands went to my hips. "Did you just threaten to rape me in a men's bathroom?" I wanted to be absolutely sure this wasn't a terrible attempt to impress me, that this guy wasn't trying to be romantic but simply didn't know how.

"That depends on you, I suppose." He started to move toward me.

He'd just fucked with the wrong bitch. I pretended I was gonna kick him between the legs so he would throw his arm down to block me and move out of the way, but instead, I slammed my right fist hard into his face.

It was hard enough to make him stagger back against gets the wall. He rubbed his face and looked shocked at the impact, as if he'd never been hit like that in his life.

Since this guy had clearly stated he intended to force me into sex, I didn't let him off easy. I kicked him in the side, slammed the heel of my shoe into his gut, and even pressed my foot into his balls.

"You fucking bitch." He tried to kick me off.

I kicked him right in the face, making him sink to the floor and free the access to the door. "Enjoy prison." I unlocked the door and walked out. I headed straight to the bar and spoke to the first person I saw. I got right to the point. "A guy tried to rape me in the bathroom. Call the cops."

I HAD to stay for a few hours to deal with the police, give my statement, and watch them put handcuffs on his wrists and take him away.

I could tell who the rest of his party was, because they stayed and watched the whole thing, giving me harassing looks like I was the asshole. They looked just as shady as he did, watching me like I was inferior to them.

I flipped them off before I walked out.

I would normally walk to my apartment, but I thought it was better to get a cab. I'd fought him off, handed him over to the police where he belonged, but I'd be lying if I said I wasn't rattled by what just happened.

I was human.

When I walked into my apartment, I made sure the door was locked before I washed off my makeup and went to bed. Once I was under the sheets and comfortable, I stopped thinking about what had happened and drifted off to sleep immediately.

If some other woman were in the bathroom, that could have ended quite differently. Maybe she wouldn't have known how to fight him off, and something terrible would have happened to her. Too disturbed by the experience, she probably wouldn't call the cops either.

So maybe that was supposed to happen to me. Maybe it happened because I could handle it, put the asshole behind bars where he belonged. I believed everything happened for a reason, and tonight was no different.

AFTER A LONG NIGHT, I was a heavy sleeper. I hadn't gotten home until two in the morning, and since I'd been dancing on the stage earlier that night, I slept so hard. The only reason I would wake up was if the guy next to me snored like a bear. Otherwise, I was totally out of it.

That was probably why I didn't hear them come in.

A gloved hand immediately cupped my mouth and pushed down hard so I couldn't make a sound. Once the hand was on my face, I threw my arms out to hit whoever had attacked me. My eyes opened and looked into the face of a man I didn't know. With dark hair and absolutely no mercy in his brown eyes, it wasn't someone I knew, but someone I faintly recognized.

It was one of the guys from the table, one of the cronies of the man who'd assaulted me.

Another guy held my legs down so I couldn't kick, and then a third came at me with a syringe.

Oh, hell no.

I fought harder, tears forming in my eyes because I knew my fate right then and there. I was outnumbered, and it was the middle of the night, so no one would even know what was happening. They were going to put me under so they could either transfer me...or something worse.

I'd never been so fucking scared.

I tried to buck them off, tried to scream, but my cries were muffled.

The guy grabbed me by the hair and yanked harshly on my scalp so my neck would become exposed. Then he stabbed the needle into my neck and injected the fluid. "Talk soon, bitch."

I'd thought I was strong enough to fight off the drug, to pretend to be asleep just as I had when Heath took me. But the chemicals were too strong, immediately dumping into my blood and knocking me right out. I tried to fight it, but I was pulled under, knowing whatever I woke up to would be truly horrifying.

THE INSTANT my eyes were open, anxiety really kicked in. My heart rate exploded, and the adrenaline nearly gave me a heart attack. My eyes took in the scene around me, darkness, cages, damp coldness.

I realized I was in a little cage, similar to the one I'd been in when Heath locked me up, but there were several cages right up against one another, and in each one was a woman.

Naked.

When I looked down at myself, I realized I'd met the same fate. Buck naked, I could see my flesh from my toes to my tits. My belly button ring glittered in the dark. I tried to keep my breathing even so I could pretend I was still asleep, but I was so rattled I couldn't control my panic.

There didn't seem to be anyone on the other side of the bars, the men who took me or any guards. I sat up slightly and realized I was lying on a bed of hay. There was a bucket in the corner where they expected me to shit, a roll of toilet paper on a stool. Hot tears burned in my eyes when I realized it wasn't a nightmare. The fact that I was there with other women made it perfectly clear what had just happened to me.

I was being trafficked.

I did my best to keep my breathing deep and even, not to appear awake, not to give in to the screams and tears. There was still hope because Damien would realize I was missing eventually. He'd track me down and find me. I knew he would.

I just knew it wouldn't be soon enough before...they did things to me.

I looked through the bars of the cage to the woman beside me. She was a blonde, her hair oily because she hadn't showered in a long time. She seemed to be a veteran, someone who'd been there a long time. "Hey..." I whispered and hoped I wouldn't be overheard.

She turned me slightly, her arms over her chest.

"Where are we?"

She looked out of the bars to the walkway, like she was checking for something, and then turned back to me and placed her forefinger over her lips as if to silence me.

I needed answers. "Please."

Someone must've heard me, because footsteps sounded before a large man approached. His dark hair and brown eyes told me he was one of the guys who'd broken in to my apartment and stolen me. He was the same one who had put the needle into my neck. They must have followed me after I left the bar, ready to exact vengeance for what I did to their friend.

He opened the blonde's cage and stepped inside. "No talking, bitch." He stepped closer, making her shrink back in fear. She whimpered instantly, tears streaming down her cheeks like this wasn't the first time she'd been punished. She even closed her eyes and dropped her chin to the floor.

He kneeled down and grabbed the back of her hair before he yanked her hard. "Bitch, you know the rules." He pulled his fist back and prepared to punch her in the face.

I couldn't let that happen. "It was me."

He lowered his arm and turned his gaze on me. He couldn't even look at me without feeling the rage in his blood. His eyes burned like he wanted nothing more than to punish me after what I'd done.

"I was the one talking...not her." There was probably a stupid mistake to stick my neck out like this, but I couldn't let this woman be punished for something that wasn't her fault. She tried to keep me quiet.

He released the blonde and rose to his feet. "I was wondering when you'd wake up, sweetheart." The nickname should be endearing, from a father to a daughter, or to a woman from a loving man. When he said it, it was terrifying, disgusting. He left her cage and moved into mine.

I pulled my knees to my chest and covered my tits with my arms, but I also didn't see the point because he'd obviously already seen me naked. I didn't feel any different, feel any aches, so I didn't think they'd had their way with me already... at least I hoped not. These guys seemed like the types that wanted to take their victims awake so they could watch them suffer.

His boots tapped against the concrete as he approached me, walking with a slow gait, like he wanted to draw this out and take his time. There was such arrogance in his countenance, but he enjoyed every second of my suffering.

He kneeled down and faced me head on.

I did my best not to shake, but the shivers were uncontrollable. Bumps were all over my arms, not because I was cold, but because I was absolutely terrified. I always held my head high and I wasn't afraid to stand up to a bully, but this was a whole different situation.

This was hell.

He reached out and grabbed me by the neck, squeezing my windpipe so I struggled to breathe. "I'm gonna make you pay for what you did to Ivanov."

I struggled to breathe and tried to kick him off, but he was too strong. I grabbed his hands and tried to pull them off my neck.

He squeezed harder and slammed my head against the wall. "Who the fuck do you think you are? You dress like a whore, then expect to fuck like a whore. Fight like a man, expect to be beaten like a man." Then he punched me hard in the face.

Then again.

And again.

FIVE

HEATH

THE GUYS OPENED THE DOORS TO THE BACK OF THE armored truck, and I threw my bag of cash inside. It fell on top of the other black duffel bags, shifting slightly as all the bills fell to the right. It eventually toppled over and rolled to the bottom of the pile. "Next." I headed to the passenger door while the guys locked up the back and moved to their seats.

Steel was behind the wheel. "Where to next?"

I pulled out my phone and looked through the list. "Popov." He was one of the members of an underground Russian trafficking group. They took girls and sold them to other countries, mainly Russia. Sometimes they sold them locally. Apparently, Russians liked Italian women.

Steel pulled onto the road and drove a few miles to the location, the laundromat with a basement underneath. The laundry place was only open until five, and after dark, it was used to bring girls in and out of the basement.

The biggest part of my job was going around and collecting money, exactly like the tax man. I had a lot of men on my roster, so I spent most of my time collecting cash, always prepared for resistance even though that almost never happened. Damien was one of the few who was dumb enough to try to get out of it.

It was the one positive thing that came out of Catalina's decision, that I could continue my murderous crusade against him. Rejection stung, especially when I continued to think about her, but I tried to see the good in it, to appreciate the fact that my situation was no longer complicated now that she was gone.

Even though she was still on my mind...a lot.

I hoped she would miss me chasing her and eventually want to chase me, but that never happened. She got what she wanted, and she was too stubborn to change her mind. No matter how much she liked my dick, her ego was far too big to go back on her word now.

We parked at the curb minutes later, unafraid to be spotted by the police or other adversaries. No one drove around in a bulletproof armored vehicle in plain sight unless they were registered with a security company.

But I didn't give a fuck.

I wanted people to see me coming. I wanted people to be afraid.

I left the guys at the truck because I usually ventured into these discussions alone. There was only one ruler, one Skull King, so I was the only one who asked for the cash. I wouldn't be the Skull King if I sent my cronies to do it. Seeing me in the flesh always made them very cooperative.

I walked into the laundromat and took the stairs to the basement. I knew they were expecting me because I came at the same time every two weeks. Once I was at the bottom of the stairs, I was in a whole different world. It was dark, damp like we were in the sewers, and the women were against the opposite wall, as far away from the doors as they possibly could be. They were naked, but I was never tempted to look.

Slaves weren't my thing.

Popov sat at the table in the middle of the room, smoking a cigar while his crew played a round of poker. The smoke rose to the ceiling, and they enjoyed a bottle of vodka without a mixer. Stacks of cash were on the table, the pot worth at least thirty thousand euro. When I approached, Popov rested his cigar in the black ashtray. "Look who it is…"

I glanced down at the table. "Who's winning?"

"Petrov." He straightened in his chair before he rose to his feet. "But we think he cheats."

Petrov shook his head before he threw his cards on the table. "Don't cheat. Just know how to play." His hand was strong, two pair, and it made him win that round.

Popov was on his feet, and he faced me with his arms across his chest. "Wanna pull up a chair?"

It was hard to believe, but I wasn't a gambling man. "I'm here for business, not pleasure."

"Oh, I know." He grabbed his cigar out of the ashtray and puffed on the wet tip. "You're the only man I know who turns down a free fuck." When he released the smoke from his mouth, he blew it right in my face as it rose to the ceiling.

Rape didn't turn me on. "Get my money."

Sometimes he looked like he wanted to resist me when that unsettling look came onto his face, but he never did. He stepped away to retrieve the cash.

Then I heard a voice I'd recognize anywhere.

"Heath...?" It was a quiet voice, afraid to be loud. It possessed so much trepidation that it seemed to belong to a person I didn't know, like saying my name was the equivalent of risking her life. But the sound of her voice was so ingrained in my brain that I could recognize it even if it wasn't quite the same.

I turned at the sound, looking through the bars to the first cage on the left. My eyes narrowed as I looked at the brunette on the floor against the wall, her face so bruised it was almost unrecognizable. Her arms were across her body to hide her nakedness, and she looked so scared that her energy was totally different. She wasn't the strong, spontaneous woman who wielded an iron fist, who had the spine most leaders lacked. It took me at least ten seconds to understand what I was looking at.

When she got a better look at me, she disregarded her naked-ness and came to the bars. "Heath..." Her voice broke just saying my name, tears flooding her voice, making a crack like a stick cleanly snapped in two. "Please get me out of here... please. Help me. Don't leave me in here." She turned hysteri-cal, yanking on the metal bars and making them shake. She wanted to break through them and escape. "Please..."

Her face was so bruised and swollen, she didn't look like herself. The green color of her eyes was almost nonexistent because her eyes were nearly swollen shut. The bruising all over her face indicated a man had beaten the shit out of her, slammed his fist into her face so many times that her features were destroyed. Her spirit was broken because she had no pride.

It was the first time in my life I was too disturbed to react, to pull myself together and move forward.

Popov returned and dropped a bag of money on the floor. "There you go."

When Catalina immediately stepped back from the bars as he came close, that told me he was her tormentor. Her arms moved across her chest and hid her breasts from view as she continued to sob uncontrollably.

I turned him. "Open the door."

He glanced at her and turned back to me. "I just got her."

I stared at him harder, furious at his disobedience. "Open the fucking door." I took a few steps toward him, silently promising retribution if he didn't do what he was told. I could burn this place to the fucking ground if I wanted to.

"She's the reason Ivanov is in prison right now."

Now I raised my voice so loud, all the bars in the cages rattled. "Open. The. Door." I didn't pull out my gun because I didn't need more than my voice to make a serious threat. The guys at the table were still, watching their leader engage me in a verbal battle. If he didn't obey, I'd shoot him and move on to the next guy.

He sighed in annoyance because she was a prized prisoner, but he knew it wasn't worth his life, along with the lives of his men. He pulled the keys out of his pocket and finally opened the door. "There."

The second the door was open, Catalina sprinted to me, getting to me as quickly as she could, as if I was the only thing in the world that could save her. She crashed into my chest so hard she actually made me shift backward slightly. Naked, sobbing, and shaking, she wrapped her arms around my neck and buried her face into my chest. "Please get me out of here." She grabbed at my shirt and cried, taking deep breaths and soaking my clothes with her tears. "Please. Don't leave me here..."

My hand moved under her hair, and I pulled her back slightly so I could look into her face. I'd imagined that naked body so many times, but now I didn't look, I didn't want to look. I pulled my shirt over my head and gave it to her.

She took it with shaking hands, as if she'd never received a gift so wonderful as the clothes off my own back. There were no words she could say to match the appreciation in her eyes. It led to a whole new batch of tears. She was shaking so much she couldn't even get it on.

So, I did it for her. I pulled it all the way down over her ass and her thighs so she would be completely covered. Then I cupped her face with both of my hands and looked at all the bruising and swelling. It made me sick to my stomach, made me feel so much pain. This woman was so beautiful, but now she was a busted fucking piñata. I whispered to her. "You're safe now."

A flash of gratitude came into her eyes before she closed them, more tears flooding.

I turned to Popov. "Who did this?"

He was silent, rigid because he knew shit was about to go down.

I turned Catalina around and pointed at her face. "Who fucking did this?"

He was too scared to look at her. "Ivanov is in jail because of her. He'll probably be in there for life because the cops have been looking for him—"

"Who. Fucking. Did. This?"

Popov looked at his men, as if he were asking one of them to take the fall.

Catalina spoke through her tears. "It was him." She came closer to my side, like she didn't want to be even a few inches apart for me. "He came into my cage and choked me while he beat me until I blacked out…"

Popov held up both hands once Catalina threw him under the bus. "I didn't know who she was—"

I pulled out my gun and shot him right in the fucking head.

His dead body fell to the floor with a distinctive thud. The ceiling was low and there was no air filtration, so I could smell the burning of my gun right away. I could even smell death because we were in such close quarters.

Catalina closed her eyes and breathed deep with relief, like she was thanking god he was dead.

I returned my gun to the back of my jeans and faced the other two.

Neither reached for his gun or rose from his chair to resist me. They didn't avenge their friend; they took the path of least resistance. The smoke from Popov's cigar still rose to the ceiling, and the rest of their poker chips sat on the table, untouched.

I grabbed Catalina's hand. "Let's go."

Instead of running for the door, she stayed put and tugged me back to her. Her face came close to mine, and she whispered, "I can't leave the others. They have to come too."

I shouldn't have been surprised by the request. "I can't do that."

She started to grow hysterical again. "You have to. I can't live with myself if I go free and they don't. Please do this for me…" New tears started in her eyes and quickly dripped down her cheeks. She must be in so much pain right now, but instead of thinking about herself, she still thought about other people.

I couldn't let these girls go right now. There were only two men standing in my way, but this was just the top layer of a much bigger organization. If I freed all their slaves, there would be consequences. I couldn't deal with it right this second. "There's nothing I can do right now."

"Heath, please." She squeezed my hand.

"We have to leave them right now. But I'll come back."

That wasn't good enough for her. She shook her head. "I know you can do it now—"

"I promise I'll take care of it later. You need to trust me." I'd never been a hero, never cared about anything but myself and my money, but right now, I would do anything she wanted. I would take off my ring for good and give it to a homeless person if that was what she wanted. My heart was broken at the way she'd been treated, and it changed me all the way down to my core. It nearly made me want to cry, knowing how hard he had to have hit her to make her face look like that.

She looked like she still wanted to argue, but she eventually gave in. "I trust you..."

I COULDN'T DRIVE the armored truck around, so I told Steel to return to the Underground with the money and I'd take a cab.

Hadn't been in a fucking cab in so long.

When we were both in the back seat, I stared at her against the opposite window, looking outside, wearing my shirt with a bruised face. "Damien's place?" I wasn't sure where she wanted to go first, but I doubted she wanted to go home and be alone.

She kept her eyes out the window with her arms across her chest. "No. My apartment."

I gave the driver the address, and we took off. It was only a few blocks away, so the drive wouldn't be long. I caught the driver glancing in the rearview mirror, trying to get a better look at the half-naked woman sitting in the back seat. She'd been through enough, and the last thing she needed was another admirer. "Eyes on the road."

His hands swerved on the wheel slightly, and the car almost crossed the center line into the other lane.

I was surprised he'd picked us up in the first place. I was shirtless and covered in violent tattoos, while looking pissed off. If he'd paid better attention, he might've noticed the gun in the back of my jeans.

We pulled up to her apartment minutes later, and after I handed over the cash, we went into the building and up the stairs to her floor. Once we arrived at her apartment, I saw what they had done to her front door. They'd worked on the keypad lock until the mechanisms broke. The door was still slightly cracked, exactly as they'd left it when they took her away.

If this had been the setting of her kidnapping, I was surprised she wanted to come back.

She was the first one to walk inside. "I want to take a shower..."

I followed behind her and shut the door even though it couldn't lock anymore. She was usually candid with her thoughts, so she would have asked me to leave if she wanted me gone, but she didn't give me any directions. "Are you sure you don't want me to take you to Damien's?" He had a big place with plenty of rooms, and being under his roof would probably make her feel a lot safer than staying here.

"Yes." She walked into the bathroom and turned on the shower. "I'm fucking starving, but I've got to get this shit off me." She pulled my shirt off her body right in front of me and tossed it onto the back of the couch. "Thanks for letting me use it." She walked into the bathroom, leaving the door open. Maybe she was so used to being naked she didn't think twice about undressing in front of me.

I kept my eyes averted and didn't stare.

When she was in the shower, I pulled the shirt over my head and entered the doorway.

The shower curtain was closed, so I couldn't see her. Steam quickly filled the room and fogged the bathroom mirror. With my arms crossed over my chest, I leaned against the doorframe, my eyes down even though I couldn't see anything. "I'll get you something to eat. What do you want?"

"Anything. I haven't eaten in days."

I took a deep breath and felt my eyes squeeze shut when I heard about her mistreatment. I had no idea how long she'd been in that cage naked, starving, and beaten while I slept peacefully in my bed every night.

"I'd just eat something here, but I don't have anything." She raised her voice over the sound of the running water.

"I'll be back." There were a few places nearby I could walk to in five minutes.

Before I turned away, she spoke. "Hurry."

I could dissect her tone easily even though we hadn't spoken in weeks. She needed me to come back as quickly as possible, not so she could eat, but so I would be in the apartment with her again. "I will."

WHEN I RETURNED, she was still in the bathroom.

She sat on the edge of the tub with the shower curtain open, a blue towel wrapped around her body with her damp hair over one shoulder. Once her shower was over, it seemed to be the first thing she did, and she hadn't moved since.

I stepped into the bathroom with the plastic to-go bag and expected her to get up and move to the dining table, but she stayed still, looking at me like she expected me to bring the food to her. "Do you want to eat here?" Eating in a steamy bathroom sounded disgusting, but right now, she could do whatever she wanted and I wouldn't say a word.

She nodded.

I took the container out of the bag and handed it to her. It was a hamburger with French fries. Then I sat on the closed toilet and faced her.

She quickly opened the lid and started to eat. She shoved several fries into her mouth at once, picked up the burger in both hands and took an enormous bite like she really was starving. The few times I'd seen her eat, she was really methodical, trying to eat as little as possible. "You're not hungry?"

I kept my eyes on the floor so she wouldn't think I was staring at her in that thin towel. "No." There was so much acid in my stomach, I thought I'd never eat again. Thankfully, some of the bruising on her face had lessened after the shower, so those skin cells were dead and fell off, but I was still disturbed by what happened to her to make her so bruised in the first place.

And I was afraid something worse happened besides those bruises.

She ate the whole thing, even the crispy burned fries. The entire hamburger was gone, and once she'd sighed in satisfaction, I wouldn't have been surprised if she could've eaten more. She closed the box and left it on her lap like a pet she didn't want to lose.

"Why don't you want me to take you to Damien's?" I didn't understand why she'd want to stay in the same place she'd been taken from. No way she would feel safe. No way the memory wouldn't haunt her forever.

"I refuse to be run out of my own home." Despite everything she'd been through, the hysterical tears and deep bruises, she still had a resilient piece inside her. "Besides, I don't want him to see me like this..."

"It'll be a long time before those bruises fade, so he's going to know eventually."

She took a sharp breath like the thought of that conversation made her sick. "I'll worry about that later. Damien might be able to handle it, but my father won't." She blinked her eyes quickly as the tears welled up once more. "It'll make my father cry." She fidgeted with the box in her hands.

Guilt suddenly flooded through me when I remembered what I did to him, that I would've executed him if Damien hadn't outsmarted me. I had other things to think about right now, so I compartmentalized it. "I'll change your door for you. Get you one that people can't get past."

"Thank you..."

I leaned forward with my arms on my thighs, unable to believe I was sitting in a bathroom with her, that I'd gone to work like any other day but saw the most disturbing thing in my life...her in that cell.

"You can look at me." Her voice was quiet, delicate.

That was when I realized I wasn't averting my gaze to protect her privacy. I did it for myself, because looking at her made me want to die. "I don't want to." I concentrated on my fingers, tried to block out the memory of her face, but I felt the hot tightness in my chest, an inexplicable emotion I hadn't felt since I was a boy.

We sat together in the bathroom a long time, saying nothing. The steam eventually filtered out and her hair became completely dry. She finally stood up and walked out.

I followed behind her and watched her throw away the box before she went to her bedroom.

I assumed she was changing, so I stayed in the living room, looking at the front door as I considered what I would use to replace it. Maybe I could put her in a different apartment for the next week, just to give her real peace of mind.

She came back minutes later, in jeans and a shirt. The rest of her body didn't seem to have injuries, but her neck was bruised too, signs of where he'd strangled her.

I turned back to the door. "Do you want me to leave?" I didn't want to stay. I didn't wanna have to look at her and imagine what had happened to her. I was no saint, but I'd never been tempted to hurt a woman just because she stood up to me. I'd never been tempted to hurt a woman at all, actually. I punished those who deserved it without mercy and spared those with petty crimes. I couldn't comfort her, do anything for her, except try to under-stand why any man would damage that beautiful face.

"No." She came closer to me but kept a few feet between us.

She glanced at the door, which was now shut but unlocked. "I'll probably get a new place, even with the new door. But for now, this is all I have."

I would offer to let her stay with me, but after everything she'd been through, staying with some man she hardly knew was probably the last thing she wanted. And offering would also seem insensitive.

"I'm so tired." She ran her fingers through her hair and closed her eyes for a moment. "I haven't really slept since...I can't even remember. I don't know how long I've been gone, I don't know how many days passed, but I couldn't sleep the entire time."

"Then get some rest."

She turned to me, looking at me with her bruised eyes. "Could you stay...?"

I stared into her green eyes.

"I know you don't owe me anything, you've done enough, but if you could sleep on the couch, that would make me feel better..." She dropped her gaze slightly, like she was embarrassed to ask.

I'd do anything she wanted. "Yes." I turned away from her and headed to the couch. "Go get some sleep. I'll be here whenever you wake up."

She crossed her arms over her chest and nodded. "Thank you..." She turned around and slowly walked to her bedroom. Instead of closing the door, she left it open, like she wanted to be able to hear the sounds in the rest of the apartment. Her body made the mattress dip when she got inside, but then she was still. When she didn't move again, I knew she'd gone to sleep instantly.

❄

SHE SLEPT FOR THIRTEEN HOURS.

I stayed on the couch the whole time, and when I had phone calls and other things to do, I stepped into the hallway and took care of it so I wouldn't wake her. I didn't sleep much because I was too upset by what I saw. That shit would probably give me nightmares, which was saying something, because nothing scared me.

I stepped into the hallway and spoke to Steel on the phone.

He asked me about what happened. "So, what was that about?"

"That's a long story." The hallway seemed to be deserted. "Remember that woman I told you about?"

"The one you want but doesn't want you?"

"Yeah. She was in there, and I had to get her out..."

He was quiet for a bit. "Well, she's gonna want you now," he said with a chuckle.

After being beaten and god knows what else, that was the last thing on her mind. "I doubt it."

"You literally saved her life. She owes you."

"She doesn't owe me a damn thing." Even if she hadn't begged me to save her, I wouldn't have left her there. Even if it had resulted in a gunfight, I wouldn't turn my back on her.

"You really like this woman."

"I'm just disturbed by what I saw..."

"I can imagine. Need me to do anything?"

"Drop off my truck outside."

"You got it."

I'd promised Catalina something else, and since I was a man of my word, I would stick to it. "We have another problem."

"Yeah?"

"We have to get the rest of the girls out of there."

He was quiet as he considered what I'd just said. He probably had to make sure he heard me right because of the ramifications of such an insane request. "Why?"

I didn't want to give the real answer because it made me sound like a pussy, but a real man told the truth. "Because she asked me to."

"So what if she asked," he snapped. "That's impossible."

"Nothing is impossible for me." Would it be a pain? Would it cause problems? Yes. But I had to do it anyway.

"They are one of the biggest traffickers in the city. They have a lot of men and a lot of girls. Even if we tell them to shut down and they agree, we're gonna lose so much money. The men aren't gonna be okay with that shit."

That was the biggest problem. "I know. But I'll figure it out."

"Heath, come on," he said with a sigh. "If you want to get laid, just tell her you did it."

She would never know if I kept my word or not, unless she physically went back there, but that would never happen. "You know I won't do that."

"Well, you're going to cause a lot of problems. Vox has never made his hatred toward you a secret, and if you do this, he's going to take advantage of the situation. He'll try to take the throne from you."

He'd always been a problem, even when Balto was in charge. But I wasn't gonna let that man change my decision. "Then let him try." I kept my word, and maybe it was a stupid promise to make to a woman who didn't even want me, but I'd already done it. I couldn't take it back. "Bring me a door too."

Steel was confused by the change of subject. "What?"

"I'll send you the measurements. I need the toughest door you can find." I hung up.

SIX

CATALINA

For the first minute I was awake, I felt peace. Memories of the last few days hadn't hit me just yet, and it felt like a regular day, the sunshine coming through my window and heating my sheets. I stretched out as I released a deep breath and woke up.

Then I remembered everything that happened.

Wasn't a dream. Wasn't a nightmare.

I sat up and looked at the time on my nightstand.

It was three in the afternoon.

Damn, how long had I been asleep? Over twelve hours?

I got out of bed and pulled on a pair of pajama shorts before I opened the bedroom door and tiptoed into the living room. I wasn't sure if he was asleep, so I tried to stay quiet.

He sat in an armchair facing the window, the sunlight blanketing his entire body. His blue eyes were bright because of the sunlight, and he looked across the city like he was entertained by the view.

When I came closer, I walked normally so he would hear me approach. I noticed his hair was different, a little flatter than normal. "Did you take a shower?"

He still didn't look at me. "I hope you don't mind."

"Not at all." I looked down at the couch to examine it, and there was no sign that he'd been there at all. Then I looked at the front door, and instead of seeing the mahogany-colored door that had been there before, I saw a gray-green barrier that looked like it was made out of something stronger than wood. There were lots of heavy bolts along the side, making it intimidating. "You did this?"

He didn't turn to see what I referred to. "No one will be able to get through that. Will have to come through a window, but I installed an alarm system, so that way won't work either." He rose from the armchair and took his time walking toward me. He purposely didn't make eye contact with me, looking at the floor or the wall.

"Thank you..." I hadn't even asked him to do that. Now I didn't know what to say.

"Do you want me to stay?" His voice was so deep, slightly broken, like there was emotion bottled up inside him that he refused to release.

I wanted this enormous man to protect me every hour of the day. He was the only person strong enough to guard me from everything, to get me out of that basement just by raising his voice. I wanted him at my side forever, but I knew he had a life to live. He'd already done enough for me that I couldn't ask for another minute of his time. "No."

He moved to the door like he'd been dismissed.

"Wait."

He sighed quietly, like the last thing he wanted to do was be in that apartment with me. He continued to look at the door and wouldn't turn back to face me, to have a conversation like a normal person.

"Why won't you look at me?"

He turned my way slightly so I could see his expression, but he still didn't make eye contact. He closed his eyes for a few seconds like he needed a moment to gather his emotions. "Because I can't."

When I understood how much it hurt him to see me in pain, I was speechless. If we'd never met, I might never have escaped that dungeon. I might even be dead right now...or worse. I moved until I was directly in front of him, close to his body.

He reluctantly lifted his gaze to look at my face, and when he did that, his expression hardened, his eyes looked pained, and he pressed his lips tightly together to suppress a grimace.

"It doesn't hurt that much anymore." It was difficult to look at myself in the mirror for the first time, to see the damage inflicted on my face. It would take at least a month for it to clear up. Right now, I wasn't sure if makeup would be enough to hide it.

"That's not what haunts me the most."

I didn't expect a man like him to care so deeply, especially when he went down there all the time to collect his money, money made off those women. He didn't care about those other girls. Why did he care about me? "I'll be fine. When I fall on my ass, doesn't take me long to get up again."

Emotion moved into his eyes, like he was both hurt and pleased by what I said. "You're incredible, you know that?"

I was broken and damaged all the way down to my core, and it would take a while for me to bounce back. But I knew I would overcome it, not allow it to defeat me—with time. "You're the one who saved me. If you hadn't come down there…" I couldn't finish the sentence because my silence implied so much. "I don't even know how to thank you for what you did." I moved closer to him and rested my hand on his arm. "Thank you." I looked up into his gaze and felt my eyes water as so many emotions hit me at once. I'd survived something so horrific that words couldn't describe it. But this man came to my rescue.

"You don't need to thank me." He pulled his arm away like he didn't want me to touch him.

"And thank you for the food, the door, staying here so I could get some sleep…"

"You can call me if you need anything. I'll be here in fifteen minutes."

It was hard to believe, but this man had captured me and put me in a cage. It was hard to believe that he'd let me go and then we tried to resist our physical attraction to each other. And now he was in front of me, visibly moved by the pain I'd endured like he had a heart bigger than mine. "You'll save those other girls…?" If he didn't, I would have to ask Damien to do it, but I wasn't sure if he would help. That wasn't his arena.

"I'm a man of my word." His blue eyes were more beautiful than they'd ever been, so clear, like words on a page. His jawline was covered in stubble, a deep shadow that matched the dark strands on his head. His shoulders were so broad and strong, and when his shirt was off earlier, I could see just how powerful he was.

"How long have you been going down there and collecting money?"

Shame moved into his eyes. "Awhile."

He'd seen that scene many times, saw those naked girls in those iron cages, and he didn't blink an eye until now. "Then why did you agree?" He could've vetoed my request. He could've told me it couldn't be done.

He dropped his gaze for a few seconds before he took a deep breath and met my eyes again. "Because I feel differently about it now..." His eyes shifted slightly back and forth as they looked into mine, staring at me in a way he never had before. There was vulnerability, passion, and sympathy.

I didn't know what to say to that. "Thank you."

When there was nothing else to say, he prepared to leave. "You don't need to be scared, not because of the door and the alarm system. Don't be scared because no one is going to bother you again."

"Because of you?" I whispered.

He nodded. "Always be aware of your surroundings. Always be careful. But something like that will never happen again. I promise. They know you're off-limits."

"Who's they?"

He took a long time to answer. "The rest of them."

So, there were more.

"Don't let it change your spirit. Because you're damn perfect the way you are." He turned away and headed to the door.

I felt a pain in my chest the second he moved to depart. I felt like I was losing something special, and even though I could call him if I wanted to see him again, I still didn't want him to leave. My opposition to our relationship hadn't changed, and if anything, it increased because I wanted nothing to do with men in general right now. But I saw him differently. I saw him as the hero rather than the villain. I saw him as a man that any woman would be lucky to have. An emotional attachment had begun, and I knew it would always be there after what he'd done for me. So, I didn't want him to walk away, didn't want him to leave my side.

I grabbed his arm and gently pulled him back to me.

He turned his head to stare down at me, his expression guarded like he wanted to cover up every emotion he possessed. He prepared himself for the real world outside my door, prepared himself to be the Skull King once again.

I rose on my tiptoes and gripped his arms for balance as I leaned in and kissed him. I was probably undesirable with all these bruises. I wasn't the beautiful woman I used to be. Now, I was a victim of abuse and assault. I wasn't the strong and resilient woman that he remembered. I kissed him because I wanted to kiss him, to feel the strongest bond I'd ever felt with another person.

Instead of turning away or being disgusted by my appearance, he slid his hand under the fall of my hair and cupped the back of my head as he returned my affection as if all he wanted to do was share this kiss.

I felt that combustive chemistry again, felt that shiver start at the top of my spine and move all the way down to the bottom. I took a deep breath because I felt more than I had before, felt something much deeper than lust. The kiss was short and simple, not a make-out session like we'd had against my car. But there was more action packed into those three seconds than there could be in three minutes.

I lowered my feet to the floor and stepped back, my hands sliding down his arms until our fingertips were the last things in contact. Then they broke apart, making me turn cold like midnight in the Arctic.

After a final look, he turned around and walked out of my

apartment.

I DIDN'T LEAVE my apartment for a long time.

It wasn't just the fact that my face was swollen like a bruised peach; it was the fact that I had no interest in seeing other people. I'd be lying if I said I was over what happened. I was nowhere near over it.

I could still picture that basement so clearly in my mind. I still remembered exactly how it felt to be punched in the face like that. To be buck naked and afraid of being raped at any moment... There was no other suffering in the world like that.

Even if I was safe now, I wasn't safe from my own memories, my own feelings.

While I'd been asleep that night, he must have put groceries in my cabinets because I had enough food to last me several months. There was more food in my apartment now than at any other time in my life, even when I had people over. My fridge was stocked with fresh meats, veggies, and dairy products, and my pantry was full of bread and snacks. Maybe he did that on purpose because he knew I wouldn't want to leave the house for a long time.

I obviously couldn't perform at the ballet, so I said I had a serious strain of the flu and I would be out for at least three weeks. When Anna texted me and asked me to hang out, I gave her the same excuse.

No one could see my face right now.

It was even hard for me to look in the mirror sometimes. It was hard to see the way that man had punched me, the way he'd physically marked me with his abuse. I wanted the bruises to fade so I would really feel clean of him.

I spent my time watching TV, eating, napping. It was lonely being isolated in the apartment like this, and since I wasn't getting paid, I started to stress about paying my bills.

But instead of worrying about that, I should just be grateful that I was here. Those other girls might still be down there, so I shouldn't complain about the lack of digits in my savings account.

I had just left the kitchen and walked to the living room when a white envelope slipped under my door. It was thick, like a wad of cash had been stuffed inside. There was only one person who would shove money under my door, so I quickly opened the door and saw him halfway down the hallway. "Hey." I stared at his broad shoulders and muscled back, the way his red shirt fit him so snugly. His black jeans were tight on that strong ass and muscled thighs.

He stopped and slowly turned around, but he was visibly aggravated that he'd been caught.

I grabbed the envelope and broke through the tape holding it closed. Inside was an assortment of bills, adding up to at least five thousand euros. I stared at the cash before I looked at him down the hallway. "What's this?" I held up the envelope.

He rubbed the back of his neck with irritation before he walked back down the hallway to me. He had a masculine stride, the way his shoulders shifted slightly with his movements, the way his heavy arms hardly moved. His blue eyes were on me, and he stopped on the threshold instead of inviting himself inside. Rather than looking at the cash, he looked at my face, gauging how much I'd healed since we last saw each other. "I know you aren't working right now."

"So?" I handed the money back to him.

He gently touched my wrist and pushed my hand back. "I don't want it."

"Well, I don't want it either. I don't need it. You already bought me a bunch of groceries, and that had to be hundreds of euros. You've done enough for me. You don't owe me anything else."

When he slid his hands into his pockets, it was clear he wasn't going to take it. "It's a gift. Keep it."

"Look, I don't need your charity..."

"If you wanna show your gratitude, you'll take it."

My hand shook as I held the envelope, and I knew he had me bested. I would be indebted to him for the rest of my life, so he could manipulate me into doing whatever he wanted. I lowered my hand and kept the cash.

He hadn't smiled once since he'd rescued me. He used to make a lot of sarcastic remarks, give me a lot of boyish grins, but now he was stone-faced. "You've improved."

I absent-mindedly touched my cheek, noticing the way I wasn't so sensitive anymore. "I heal quickly..."

"Good." He gave me a slight smile before he turned away.

I didn't want to watch him go again. He gave me this money because he still wanted to take care of me even though I wasn't his problem. "Heath?"

He turned back around and look down at me.

"I think I'm gonna tell Damien what happened."

"Do whatever you want. But I said I'll take care of it."

"That's not what I meant...and you haven't yet?" It'd been a week, and I'd hoped all the girls had been released days ago.

"It's a lot more complicated than you understand."

"Then make me understand." I should only be kind to him

after what he did for me, but I couldn't stop the accusation from entering my tone. It was important to me that those women go free.

"Alright." He nodded to my door so we wouldn't continue this conversation in the hallway.

I walked inside first then tossed the money on the table.

He shut the door behind him. When he stepped closer to me, he slid his hands into his pockets. "The Skull King collects money from every underground business in the city. That's why I was there in the first place."

"I know that."

"If I put a stop to their business, that means we stop getting paid. And we're talking millions of euro here."

I crossed my arms over my chest, turning vicious. "We're talking about innocent people here."

He raised his hand to proactively silence me. "I get that. But if I shut them down, my men won't be happy."

"So? You can make money doing other things."

"And that's what I'm trying to figure out. If I take this away, I need a substitute. And if I go in there and shut them down, they could always retaliate. I know I'll win, but it would still create lots of other problems. And there're a few men under my rule who would love to take my place. The instant I'm unpopular, they might try to overthrow me."

"It sounds like a medieval drama."

"When you live without rules, it can be. So give me time to figure this out."

"The longer you wait…"

He lowered his hand. "I'm doing the best I can, and I will fulfill my promise to you." He looked at me with his fierce blue eyes, turning into the leader he claimed to be.

I backed off. "Alright." I knew he deserved my trust, the benefit of the doubt, but I was so passionate about this, it was hard for me to stay calm. "The reason why I want to tell Damien the truth is so he'll know what you did for me...and he'll drop this feud." If Damien knew that Heath saved my life, saved me from a life of slavery, he could leave the past in the past.

"You would have to explain how we knew each other to begin with. Because there's no way I would look through those bars and decide to save you out of the goodness of my heart. He knows that's not who I am."

"Well...then, I'll tell him how we know each other."

He shook his head slightly. "That I kidnapped you and intended to use you as a bargaining chip to kill him? And if you refused to cooperate, I would kill you?"

"But you let me go..."

"Doesn't matter. Doesn't change what I did in the first place."

"But if I talk to him, I could convince him to understand." My brother would do anything for me, listen to me even if he didn't like what I had to say. If he could hear the emotion in my voice, he would drop his need for vengeance.

He shook his head slightly. "I appreciate what you're trying to do, but I've done too many terrible things to him. I've done things you don't even know about. It's not gonna happen."

I bowed my head in disappointment.

He stood there for a long time, just staring at me. "Nothing has changed between us. Just because I saved you doesn't mean you are indebted to me. You know where you stand with your brother, and I respect that."

I didn't want to try to make this work because I owed him. I wanted more of him because now that I'd had a piece of him, I realized just how damn good he was.

"I won't bother you again."

My voice came out as a whisper. "You aren't bothering me..."

He averted his gaze. "I just wanted you to have that money. I know that you needed it. And you seem to be on the mend now, so I'll leave you alone." He turned around to walk out again.

I hated watching him leave. It was like watching someone special walk out of your life forever. Now I had a strong connection to this man, and every time he left, it hurt so bad. I moved into him, wrapping my arms around his waist, my face pressing into his back.

He stilled when he felt me. He was motionless for a long time, letting me squeeze him and hold him close. He eventually turned around so we could be face-to-face.

My arms moved around his neck, and I placed my forehead against his. Then I closed my eyes, hugging him more intimately than I'd ever hugged anyone else. How could I say goodbye to the man who saved my life? Say goodbye to the only person who knew what happened to me? I held him for a long time because I didn't want to let him go. It was easy to forget that he'd done unforgivable things to my family. How could a man so good be so bad?

He was the one to pull away first, like he had been the one crossing the line. "I'll take care of those girls. Consider it done." He gave me a final goodbye with those blue eyes before he left my apartment for the last time.

SEVEN

HEATH

"This is a fucking mistake." Steel was still trying to talk sense into me before I kicked the beehive. "You think the Skull Kings are going to agree with this plan? You're taking one of our biggest businesses and throwing in the garbage."

I sat beside him at the table, knowing I had no other choice. "We already bring in enough money. It's not gonna make that much of a difference in the long run."

"But you aren't substituting it with something better."

"Because there is nothing more lucrative than free labor." Slavery would always be the hottest commodity in the world. Running a business with no overhead and no taxes was the dream. "But we can't do this shit anymore. It's wrong."

"You think those assholes are going to care?"

I was going against the grain, and while I was annoyed with the endeavor, I was determined to make it happen. "We'll turn it into a brothel. Ash brings in high revenue with his girls. We can still make a ton of money doing this another way."

"But those girls aren't going to sign up for this. They're gonna want to leave."

"Then we'll find other girls. I'm sure Ash can help us with that."

Steel shook his head. "So, you take down this crew? Then what? We have other clients that do the same thing. Don't you think that's going to cause problems? The Russians are the only ones being punished for the same crime."

I'd anticipated that problem. "Then we'll ban it altogether."

Now both of his eyebrows rose up at the same time. "You've got to be kidding me."

"NO." Balto had banned the practice from the Skull Kings when he was in charge, and while some of the men were pissed, they got over it. But this undertaking was far more complex. "They can follow in the same footsteps. They'll all be on a level playing field, with fewer girls, they can charge more money. It's basic economics."

Steel still looked appalled. "This is not gonna be as simple as you think it is."

"Trust me, I don't think it'll be simple." I knew there would be resistance, anger. I knew some of my men would question their loyalty to me. I had to bring in more money quick. Otherwise, they would never forget it.

"Vox isn't gonna let this go. Even if you're successful, which I doubt, he's still going to come after you."

I shrugged. "Then let him come."

I SAT on the wooden throne, skulls carved into the black wood. I'd moved it to the main room when I took over. The beer was on the table beside me as I looked down at the room, seeing them all gathered around. They drank their beer in front of the fire, the pretty girls handing out drinks while the men talked loudly.

Steel looked at me from his seat at the bench, wearing a cold expression warning me not to go through with this, that I should let it go because there was still time to change my mind.

But I couldn't change my mind.

Vox was in the back with his crew, with dark hair, dark eyes, and a muscular size that rivaled mine. He spoke to his men quietly, and the moment I stood up, his attention shifted to me, anxious for whatever announcement I had to make. He was waiting for the perfect moment for me to trip so he could pound on me. He'd been the same way with Balto, and he would always be that way until he got what he wanted.

"You guys know I'm a capitalist. Entrepreneur. And sometimes a thief." My chair was at the top of the platform, so I could see everybody easily even if I were sitting down. "I found a better way to make money. I found a way to increase our profits by at least 50%."

The men started to clank their mugs against the table, their voices growing loud with excitement because something new was happening. Someone randomly shouted, "What is it?"

I continued. "One of our clients turned over his monthly royalties, and I was impressed by the amount. He's a pimp, and he's making a killing in Rome and now Florence. I've decided to do the same."

"Good. The girls are back!" Someone spoke from the corner of his table. He held up his mug and clinked it against his neighbor's.

"Fewer girls, actually." I arrived at the hard part, the difficult conclusion. "Increase the demand for a limited product, and you increase the price per unit. Trafficking will be outlawed in this country, and brothels will replace it. With the lower inventory of women, we'll charge ten times the amount."

That was when the men fell quiet, like they didn't agree with his new business venture at all. Vox looked exactly the same, but the murderous intent in his gaze showed how much he disagreed with my new vision.

"We start with Petrov's crew tomorrow. Consider it a remodel."

Questions started to fire off. "What do we do with the girls?"

"Offer them a job. A high-paying job. They won't be able to resist." Ash told me his girls were paid half the total profit, allowing them to live a lavish lifestyle that made being a whore worth it.

"And if they say no?"

I stared at the disappointed faces of my men. They wouldn't openly revolt against me, because disobedience was punished by death. But once I turned my back, they would whisper to each other, talk about the sudden changes in our organization. Hopefully they trusted me, and when they saw the money, they would forget about this. Hopefully this wouldn't grow into a bigger problem, resentment spewing into anarchy. "We let them go."

I TOOK the stairs down to the basement, arriving at four in the morning, completely unexpected. I went in alone, only my pistol in the back of my jeans. When I reached the table in the center of the room, Petrov sat there smoking a cigar, scrolling through his phone even though the internet must have been spotty way down here. "Why are you here?" He put his phone down then put his feet up on the other chair.

Instead of looking at him, I looked through the bars at the women either sleeping on their hay beds or leaning up against the opposite wall with wide eyes. I'd been down there so many times, but I'd never honestly cared about the women who were stuck there. "We need to talk." I sat in the chair across from him.

"I thought you would come back after what happened with Popov." He picked up the cigar and took a deep inhale before he released the smoke. Then he rolled a cigar across the table toward me, offering me one.

"No." I wouldn't pay for his death. Definitely wouldn't apologize for it. "I've decided to outlaw trafficking in this country." I wasn't the prime minister or any other government official, but I could do anything I wanted. This was the first item on my agenda. "That means you're going to turn this place into a brothel. The women who want to stay get paid. And they have the freedom to come and go as they please."

He left the cigar in his mouth without taking a breath. After his momentary shock, the smoke slowly drifted to the ceiling. Once he'd gathered his bearings, he pulled the cigar out of his mouth and smashed it into the ashtray. "Don't tell me this is all because of that stupid girl?"

"We can make a lot more money this way."

"More?" he said incredulously, his Russian accent growing thicker the more distressed he became. "There's no way we'll make more by abandoning this plan. None of the girls will stay. We'll have to let them go. We'll lose international buyers..."

"I don't care." In order to make this work, I had to put my foot down and hope it was enough. "With fewer women in our inventory, it'll drive up the asking price for every man who walks in here. You can make a lot more money doing it that way instead of selling these girls for a few bucks."

Petrov looked like he was debating whether he was going to kill me or not.

"I'm not taking your business away. I'm simply changing it. Improving it."

"You're improving shit, and you know it."

I pulled the gun out of the back of my jeans and set it on the table. I didn't even aim it at him, because the gesture seemed to be enough. "I've come prepared, Petrov. Whether you cooperate or not, the outcome will be the same." I grabbed the gun and clicked off the safety. "So, you have to decide. Do you want to be alive or dead?"

He breathed deeply while he ran his fingers through his hair, trying to process his frustration all the way down to his bones. He glanced at my gun again before he reached into his pocket and withdrew a ring of keys. He threw it at me. "You'd better be right about the money. Because if you're not, someone's gonna make you pay for it."

I went to the first cage and unlocked the door. Inside was a blond woman. She was up against the wall with her arms over her chest, and instead of looking at me like her captor or savior, she just stared like she didn't know what to do. "You're the guy who was here a few weeks ago..."

I opened the door. "You're free to go."

She didn't sprint out of there the way Catalina had She stayed in her spot, like it was home to her because she'd been there so long. "You rescued that other girl. She told you to come back for us, didn't she?"

Yes, Catalina was the only reason these women would go free. I had the muscle to get it done, but she was the one who had the heart to make it happen. I wasn't the hero. She was. "Yes."

EIGHT

CATALINA

Once my face had improved enough, I started to go out again. My makeup successfully masked the bruising, so my injuries weren't visible under the stage lights. Sometimes people asked if there was something wrong, as if they definitely noticed the discoloration around my eyes, but I always said it was a side effect from having the flu.

The girls asked me to go out a few times, but I always said no. I knew I shouldn't be afraid to live my life, especially after Heath told me nothing like that would ever happen again, but it was just too soon.

I wished I could explain that to my friends.

After being alone in my apartment for a few weeks, I felt more comfortable in my home. My new door was good enough to protect a bank with a vault full of money, and my alarm system was always on, whether I was at work or at home. It gave me the peace of mind I needed so I wouldn't have to search for another apartment. That was a blessing because I really couldn't afford much else. My lease had rent control, so until I could afford another place, I was staying put. But that seemed unlikely because I would never make much as a dancer.

Heath's money got me by so I wouldn't have to stress about my bills and necessities. It was more than enough for anything I could possibly need, and I hated enjoying all that the cash provided. It did make me feel better, made me grateful he gave it to me. I never took charity from anybody, always stood on my own two feet. My father had offered me money many times, but I always declined. Damien had offered to buy me an apartment that was much nicer than what I had, but I declined that too.

But I held on to Heath's money. I told myself he didn't need it, that if he went to every underground organization and collected bags stuffed with cash, he probably had more money than I could even understand. He was probably richer than Damien and Hades combined. He probably found this cash at the bottom of a drawer somewhere.

As weeks passed, I improved enough that I didn't need makeup at all. My face started to fade back to its original color, olive-toned skin with a slight fairness. All the swelling had gone down, and the darkness around my eyes vanished. Now, I started to look like me again.

Feel like me again.

I wanted to know if Heath had done what I asked, and I considered calling him a few times to check if those girls were free, but I also didn't want to talk to him again...because I knew what would happen. Now that I'd had space from him, it gave me the opportunity to remember why I'd turned him down in the first place, to remember what was important to me. Even if we just had a short-term fling that lasted a few weeks, it was still a bad decision. That was why I didn't call, why I had to trust that he'd fulfilled his promise.

"YOU SEEM DIFFERENT." Anna looked at me across the table. She grabbed the folder with her bill at the edge of the table and slipped her card inside.

I'd blanked out for a second, so I hadn't been paying attention to the last fifteen seconds of our conversation. I picked up my bill and used the money Heath gave me to pay for it. "In what way?"

"I don't know...more serious?"

It'd been a month since I'd been down in that basement. It was a traumatic experience, being taken from my bed in the middle of the night and placed in a dirty cell. Waking up completely naked was the worst part, knowing someone stripped off all my clothes when I wasn't even aware of what was going on. Then that bastard stepped into my cage and beat me senseless. My bruises had healed, so I shouldn't let my emotional scars mark me forever. I needed to carry on, continue to be me. When that man had assaulted me in the bathroom, I'd told myself it was meant to happen because I could handle myself. That attitude changed once I was in the basement. But now, when I looked back on it, I wondered if my first instinct was right. Because if it hadn't, those girls wouldn't be free.

If it were somebody else, it might not have turned out that way. That was what I chose to tell myself to get through it, to consider it an accomplishment rather than a regret. Getting my ass beaten was worth it if it saved lives. "I think I'm still recovering from that cold..."

"That was like a month ago. And wasn't it the flu?"

"Yeah. Same difference."

Anna handed the tab to the waitress so she could charge the card. "Uh, not the same thing at all..."

I needed to change the subject quickly. "What's new with

you?"

She shrugged. "I've had a lot to do at the hotel since Sofia went on maternity leave. She's due any day...really exciting. Sometimes I think Hades is more excited than she is."

"That's sweet." I'd been around Hades a lot for the last ten years, and it was interesting to watch him evolve from a heartless man into a loving husband and devoted father. "You and Damien talk about having kids?"

Her demeanor completely changed at the question. She had been happy a few seconds ago, but now a heavy rain cloud cast a shadow over her face. "Yes. But I'm not sure how easy it will be for us to conceive since I had a miscarriage with Liam."

"I'm sorry, Anna." There was nothing I could say to heal that kind of wound.

The waitress set the bill at the edge of the table and walked away.

Anna grabbed the paper and signed the receipt. "You'd think I would get over it because it'd been so many years now, but I never have. I don't think I ever will."

"You're not the only woman to feel that way. And I wouldn't be afraid to have children in the future. Miscarriages are common, a lot more common than people realize. So, don't assume the worst."

She nodded.

"Does that mean you'll get married soon?" This was the question I'd been waiting to ask. I had been waiting for the perfect time to strike.

She released a slight chuckle. "Well, that's up to him."

"Bullshit, it's up to him." I shook my head dramatically. "If you want to get married, tell him that. Or ask him yourself."

She released a chuckle. "No...Damien would *not* like that."

"So, then are you ready?" This was the answer I needed.

She shrugged. "I wanted to wait awhile before I got remarried, mainly out of principle, but I've been living with Damien for months now and it just feels right. My previous life with Liam...it's like it never happened. It's strange. I feel like Damien is the person I was supposed to be with all along."

That was the most romantic thing I'd ever heard. "That's heavy stuff."

"I wish I could take it slower, but I don't think I can control what we have. There's no hurry, but I'm in a rush to be with this man forever, like we're going to run out of time or something."

"It took you so long to really be together, so maybe you're scared something's gonna happen...but it's not."

"Yeah." She gave a slight smile and returned her card to her purse. "Whether he asked me now or later, it doesn't matter. I'll say yes. For now, at least we're together."

MY FATHER WAS an excellent chess player, and he taught me everything I knew. But I had youth and a strategic mind, so it was easy to kick his ass every single time. But since I was a good daughter, I threw the game half the time so he wouldn't feel defeated.

He stared at the board as he tried to decide his next move. I already knew what he was going to do because he only had two good options. But I had a rebuttal against each one, and the result was the same.

I'd win.

That was why I was such a good chess player.

I knew all the moves of my opponent before he made them, so I was always ready to demolish them. It was like being a warlord, anticipating your opponent's moves and destroying them the second they took a step. He continued to stare at the board without blinking.

I glanced at my watch on my wrist to see the time. "Daddy, come on."

He held up his hand to silence me.

I rolled my eyes and looked out the window.

"I'm an old man, sweetheart. Takes me a lot longer to think things through than it does for you." His once-handsome face was covered with wrinkles, and his dark hair had turned gray once he hit seventy. He was still a good-looking man, but his youth had vanished completely. It was hard to see him like that because I knew he didn't have much time left on this earth, at least not with his full faculties. He was much older than my mother and had us late in life. It was one of the reasons I wanted to have my first kid at thirty, to be young enough to enjoy them as adults.

It was also the reason I would never marry an older man. I wanted a husband who would be around for as long as possible. Unfortunately, I did find older men much more attractive than men my age, but I would keep looking until I found someone decent. "You aren't an old man, Daddy."

"Stop interrupting me."

"You're taking ten minutes to make a move when you know you're gonna lose anyway."

He finally made his move, the better choice of the two.

And then I demolished him. "Checkmate."

He was visibly disappointed. "I never should've taught you. I've created a monster."

"No. You've created another you. When I have my children, I'll teach them this game, and they'll kick my ass when I'm your age."

He smiled slightly, pleased by that legacy.

Damien walked inside. "Who won?"

"Your sister," he answered. "But I'll get her next time." He slowly rose out of his chair and came to my side of the table to kiss me on the head. "Good game, sweetheart." Then he moved away to the dining table, where Patricia had placed coffee and muffins.

Damien took the vacated chair. "You didn't let him win?"

"Not this time." My hair was in a messy bun, and I played with the earring that hung from my lobe. My father and brother had never noticed anything unusual about my face, and since my brother was so attentive to detail, the only reason he didn't comment on it now was because my face had truly returned to normal. He would have been able to tell if I were trying to cover up something with pounds of makeup.

"How was lunch?"

"Good. So, Sophia is going to pop soon?"

He shook his head slightly at the description. "She's supposed to go into labor in a few days. If not, they'll induce her."

"Hades must be excited."

"I guess Sofia is really uncomfortable right now, so I think he's more excited for that to be over, to be honest." He smiled slightly, like he was remembering a story Hades had told him.

"Anna and I talked about marriage and babies and stuff..."

His eyes narrowed. "What? Are you gonna keep me in suspense?"

"Yep." I continued to play with my earring and let the silence stretch out, loving the fact that I had something to hang over his head.

He crossed his arms over his chest, shaking his head slightly with irritation.

"Okay, I've let you suffer enough... She's ready."

He leaned forward, his eyes a little wider with excitement. "She said that?"

"She said she was trying to take it slow, but it's too hard. She believes you're meant to be and it seems stupid to wait out of principle."

He leaned back into the chair and didn't give any obvious reaction, just the subtle cues in his eyes and lips. He looked away for a second, thinking about something that made his eyes light up a bit. "Well, that's good news since I already have a ring."

"You do?" I threw my hands down onto the table, making my palms smack against the surface. "Oh my god, show me. Princess cut? Solitaire? How many carats is it? It's got be at least three."

He rolled his eyes and pulled out his phone. "Here's a picture." He slid the phone toward me.

"Why do you have a picture of it on your phone?" I asked him incredulously. "If she sees this, it's going to be obvious what it is. You don't even need to be smart to figure that out." I waved the phone in front of his face. "Are you stupid?"

"We don't have that kind of relationship," he said, speaking confidently. "She would never go through my phone like that, and I would never do that to her either."

"Damien, accidents happen."

When he grew frustrated, he pushed the conversation forward. "Just shut up and look at the picture." I grabbed the phone and brought it closer to my face. I tapped my fingers against the screen and spread them apart to pull the image closer, to inspect the diamond with a trained eye. I examined it like a jeweler. "White gold...solitaire...two carats. It's nice..."

"It's nice?" he said in offense. "That's a beautiful ring. What's wrong with it?"

"It's a little small." I put the phone down because I'd gathered all the data I needed. "I thought you were rich?"

"I am rich. But she's not the kind of girl to walk around with a ten-carat diamond ring." He raised his voice in protest, knowing my father was practically deaf at this point and wouldn't have any idea what we were talking about.

"How do you know? Have you asked her? Has business been bad? Please don't tell me you guys are gonna have to move in with me..."

He pressed his lips tightly together, annoyed with me. "There's nothing wrong with my business. And I'd rather be homeless than move in with you."

"Good. I'd rather you be homeless too."

He released a deep sigh, his nostrils flaring.

"Sofia has a huge ring. That diamond is bonkers. This looks like fake jewelry that came out of a gumball machine. Do you shop at H&M?"

He snatched the phone from the table. "It does not. And since when did you become so materialistic?"

"I'm not. But you're like, what, a billionaire? Can't you buy her a big-ass ring? Open your wallet a little bit..."

"Annabella isn't the type of woman that cares about the size of the diamond. She cares about the man giving it to her. She'll love it."

"Fine." I leaned back in the chair and crossed my arms over my chest.

Damien opened the photo on his phone again and stared at it before his eyes were back to mine, like he wasn't as confident anymore. Then he released a deep sigh. "Fine, what do you think I should get?"

"How about we just go shopping? Anna is going to be my sister-in-law, so I don't want her walking around without a big-ass rock."

He put his phone back into his pocket. "Alright. But when you fall in love and the guy asks you to marry him, you aren't going to care what the ring looks like. If it's not a huge diamond, you're still going to be just as happy."

I shrugged. "Maybe. But if he was rich and knew me at all, he'd probably know what to get me."

"Why does it matter to you?" he asked, turning serious.

I considered the question and the best option for a response. "It's hot," I said with a shrug. "If I'm walking around with a huge rock, every guy who looks at me is gonna steer clear because they'll know I belong to one hell of a man. And every woman who looks at my hand is gonna be jealous, especially if she sees us together, because she'll know that fine man is really devoted to me, ain't gonna cheat on me, ain't gonna even look the other way."

Damien was quiet for a while as he considered everything I'd just said. His face was a blank canvas, as if he was replaying my words in his head. But it must've hit close to home, because he rose out of his chair. "Let's go now."

I grinned and followed him out the door.

NOW THAT SIX weeks had come and gone, my life had returned to normal. I would never forget what happened because the memory still came back to me in my nightmares, but I definitely started to move on. Staying at home and moping around didn't help at all. When I got back to work, hung out with my friends, spent time with my family, those things seemed to help me the most. I hadn't been with anyone else since before the incident, but I thought it was time to get back on the horse.

I pushed Heath from my thoughts even though he'd never really left. As time went on, his presence in my mind begin to fade, and there were days when I didn't think about him at all. But he always popped up again...eventually. Sometimes I thought about him when I was in the shower because I remembered that painful conversation in the bathroom. If I ever ate a hamburger, I remembered how he'd brought one to me when I was starving. Whenever I opened that white envelope stuffed with cash, I remembered him.

But in time, I would forget.

After a performance, the girls and I went out. It was my first time going to a bar since that night of the confrontation in the bathroom. I was in a short purple dress with my hair in curls, and it took me an hour to settle down after we arrived. I was aware of my surroundings more than usual, checking to see if there were any creeps similar to the one who cornered me in the bathroom. As if danger lurked everywhere, I kept my eyes peeled, and I guarded my drink like someone might spike it.

Tracy noticed my behavior. "Are you okay?"

"Absolutely." I knew my answer was a little too enthusiastic, as if I was trying to compensate for my unease. "Why?"

"Because there're so many hot guys staring at you, and you haven't noticed."

I only noticed the men who looked like a potential danger to me, and they didn't seem interested in me at all. It made me forget the whole reason why I was there in the first place. "I guess I've been out of the game. I was sick for so long, and I just needed some time to get my feet back in the water."

She patted my back. "Well, jump in. The water's warm."

AFTER A FEW DRINKS were in my system, I wound up at a table with a nice guy. He was tall, blond, with fair skin and blue eyes—not my usual type, but nice enough. He had a position in a hotel, accounting or something, and he was absolutely nonthreatening.

I drank from my glass and tried to focus on the conversation, because he seemed to be really into me, finding my ballet career interesting rather than quizzical. We shared a few laughs, got along pretty well, and I thought my reintroduction to the dating world wasn't bad. But I couldn't imagine telling this guy what had happened to me six weeks ago. I couldn't imagine telling anyone that, even if I were in a serious relationship. I wasn't sure why.

A dark energy filled the room, like something dangerous was about to happen. I could feel the heavy stare on my face, just couldn't figure out where it was coming from. The guy kept talking, but I pulled away from the conversation to locate the source of my unease.

That was when I saw him.

He stood at the edge of the bar with his body facing me. He didn't have a drink, so he seemed to be waiting for the bartender to finish making his cocktail, probably something with vodka. He was in a gray shirt, the sleeves tight on his biceps and triceps, and he wore black jeans. He stared at me without blinking, his blue eyes beautiful and terrifying.

That was when I withdrew from the conversation entirely. This man was no longer interesting to me at all. It didn't matter how nice he was. It didn't matter that he seemed completely harmless. Seeing Heath stirred a million emotions inside my chest, making me feel unbridled lust, overwhelming longing. Memories of our previous kisses came back to me, the feeling of his hard shaft between my legs. He was a flavor of man I had never tasted before, and now that I had the best, it was hard to settle for anyone else.

When the bartender handed him his drink, he held it around the top of the glass and headed my way, right for my table with clear intentions.

My date kept talking. "We're right next door to the Tuscan Rose, so we always have to compete with this chain that's been around for decades..."

"I'm sorry, but could you excuse me?" I thought it would be better if I got rid of him before Heath arrived and scared the shit out of him.

He stared at me quizzically, like he had no idea what he did wrong. "Did I say something...?"

Heath reached the table and set his glass down, marking his territory in silence.

The guy looked up at him, and that was all it took for him to vacate the seat. "Nice talking to you." He grabbed his drink and left, and once he was out of my line of sight, I didn't think about him again.

Heath took a seat and stared at me. He didn't apologize for interfering with my date, probably because he knew I wasn't enjoying it anyway. Resting his thick arms on the table, he watched me with an intense expression, his diamond skull ring on his right hand. It was so flawless that it illuminated the area, refracting tiny particles of light.

Now that my eyes were on him, I couldn't look at anything else, think about anything else. My pulse quickened in my neck, and I discreetly crossed my legs because the overwhelming need to change my position came over me. I was suddenly both uncomfortable and so comfortable at the same time. It was refreshing to be with a man without having to talk. He could handle silence, feel my emotions rather than question me about them.

After what felt like minutes, he spoke in his sexy, deep voice. "I took care of it."

Without needing to question him, I knew exactly what he referred to. "Thank you." The second I saw him, my eyes had latched on his. Even now, I didn't look away. Now that this man was in the room, I didn't care about anyone else. Without thinking twice about it, my hand moved to his, and I locked our fingers together.

He didn't react or look down at our joined hands. He kept his eyes on me, staring at me like there was no other woman in the room who deserved his attention...except me. He gave me a gentle squeeze in return.

I knew I didn't want to go home with anyone else in that bar—or in the whole world, actually. When I wasn't around him, I could forget about him, but the second we breathed the same air, I was lost. My emotions took over, my blinding need consumed me. My relationship with him was so complicated, because a part of me still resented him for what he did to me, but I wanted him still...wanted him so much.

I brought his hand to my lips and kissed his knuckles. His hands were so big that a single one could cover both of mine at the same time. I kissed each knuckle, physically thanking him for what he had done for me.

He watched me, his eyes still focused on mine.

I knew every woman in the room wanted to be me, was disappointed they didn't even get the opportunity to buy him a drink. He came right over to me, and this time, I didn't let him slip from my grasp. I touched him because I wanted everyone to know he was off-limits, at least for tonight.

He pulled his hand away then reached under the table to grab my chair. Effortlessly, he dragged it across the floor toward him, maneuvering it around the corner of the table so I would be right by his side. He was so heavy in his chair that it didn't move, only mine. Once I was in place, his arm slipped around my shoulders and his fingertips lightly touched my hair.

My face moved into his neck, and I breathed in the scent of him, the mixture of his cologne, his laundry detergent, and his soul. My hand went to his thigh, and I gripped him through his jeans, feeling just how muscular and strong he was. I didn't know what had come over me. I was so relieved to see his face, to be with a man I had forged such a strong bond with. It was like being with an old friend, but so much more. "I missed you..." I whispered into his ear even though no one could overhear us. We were in our own world where there were no other people, no music.

He turned his face closer to mine, his cheek against my lips. "I missed you too."

I sat that way with him for a long time, just appreciating the affection. I loved being smothered by his large size, feeling a strong man wrapped around me like an indestructible cage. I pressed my forehead against his neck and just sat there. It'd been over a month since we'd last spoken so there was plenty to talk about, but I still didn't have a single word to say.

Neither did he.

WE SAT TOGETHER FOR HOURS, saying nothing, and by the time it was almost one in the morning, most of the people had already left. My friends went home because I was obviously busy, and the only people who remained were the people who hadn't found anyone or who had nothing to go home to.

He pulled his face away slightly to look me in the eye, which he hadn't done much since we were so close together. "You look beautiful." His hand slid across my cheek and into my hair, keeping it from my face so he could take a good look at me.

"Thank you."

"I miss being able to look at you." With his intense gaze, he showered me with his focus, looking at me in a way every woman dreamed about.

"Me too."

"How are you?" He asked the question like we were friends, like he cared about my well-being, like he had been thinking about me even when we were no longer in each other's lives.

"It took a long time for me to get out of the house. This is my first night out..."

"And how did it go?"

"Rough in the beginning. But it ended pretty great." My hand squeezed his thigh. "How about you?"

"Fine."

"Releasing those girls cause any problems...?" He told me it would be complicated because of the reaction of his men, because of the way his operation ran, but if there were problems, he probably wouldn't tell me about them.

"I had to change their business plan and it's taking some time, but I think it's working. Now I have to do it with everyone else..."

"What do you mean, everyone else?"

He held his drink with one hand. "They aren't the only business in the city..."

My mind tried to process what that meant. "So, you intend to stop them all?"

He nodded.

I was speechless for a moment. "You're doing that for me?"

"No. I told you I feel differently about it now."

"But that's because of me..."

He never replied.

I leaned into him and placed a kiss on his neck, my attraction deepening. His actions didn't vindicate his crimes, didn't fix what he did to Damien, but it still resonated all the way down to my soul. "Thank you." We'd been holding each other close all night at the bar, but Heath hadn't asked me to go home because he assumed my answer was still no.

I wasn't sure what my answer was anymore.

He finished his drink and left the glass on the table. "I should go." He sat still for a moment, not pulling away, like he was waiting for me to object. "Do you want me to walk you to your car?"

I was disappointed that he was going to leave, take his touch away and give it to somebody else, but there was no other outcome for us. Without really thinking about what I was saying, I answered. "No, I'm parked right outside." I'd managed to grab a spot at the curb right outside the entrance.

He was still for a while, not knowing what to do other than leave me there. "Alright." He rose to his feet and pulled his body away from mine. He didn't look at me again before he walked out of the nearly deserted bar and through the front doors.

I stayed in my chair and felt so empty inside once he was gone. I was back to my usual existence, feeling numb and empty. Nothing excited me; everything was normal. He was the only thing that kicked me into gear, that made all my nerves tingle with electricity. That man was the only one who could bring me to life anymore. He was a spectrum of color in a sea of gray.

I turned back to the door when I knew he was gone, but an impulse overtook me, a desperation so profound that I stopped thinking about the consequences, the morality of the situation. I just wanted what I wanted...unapologetically.

I left my seat and ran after him.

I'd probably waited too long, sat in the chair and did nothing when I should have taken action. He was a fast walker, and I had no idea where he'd parked. I could call, but that somehow felt shameful. I left the bar and emerged onto the sidewalk. I looked to the right first but saw nobody. There were only a few cars on the street, but none of them was his truck. Then I turned to the left.

He stood there with his hands in his pockets, regarding me with fierce coldness. Six foot three of all man, he carried himself like a king, with a strong back and shoulders so heavy only a powerful man could carry them. "Took you long enough."

His arrogance was infuriating, but in that moment, I didn't care. I ran to him in my heels, jumping up into his arms because I knew he would catch me. I hit his chest like a car crashing into a concrete wall, and I wrapped my arms around his neck. My lips crushed against his, and I felt a surge of joy flush through me. It was everything I wanted in a kiss—lust, trust, and a fierce passion. I knew I would never find it anywhere else, and I should just enjoy it before it was gone. Between our kisses, I spoke. "You asshole..."

MY HEART WAS BEATING SO WILDLY, I thought it would explode out of my chest and onto the floor. It was the feeling I'd had as a teenager, being so nervous to kiss a boy, to do things that were forbidden because I was too young. But I felt those sensations a million times stronger with this man.

He stood in front of me at the foot of my bed, his hand snaking up my back to the zipper at the center of my spine. When his fingers grasped it, he pulled down slowly, going over my ass until he reached the very bottom. Instead of kissing me, he chose to stare at me, making the arousal much more intense. He wasn't afraid of eye contact, whether it was a sign of aggression or intimacy. When my dress was loose, he pushed the straps over my shoulders and allowed gravity to do the rest.

It fell off my body into a pile around my ankles. So I wouldn't trip, I pushed it aside, and now I was nearly naked but somehow completely comfortable. My tits were pointed because of the nerves and excitement, and my tummy was tight because I wanted to look as sexy as possible.

He'd been in my presence when I was naked before, but he'd never looked. But now that he'd been explicitly invited, his eyes slid along to my neck, to my chest, and went all the way down to my thighs. And then the sexiest moan came from his throat, a moan only a real man knew how to make. He didn't have to tell me he thought I was beautiful, didn't need to describe what he was about to do me. That little noise was more than enough to explain every single thought inside his brain. He grabbed his shirt and pulled it over his head.

I'd seen him shirtless before, but I hadn't really paid attention because I was in the midst of the most traumatic moment of my life. My gaze dropped, and I examined him the way he examined me, looked at the dark tattoos that covered his rock-hard body. The deep color of the ink couldn't mask how strong he was, his massive pectoral muscles and his chiseled, tight abs. I wasn't sure what was sexier, his ink or his body. My hands flattened against his abs and slowly moved up over his powerful chest. My fingers felt resistance immediately, because there was nothing under his skin except muscle. I moved into him and tilted my chin up to look into his gaze. "Just tonight..." I couldn't resist him anymore, and I wanted to have this moment, to submit to the lust that had drowned us both. We could have an incredible night together and then move on, not have to spend our time wondering what could have been.

He didn't say anything. Not a word. He unfastened his jeans and got them loose before he pushed them down along with his boxers, sinking lower and lower over his tight stomach, revealing the thick vein that traveled down past his hips to his crotch. And then his big fucking cock came out.

"Oh fuck..." It was even bigger than I'd imagined, bigger than what I'd thought I felt when he ground against me. Dicks were dicks, nothing spectacular, but his cock was damn beautiful, like the inspiration for every dildo in the world.

When his bottoms hit the floor, he kicked them away. "We'll see."

The last thing I was going to do was argue with the sexiest man in the world while he looked like that, like a Greek god came to life from marble just to please me. He didn't just look kingly, but he behaved like a king, owned the room like one.

His hands went to my hips, and he grabbed my black thong before he pushed it over my hips and ass and down my legs. He sank down with the material, his face right at my stomach. He pulled it away from my ankles so I could step out without getting tangled in the fabric. Then he placed his massive palms over my stomach, his fingertips wrapping around my rib cage. He squeezed me like he wanted to feel me, feel exactly how my frame was built, and then he dragged his hands down over my hips, over my ass, down my long legs to my knees.

I'd never been touched like that.

One of his powerful arms grabbed my leg and placed the other over his shoulder.

I clutched his broad shoulders for balance because I thought I was going to topple over having to stand on one foot.

Then he pressed his mouth between my legs and kissed me.

Oh my god.

I closed my eyes at just the first touch, feeling those powerful lips kiss my clit like they knew exactly what they were doing, like they had pussy for breakfast every day. I winced because it both felt good and bad, bad because I hadn't been touched like that in so long my nerves were too sensitive. I grabbed his shoulders, and my nails clawed into his tough skin.

When I opened my eyes, I saw the large mirror I had propped against the wall. It was the place where I tried on clothes and examined my appearance before I left the house. Now, I saw a gorgeous man on his knees, kissing my sacred place, his powerful hands supporting me and gliding over my body. His hand squeezed my thigh and then my ass before moving up and touching my stomach. His ass was muscular and tight, and his back was so ripped, he looked like the strongest man in the world.

I stared at the most erotic scene in my life, and I could hardly believe I was living it. I was even turned on by my own appearance, the blush in my cheeks, wetness in my eyes, the way my mouth couldn't stay closed because I was breathing so hard. My hand dug into his hair, and I moaned while he did amazing things to me. Every time I took a deep breath, my tits rose and pointed to the sky. My stomach tightened, and my little abs became more distinct. My skin was tanned and olive-toned naturally, much darker than his beautiful fair skin.

"Heath...my fucking god." It had already started off unbelievable, that hard mouth so good against my body. He had a shadow of hair over his jawline, and I could feel the coarse hairs rub against my cunt when he kissed me, and I liked that even more. I loved feeling a man's facial hair against the most erotic part of my body. I could tell I was already wet, ready for that fat dick whenever he wanted to give it to me.

He kissed me for a while, doing it slowly like he wanted this to be foreplay, not the first climax he gave me. Sometimes he pressed into me harder just to tease me, but the rest of the time, he was soft, pulling me into his face and grinning as I ground against him.

It was so fucking good.

He slowed down his kisses until he gave me a few final embraces, gentle pecks that told me he was finished and ready to move on.

Couldn't wait to see what came next.

He stabilized me while moving my leg off his shoulder before he rose to his feet and looked down at me again, a distinct shine to his lips that came from me. His hand slowly slid into my hair, and he grasped a handful as he guided me backward to my bed. His other arm gripped my ass as he brought our faces close together, our foreheads touching. His hand squeezed me over and over as he let the intensity grow, made me wait for the moment when he finally kissed me.

Then he did.

I could taste myself, but I didn't mind. I just got to taste his own desire for me, think about the way he'd just kissed me like there was nothing else he wanted more than to adore my most private area. He wasn't afraid to please a woman the way she liked, to do something most men avoided at all costs. He did it...and he fucking loved it.

His arm gripped my waist as we moved toward the bed. He supported my frame with his arm, holding me as he lowered himself down with a single arm. He positioned me on the bed underneath him, sliding his arm out of the arch in my back once I was in place.

His thighs opened mine as if he intended to take me like this, his heaviness making my mattress creak because it was old. With every move he made, I could feel his weight, feel two hundred and thirty pounds of pure man on top of me. He opened my legs wide like he needed the room to get his fat dick inside me.

He helped himself to my nightstand and fished out a condom as if he already knew they were there. With experienced movements, he ripped into the package and rolled on the condom that was a little tight for his big dick.

It only took him a few seconds, but it felt like an eternity. I grabbed his arm and pulled him on top of me, my lips landing on his. I cupped his face and brought him close to me, our lips moving together with perfect languidness.

His arms hooked behind my knees once his dick was pressed to my entrance. Then he slowly inched inside, pushing deeper and deeper into my wetness, through my tightness, and moved until there was nowhere else for him to go.

I stopped kissing him because I needed a moment to breathe, a moment to appreciate all the sensations inside me. I'd never been stretched like that, never had a man so big inside me. I didn't even know dicks could be this big. "What a man..." My fingers were still in his hair, and I looked him in the eye as I gave him the compliment.

He stilled inside me and looked into my face, his muscular chest pressing me deeper into the sheets. There was a bit of hair in the center of his pecs, exactly as I liked. He held my gaze for a while, as if he wanted to look at me and enjoy the victory before he actually started to fuck me. I'd told him no so many times, but he never gave up on me. He knew I would cave, waited patiently until the moment I could no longer resist this fine piece of man.

He rocked his hips inside me, his big dick sliding in and out of my small channel. I was an average woman with an average size, but he was so large in every way that he made me feel tiny. Sometimes he pushed inside a little too hard and it made me wince because he pressed right up against my cervix, but I enjoyed being with a man who was big enough to even hurt me.

When he got used to my body, he never made me wince again, his dick memorizing exactly how deep I was. His neck bent down, and he kissed me as he rocked, exchanging a few hot kisses before he pulled away to look at me, to see the burn in my cheeks, emotion in my eyes. Then he kissed me again, breathing into my mouth, giving me his tongue.

Whenever I brought a man home, the sex was usually disappointing. And even when it wasn't, it still wasn't anything like this. He fucked so good, he seemed like a professional, like I'd thrown a stack of cash at him and paid him to do this. I already felt the small explosion begin at the bottom of my belly, but it took me a second to recognize it because I couldn't believe that it was happening so quickly, that he could bring my body and mind to the threshold within seconds. My hands reached for his chest for something to hold on to, and my nails slightly dragged down as the explosion hit me, making my toes squeeze and cramp, making my hips buck against him uncontrollably. I bit my bottom lip so hard, I nearly drew blood. But the screams inside my chest were unable to be suppressed, so I moaned loudly for him, coming with such intensity, it was an out-of-body experience. My head slammed back onto the pillow, and I dug my hand into my hair because I was writhing, making sounds I didn't even know I could produce. Tears began because it felt so good to release like that, felt so good I thought I would die.

He'd made it happen in less than a minute.

It was a long climax, nearly thirty seconds of unbridled goodness. My nails released from his chest, and I lightly touched his abs as I came down from the stars. I looked into his face above me, and the moisture had built up in my eyes so it had to escape as two tears running straight down to my ears.

Watching me come turned him on but didn't make him explode. He continued at the same pace because he knew I enjoyed it. "That was easy." He'd conquered my pussy, conquered all of me. He didn't smirk with arrogance, but the confidence in his voice was infuriating.

My emotions were strong and at the surface, especially in this animalistic state. My hand slapped across his face, hitting him hard in the cheek because it was an asshole-ish thing to say.

He turned with the hit but didn't slow down his thrusts. He kept moving, digging at me a little deeper to remind me just how big he was. Those blue eyes were dark with concentration, but also filled with intense arousal. He grew a little harder inside me, like I'd successfully turned him on a bit more.

I cupped his face and brought him in for another kiss, my fingers digging into his short hair. I breathed into his mouth as I fell deeper into him, unable to understand my own emotions, my own desire, my own intensity. One moment, I hated this man, and then the next, I thought I couldn't live without him.

He moved one hand from my knee and gripped a big chunk of my hair, pulling on it hard as he fucked me even harder. That fat dick pounded inside me, his balls starting to tap against my ass. He could give it to me good and hard without needing to come, like he was a professional at fucking.

I entirely forgot that I had been mad at him just seconds ago and pulled him closer into me, praising him like a gift from the heavens. "Heath...yes." I spoke against his lips, my other hand on his ass as I pulled myself into him over and over. "Fuck." Sex had never been this hot, sweaty, passionate. It was the best sex of my life, the deepest connection I'd ever had with a man. Just one hit and I was addicted. How could I go back to the men I met in bars and restaurants? How could I ever go out with someone and even hope for a night like this? I already knew I would never have this kind of passion with my own husband. It just didn't exist. I'd told him we would just be

together for tonight, but that was before I got fucked so good
tears fell from my eyes. "You're gonna make me come again..."
I couldn't believe it. Not only would I get to come once, but
twice, and in the same session.

His expression was exactly the same during sex as it was in a
public restaurant or a bar. That constant intensity accompa-
nied him wherever he went, whatever he did. He was focused
and precise, but he had the discipline to fuck a woman for
herself before he fucked her for himself. "I know." And just
like that, he showed how egotistical he was, how arrogant he
was with his fucking abilities. He knew he had me now and
didn't want me to forget it.

"Asshole." I slapped him harder this time.

He moaned and grabbed both of my wrists and raised them
above my head, restraining me and pinning me down to where
I could barely move. He was strong enough to hold both of my
hands with a single one of his and to continue thrusting inside
me like there'd been no interruption. "Come."

I wanted to refuse simply out of defiance, but I had no control
over my body anymore. He owned it, controlled it, and being
in the presence of his confidence made me lose the game. I
fought against his command, but the fact that he had total
control over my body was a turn-on I couldn't fight. It only
took me a few seconds to give in, to bring his face close to
mine and come all over again. My hatred was gone instantly,
and I clung to this man who had taken me. With nails deep in
his flesh, I exploded again, finally pleased by a man the way I
fantasized about when I was alone with my vibrator. "Babe..."
The bond I felt with this man increased as our emotional
connection turned into a physical one. "Yes..." My toes
curled, and my pussy couldn't even constrict around him
because I was already stretched to full capacity. My hands
dug into his hair, and I kissed him deeply, unable to believe

that this man was real, that he could really make me feel this way. I'd never felt this level of desire, this soul-crushing connection.

He pulled away so he could look into my eyes, still pounding into me like he wanted to fuck me as hard as he could. His thrusts became deeper and harder, the brightness in his eyes darkening as he approached his climax.

I wanted him to feel just as good as he made me feel, so I ran my hands up his chest and bit my bottom lip. "You have the best dick." My fingers moved up his neck, feeling the cords swell against his tight skin. I'd slapped him twice because of his arrogance, but a few seconds later, I willingly inflated his ego, wanted him to come with the same intensity that I had.

A look of approval moved into his gaze, like he appreciated the words I'd just whispered, and her tilted his hips slightly as he moved into me deeper, hitting me harder as he prepared to finish.

It started to hurt because he gave me a little more than I could handle, but I wanted him to get the full effect of this unbelievable sex. My hand gripped his ass and kept pressing him into me, wincing and moaning until my eyes spilled over with tears.

His thrusts increased until the very end, when he inhaled a deep breath and came, his hand yanking my hair forcefully, like I was an animal under his control. He groaned as he came between my legs, leaving a permanent mark no other man could erase. With his dick completely inside me, he finished, moaning the entire way.

I was satisfied and so was he, but my hand gripped the back of his neck and I pulled him in for a kiss, giving him my tongue like we were starting over from the very beginning.

He kissed me back as he softened inside me, just as hungry, just as anxious. "Just one night, my ass..."

NINE

HEATH

I leaned against the headboard with the back of my neck resting on top of the wood. With my hands on her hips, I watched the sexiest woman bounce up and down on my dick.

She grabbed her own tits, dug her fingers into her hair as she moaned, and bit her bottom lip like she hadn't already come so many times that night. Her palms flattened against my chest, and she rolled her hips in the most seductive way, taking that dick over and over, sweaty and out of breath.

Fuck.

She grabbed my hands and pinned him against the top of her bed frame, right next to my head. Her fingers locked with mine, and she squeezed them. "How do you like it?" She had such a strong core that she continued to ride my dick up and down, rolling her hips to take my length.

I fucking loved it.

I squeezed her hands back in response.

With her fingers still linked with mine, she moved my arms around my head so she could lean in and kiss me, continue to take my dick while sharing soft and sexy kisses. She moaned into my mouth from time to time, using my body to get off over and over.

The only reason I held on to my load was because I'd already come a few times. If I hadn't, I wouldn't be able to keep this up, be able to watch the most beautiful woman take me over and over like this.

She was thin enough that her collarbone was clearly visible under her skin, and she had a deep hollow in her throat. She had small shoulders and slim arms, and her tanned skin made her look irresistible. She had little tits, but her body was so petite they were big for her frame. Her stomach was so sexy, flat with slight grooves of muscle because she was so strong. And there was a glittery belly button piercing in her navel.

Hot.

She had one hell of an ass, thick and muscular, and I couldn't wait to stare at it when I fucked her from behind. And she had strong, toned legs. They were slender, but so muscular. I didn't have a specific type of woman I liked, but I'd realized I liked her type the most. I liked a strong woman. Couldn't wait to have those legs wrapped around my head.

She lost herself and started to grind into my body uncontrol-lably, dragging her sensitive clit against my pelvic bone as she brought herself to orgasm. She tried to pull her hands out of mine, but I gripped tightly so she couldn't pull away. I watched her eyes close, her mouth open, and listened to her moan just for me.

"Heath..."

You would think I'd get tired of hearing that, but I never did.

When her climax had passed, she slowed down her move-ments and breathed through her exhaustion. Her skin was shiny with sweat, and her hair stuck to her neck because she was so heated. She moved into me and kissed me again, like she was thanking me for all my hard work while all I did was sit there and watch her fuck me.

I gripped her ass and grabbed each cheek, my fingers digging deep into her flesh. She had a mirror on the opposite wall so I could see her figure in the reflection. I pulled her cheeks apart so I could look at her asshole. Then I started to guide her up and down, showing her exactly how I wanted her to make me come.

She balanced herself on the balls of her feet, moved herself up and down at the pace I set. It was an athletic thing to do, to use her legs in that way, but she was so conditioned she could do it and only become slightly out of breath. Her palms flattened against my chest for balance, and she rose and lowered, taking me to the tip before bouncing back down to the base of my cock.

I released her ass and folded my hands together behind my neck, watching her do all the work.

She was a good lover because she showed her appreciation for all my hard work. She got hot and sweaty, worked her ass off to fuck me with equal measure after she had her climaxes. It didn't matter how long it took or how exhausted she became, she kept going until I was done.

My kind of woman.

I watched her perfect figure move up and down, her tits shaking because she moved so fast. She was in such phenom-enal shape, such a strong and limber woman.

I felt a spark of pleasure begin in my hands and feet before it moved to my core and made me burn. It was a whole different way to experience an orgasm when all I had to do was sit there and enjoy it. I could sense every single rise of pleasure, every subtle change, and I could anticipate the explosion before it happened.

At the moment of release, I grabbed her hips and pulled her down, making sure every inch of my dick was deep inside her as I came. I looked into her eyes as I finished, exploding inside the pussy I'd been thinking about for a long time. I built up these thoughts in my head, assuming our sex would be unreal, that it really would be as combustible as our fights. But I'd feared that I might be disappointed, that it would never live up to my fantasy.

Fuck, was I wrong.

When I was finished, I relaxed against the headboard, staring at the beautiful brunette on my lap. When I'd gone to the bar that night, I hadn't known what would happen. When I approached her table, I wasn't sure if she'd want to talk to me. Instead, she was all over me like I was her man.

I felt like her man.

She gave me a sexy kiss before she rolled off me and onto the sheets. She was warm and sweaty, so she kept her distance to let her body cool down.

I went to her bathroom and cleaned off, adding another used condom to the bin where all my others lay. I splashed cold water on my face then dried off with a towel before I returned to the bedroom.

She finally seemed satisfied because her eyes were closed like she was ready for sleep.

I looked at the time on her nightstand and saw it was five in the morning.

I could go home and she probably wouldn't stop me, but I

wanted to stay. I got in bed beside her and lay back on the pillow, my dick a little sore from all the fucking. I stared at the ceiling and listened to her breathe.

She suddenly moved toward me across the bed, half asleep. Her face rested on my shoulder, and her arm hooked around my waist. She snuggled into me like I wasn't just someone one-night stand, but a very special man.

My arm lay over hers, and I turned my face toward her so I could smell her hair, smell the scent of her shampoo mixed with sweat, sex, me.

Then I went to sleep.

HER KITCHEN WAS STILL STOCKED with groceries even though it'd been six weeks since I put most of the stuff there. She must've been using the money I left for her to keep her kitchen stocked. I'd given her way more cash than she needed, but I did that on purpose and hoped she would use it to take care of herself. I made French toast and bacon, the kitchen smelling like breakfast time.

Just as I finished, Sleeping Beauty came from her bedroom, wearing silk pajama shorts and a shirt that barely covered her sexy skin underneath. The swell of her breasts was visible, and hard nipples poked through the fabric like they were desperate to burst through her shirt and into my mouth. She ran her fingers through her hair, yawned, and her sleepy eyes were only partially open. "What are you doing?"

I grabbed a couple plates from her cabinet and served the food. "Breakfast."

She came to my side and looked down at the hot food I'd prepared. "I don't usually eat breakfast."

"It's noon, so it's lunch." I opened one of the drawers and grabbed two forks before placing them on the dishes. I was in my clothes again, the jeans and shirt that I'd worn when I walked in the door last night.

"Shit, it is?" She turned to look at the time on the microwave, squinting. "Wow…" She ran her fingers through her hair again, her eyes tired because the few hours of sleep we'd gotten weren't enough for her. When she turned back to me, her eyes focused on my face like she found my blue eyes as pretty as all the other girls did. She tilted her head to the side so her hair fell down one shoulder, and the desire that sprang into her expression was unmistakable. She grabbed my arm and moved into me, her face pressing against my chest. "I don't give a shit about breakfast." She rose on her tiptoes and locked her arms around my neck, pressing her perfect tits into my body. She rubbed her nose against mine before she looked down at my lips.

"Yeah?" I'd stuck around just for this reason, to watch this beautiful woman want me as if I hadn't already stuck it to her good last night.

"Yeah." She gave me her confident gaze as she guided my face down to hers so she could kiss me. The kiss was soft and warm, her lips aggressive and authoritative. Her fingers cupped my face and neck and slipped into my hair while she moaned gently against my mouth.

I pushed her sexy little shorts over her hips so they fell down to her ankles. There were no panties underneath, so she was ready for my dick.

She grabbed my shirt and pulled it over my head before she planted her palms against my chest, just to test how hard I was, to feel my searing-hot skin and the power of my muscles underneath. "Jesus, you're so fucking hot."

I reached into my pocket and grabbed a condom. "I know."

She released an annoyed chuckle, furious with my ego. "If I didn't want you so much, I'd throw you out of my apartment."

"Why don't you just slap me instead?" I dropped my jeans and rolled on a condom, looking into her eyes as I did it. She'd slapped me so many times I'd lost count, and I liked it every single time. It wasn't something I was used to because no other woman had ever dared to strike me, but I loved it when she did it, loved her nerve.

"Oh, I'm sure I will."

I grabbed her hips and lifted her onto the counter before I pulled her close to me and shoved myself inside with a hard thrust.

She gripped my shoulders as her head rolled back. "Oh god..."

I didn't take my time like I had last time. Now, I just fucked her hard and fast, holding her close to me on the kitchen counter while we desecrated the area with our fucking. The food went cold while we got hot, the two of us clinging together as we got lost in each other.

Her arms remained around my neck while her legs wrapped around my waist. She was flexible enough to tilt her hips and hold the position while she took my aggressive thrusts. Her face stayed close to mine as she moaned against my lips. "Don't stop..."

I breathed against her lips and demolished her perfect cunt. "Never."

WE SAT TOGETHER at the table and ate a cold breakfast. Only the coffee was warm.

Now that she was fulfilled and satisfied, her mood dropped, as if she realized this had all been a really good mistake. She took a few bites of her food but mostly sipped her coffee, probably because she was obsessed with not eating. I loved her body, but I thought another fifteen pounds could only make her look better.

I ate all my food, not giving a shit if it was cold. I was a grown man who needed to eat. When I was finished, I stared at her beside me at the four-seater dining table. Her shorts were back on, and her shirt had never left her body.

I loved the way she looked the morning after our night together, after all her makeup had been washed away and sleep rejuvenated her appearance. Unlike most women, she didn't need makeup to be beautiful, but when she did wear it... damn. She had big, almond-shaped eyes with thick lashes, a cute nose, and such full lips that her smile was overpowering. With her fingers wrapped around the handle of the mug, she looked into the black contents and watched the steam rise to the ceiling.

I already knew what conversation we were about to have. Her mood was completely opposite of what it had been when she first woke up. Now she was melancholy, her rambunctious personality long gone. She possessed the energy of someone about to dump somebody else.

I'd like to see her try.

I cleared the plates and left them in the sink. "I should go." I had shit to do and I should've left last night, but I'd purposely stayed because I needed to set the tone for this relationship. If I departed quickly, it would make it seem like a one-night stand. But if I stayed until breakfast, that implied a lot more.

She rose from the chair and walked me to the door, the door I had installed to keep her safe, at least keep her safe from her fears. With her arms across her chest, she would hardly look at me, like she dreaded whatever she was about to say, not dreaded me leaving.

I wouldn't put up with that shit. "We aren't doing this."

Her gaze finally lifted to mine, her body a little less tense because my words caught her off guard.

"You're going to tell me this is over, that it was just one night, but we both know this is going to happen again...and again. So, let's just skip that part." I didn't say those words because I wanted to keep her; it was just what I believed. The sex was too good to ignore, to downplay, and I was a man who was blunt like a hammer. "We don't need to label this relationship or even talk about it. That's what I prefer, actually." We just had to keep fucking.

Her eyes tilted to the floor for a moment as she considered what I said, and then she moved her hands to her hips and took a deep breath and straightened. "I just need to think this over..."

My eyes narrowed with displeasure. "Think what over?"

"Everything." Her gaze was guarded, and she refused to let me in. Last night, she was all over me at the bar like there was no other man she wanted to be with. And when the sex was over, she still wanted to be near me, still wanted to cuddle with me. She could tell herself this was all sex, but it was obvious there was an emotional connection she couldn't deny. Her stubbornness infuriated me the way my confidence irked her. I wasn't a patient man, not for bullshit, so I lost my temper. "While you figure it out, don't expect me to keep my dick in my pants." I opened the front door and walked out.

Truth be told, I wasn't interested in other women right now. I hadn't even been with anyone in a long time because I was chasing that little brunette. I could pay for sex, but I continued to wait, continued to wait for the woman I really wanted. It was an idle threat, but I was pissed off, just wanted to say something to get under her skin.

She came after me in the hallway and grabbed my arm. Her ass was hanging out of her shorts and her tits were basically on display, but she came after me anyway because those words dug deep—just as I'd intended. She turned me to face her, a different expression in her eyes. "Wait."

I pulled my arm away from her grasp.

She looked into my face a long time, emotional the way I preferred. I liked it when she was spontaneous, when she lived in the moment, showed who she really was, and I liked exactly who she was. "That dick is mine." She cupped my cheek and rose on her tiptoes to kiss me, to give me a hot kiss that left her mark on me so no one else would take me away. She breathed deep into my lungs, her nails scratching me like she wanted to give me a permanent scar so everyone would assume I was taken, or as she put it, my dick was spoken for.

My arms wrapped around her body, and I pulled her hard into me, giving her a bear hug like I could crush her if I squeezed too hard. One hand covered both of her ass cheeks, and I squeezed, loving that strong ass. When I pulled away, I shot her a victorious look. "That's what I thought."

BALTO WAS in the same place he'd been for years, a multistory building that looked more like a military complex. I used to live with him a while ago, right after I was released from prison. He had armed guards on duty twenty-four hours a day, even though no one was coming for him anymore. He'd officially retired and didn't intervene in any events from the underground world.

Well, except for that one time with Damien.

He sat in the living room with me, drinking his scotch while the soccer game played on the TV. We were twins who looked so much alike, except he didn't have any tattoos and I was covered in them. Other than that, people claimed we were identical. He was a little burlier and I was a bit smarter, so we were apples and oranges in my eyes.

I didn't see any resemblance.

Our personalities were just so different. He was a lot quieter, subtler. And I was the biggest smartass on the planet. It was late in the evening, almost midnight, and it was the time I usually got my day started.

Balto was a domesticated animal now, so he went to bed at a reasonable hour, but he didn't struggle to stay up with me because he was used to my late-night visits. He finished off his glass before he set it on the coffee table, cutting back and drinking a third of what he used to. "So, you outlawed trafficking everywhere?"

I nodded.

He shook his head slightly. "Wow...you're a braver man than I ever was."

"I've been saying that for years."

Now he shook his head for an entirely different reason. "You're going to get a lot of pushback for that."

"Oh, I know." I set down my glass. "I'm trying to turn it into a prostitution business. I'm hoping we can charge more for each girl so the businesses will still thrive, maybe even make more. It's a slow process, and everyone is watching every little thing I do."

"Has Vox been a problem?"

"Not yet. But I think he's waiting for me to crash and burn."

"Never drop your guard around him."

"I never drop my guard around anyone." I would just kill Vox if it wouldn't upset the rest of the Skull Kings. I couldn't kill one of my own without justifiable cause. Vox not liking me wasn't a good enough reason, and it would probably result in my own death.

"Why are you doing this?" He took his gaze off the TV and looked at me, possessing blue eyes that were identical to mine. "When I outlawed it in our organization, you weren't thrilled about it."

I dropped my gaze, and I actually felt ashamed for that. "People change."

"Not people like you...not without reason, at least."

I shrugged in response.

As the silence passed, he read the expression on my face as if he had access to my thoughts. He'd always been that way, studying someone like he could see what was underneath. It made people writhe, made people break under the intensity and admit their sins. Maybe it really worked. Or maybe it was just a ploy. "There's a woman, isn't there?"

I forced myself to laugh. "Woman? Me? No." I took a drink.

My brother continued to study me, reading between the lines. "There's no shame, Heath. Look at me." He nodded to the wall, where a picture of him and his wife was hanging. She was in a wedding dress, and he was in a suit. "I gave it all up. She was the thing that changed me. I have a feeling the same thing changed you."

I hadn't told the Skull Kings the real reason I was making so many changes. I pretended it was all business, because if I spoke the truth, I would lose the respect of every man underneath me.

"What happened?"

I didn't feel like telling every single detail of the story, so I recounted the shorter version. "Yeah...there is someone. She was captured by Popov's men, and when I saw her down there in the cage, I let her go. She asked me to free the other girls, and I promised I would. Then I started to feel sick, collecting money off girls like that everywhere else, and I just couldn't do it anymore." I bowed my head in shame, feeling like less of a man because of what I used to do. "I decided to make a change."

Balto stared at me with an unreadable expression, taking time to gather his thoughts. "I think you did the right thing."

I met his look. "You don't think I'm a pussy?"

"FUCK YES, I think you're a pussy. You were smart to mask your true intentions as a business venture, at least. But I'm a pussy too." He grabbed his empty glass and clinked it against mine. "When do I get to meet her?"

"It's not serious."

"Changing the infrastructure of your organization says otherwise."

"Like I said, I didn't do it for her. I just feel differently about it now. She and I... It's really complicated. It's never going to go anywhere. I'm just going to enjoy it before it blows up in my face."

"Why does it have to blow up in your face?"

I grabbed the bottle of scotch and refilled my glass because I thought I needed a bit more. "Damien is her brother..."

Balto didn't react right away, staring at me for a few seconds as the weight of the situation hit him. "Then she's aware of the problem."

"For the most part." I swirled the liquid in my glass. "She turned me down many times because she's loyal to her family, but after I saved her...she felt differently. She finally gave in, and it was amazing." I shrugged. "You know me, I always deliver."

Balto didn't react to my joke.

I kept going. "She doesn't know everything..."

Balto figured out the rest on his own. "She doesn't know you almost killed her father."

I dropped my gaze and shook my head, feeling the past haunting me. There was nothing I could do to undo what I'd already done. I couldn't lie and say I never intended to kill him because that was bullshit. If Hades hadn't been there, her father would be dead in the ground right now. That was something she would never look past, something she would never forgive. "No."

I WAS at home when she texted me. *I want to see you.*

I smiled when I read the message on my phone. I loved the way she didn't ask for things, just demanded them. She spoke her mind so plainly that she was easy to understand. She wasn't a closed book, but an open story that was so addictive and easy to follow. *I bet you miss me.*

Fuck off. You miss me too.

Baby, I always miss you.

Her anger immediately evaporated. *Come over. We need to talk.*

I rolled my eyes because I didn't want to talk. I knew she wanted to talk about our situation, I just didn't know what there was to say. She wasn't gonna try to end the relationship because she wouldn't have texted me in the first place. So, I would have to suffer through it and get to the good stuff. *I'll be there in fifteen minutes.*

SHE OPENED the door for me, wearing a dark blue sundress with her curled hair pinned to one side. Mascara made her eyelashes thick and beautiful, and the purple eye shadow just made her eyes more exquisite. She wore a profound shade of red lipstick, her lips plump and sexy.

When I'd arrived at the door, I was in a bad mood because I wanted to get this conversation over with, but now that I saw her, my attitude changed completely. She was worth the annoyance, worth thirty minutes of idiotic conversation. My hands cupped her face and slid into her hair as I leaned down and kissed her.

She had been in a somber mood when she opened the door, so she went a little rigid when I kissed her, but once her lips met mine, her hands went to my stomach and she kissed me back, falling into our unbelievable chemistry.

When I pulled away, her eyes looked a little dazed, like she couldn't believe all the feelings my touch provided. Her fingers wrapped around my wrists, and she closed her eyes for a moment, like she wanted to keep kissing me.

Oh fuck, she was so perfect.

She rose on her tiptoes and gave me another soft kiss, as if she needed a little bit more before she turned away. She walked to the small table in her kitchen and took a seat.

I closed the door behind me and moved to the chair I'd sat in a few days ago and slouched, wishing we were doing something better with our time than having this conversation. At least she was beautiful to look at, and I could think about how I would fuck her when this was over.

"Do you want water or coffee?"

I shook my head. "Just say whatever you want to say." My hands came together in my lap, and my shoulders sank as I got comfortable.

She had her knuckles propped under her chin while her other arm rested on the table, and she dropped her eyes to the surface as she considered what she was going to say first. Her hair was big, with soft curls that framed her face, and when she looked so beautiful, she made it difficult to focus on her words rather than her appearance. "You're right. This is going to keep happening even though I wish it wouldn't. I thought one incredible night together would be enough for us both to move on... but it had the opposite effect." Her gaze remained on the surface of the table, and she didn't want to look at me as she spoke. "Nothing has changed. Our situation hasn't changed."

She stated the obvious, which I thought was a waste of time. This wasn't gonna last forever. We both knew that.

"But I want to be with you." After a deep breath, she lifted her gaze and looked at me. Her green eyes were filled with so much emotion, so much passion, and I was the cause of all of it. "It'll be a secret. Short term. A fling."

I wanted this fling to start right now.

"But you have to promise me something." She dropped her

eyes back to the table, like she needed a moment to gather her bearings before she said the next thing. "You said you keep your promises...so I trust you."

This was taking a turn I did not expect. "What is it?"

She looked me in the eye, fear in her gaze. "You can't fall in love with me."

It took me a few seconds to process her request, because no woman had ever said anything like that to me like before. "Does that happen a lot?" Did she have many relationships with men that ended that way? I could believe it because she was incredible, but I was also a bit incredulous that a man would throw himself at her if she clearly didn't feel the same way.

"Doesn't matter if it has. This is about us, no one else. And I need you to make that promise." Her eyes shifted back and forth as she looked into mine, anxiously waiting for me to say those words to give her peace of mind.

"And what if you fall in love with me?" I didn't expect her to, but I didn't understand why she treated this as a one-way street.

"I won't allow myself to. And even if I do, I'll never admit it."

"Why?"

She tucked her hair behind her ear and shook her head slightly. "Because it just can't happen. So, I need you to make that promise to me. I need this to have an expiration date. I need you to use me and disappear. I need you to get tired of me and forget about me."

In my experience, women wanted the exact opposite. They wanted to be remembered, wanted to be worshiped. She wanted nothing from me, and for some reason, it was a little offensive. "I didn't realize I was so terrible—"

"That's not why," she said quickly. "It's not you…"

"Then why?" Why did she believe this relationship would turn into love? Maybe it was just inexplicable physical chemistry. Maybe we would fuck the way we fought, but then that would fade and we'd become indifferent to each other.

She ran her fingers through her hair and turned her face so she could look out one of her windows. She seemed to debate with herself in silence, to wonder if she should tell me about her thoughts. "I don't want to sound crazy…" She turned back to me, releasing a sigh of resignation. "Do you believe in prophecies?"

That was the last thing I'd expected her to say.

"Like fate, fortune readings, stuff like that…"

I was silent because I didn't know what to say. No, I'd never given thought to any of those things. "I believe we make our own fortune." I didn't believe the universe had a master plan for each of us, that we were stuck with whatever hand of cards we were dealt. We had choices, and those choices dictated our future. She seemed too smart to believe that nonsense, but even if she wasn't, I didn't know how that applied to our situation. "Why?"

She pulled her hands closer to her body, her fingers intertwining and fidgeting. "Forget it. It's stupid. I'm just being paranoid…"

"Being paranoid about what?"

She shook her head quickly. "Forget I said anything."

I wanted to know more, but it probably was stupid, so I let it go. "Forgotten."

"I still need you to make that promise to me, though." She lifted her gaze, patiently waiting to hear me say the words.

I was surprised it was so important to her. "I promise." I'd never been in love, and I didn't intend to be at any time in my life. I did want a deep and passionate relationship with this woman because it satisfied me, gave me a kind of excitement I hadn't felt with anyone else. I wanted to be with her, completely, until it ended.

But that was it.

She breathed a sigh relief as if those words meant the world to her. "That makes me feel better. You don't seem like the kind of man who would love a woman anyway, so it probably doesn't matter."

"Why do you say that?"

Once she'd heard my promise, she visibly relaxed, as if she'd just gotten the best news she'd ever heard. "You are so damn hot and rich. Men like that never settle down. There's no reason to. There's always another beautiful woman after the last beautiful woman."

That accurately described my life. "I might settle down."

She grew uncomfortable again. "Yeah...?"

"I'm not against the idea of being with one woman for the rest of my life."

A slight look of surprise came into her face. "Really? Even as the Skull King?"

"If I really found a woman that I couldn't live without, that I didn't want to share, I wouldn't be stupid enough to let her go." I wasn't sure why I said that to her when I hadn't even said it to myself, but I knew how I felt about it. "I've been with a lot of women, but none of them mattered. If one of them did come to matter..." I shrugged. "I wouldn't let her walk away."

She seemed stunned. "I didn't expect you to feel that way."

"And I probably wouldn't if my brother hadn't gotten married."

"You have a brother?"

I nodded. "He's my predecessor, strongest guy I know, and he gave up everything when he met his woman. He married her, knocked her up, and that's his story. Watching him love someone and her love him back changed my opinion about the whole thing. I'm not saying that will happen to me or that I want it to happen to me, but I'm not gonna sit here and say it will *never* happen to me." I watched her reaction, watched her hang on every word I said.

She stared at me a bit longer, like she needed extra seconds to process what I said. "Well, that woman you can't live without will never be me because that's what you promised."

My lips rose slightly when I stared at her. "And you think I'm egotistical..."

She released a faint chuckle and covered her face with her hands in embarrassment. "Oh, I know I must sound crazy... I don't blame you for thinking that. I just have to cross my T's and dot my I's." She stared down at her hands. "I feel better now, but there is one more thing..."

"I'm listening."

"We have our own allegiances. Mine will never change, and if I ever knew Damien would hurt you, set you up in some way, I would never tell you. If I knew he was going to bomb your entire home and kill you, I still wouldn't tell you. Just because we're sleeping together doesn't change the way I feel about our predicament. I will never have any loyalty to you, and if there's anything I can do to help my brother, I will."

Her coldness actually turned me on, because she had the hardness of a man, the pragmatism of a devoted soldier. We were on two sides of a war, and when we met in the middle, it was for one purpose—that was it. The rest of the time, it was just business. "That's fine with me."

"I mean it. I'm close with Anna, and she tells me stuff..."

I gave a slight smile. "Baby, I don't need your help. I'm a grown-ass man."

"So, if he has plans to kill you, I could be fucking you the night before and still not say a word. I just want to be clear." She was the woman in my bed, but she was my enemy. She would betray me first chance she got and not feel remorseful about it.

Fuck, that was hot. "You're absolutely clear."

When she had nothing more to say, she turned quiet, still tense after that long conversation.

"We don't fuck other people. That's my one stipulation." My tone was firm.

"You don't seem like the jealous type."

"Because I'm not. You're the jealous one."

Her anger started to rise. "I am not."

I grinned at the memory of our conversation in the doorway. "You said my dick is yours. If that's not jealousy, I don't know what it is. And don't apologize for it because it's fucking hot."

Her anger evaporated.

"I just don't want to wear a condom." I didn't want to go

through her drawer where other men had dug their hands in the past. I didn't want to take the time to roll the piece of latex over my dick before I could finally get inside her. I didn't want some rubber shit separating our bodies, numbing the amazing sensations between our bodies. I wanted to come inside her over and over, night after night.

"Then I expect you to get checked out."

"Fine with me."

She turned her gaze back to me, studying my expression. "And what about me?"

"I assumed you would get tested or have already been tested." I knew she slept around based on what I'd witnessed at the bar, but I also knew she was smart and would protect herself at all times.

"That's not what I mean..." She turned away and looked at her sink, as if this new topic made her more uncomfortable than all the rest.

"Then what do you mean, baby?" I called her baby because she was mine. For however long this lasted, she belonged to me; she was my woman. I wanted to savor every aspect of ownership, to enjoy all the passion we could find.

She couldn't look at me as she spoke. "You never asked if I was raped..."

The thought had crossed my mind, but I didn't want to know. The bruises on her face were enough to make me hurl into my toilet when I got home. I did my best to disassociate from that reality, not to let my nightmares go that far. "It's none of my business. And even if you were, doesn't change how I feel about you...which I've already proven." My attraction to her was still enormous, regardless of where she'd been before me.

Maybe other men would be uncomfortable by the fact, but not me. I wanted her as she came, scars, bruises, and all.

She turned back to me, and this time, she gave me a look I'd never seen before. She was somewhat incredulous at what I'd said, but she also seemed deeply moved by it, like her opinion of me just rose. She stopped fidgeting with her hands and looked at me like she'd never really seen me before. "I wasn't expecting you to say that."

She still hadn't told me whether she had or hadn't been hurt, but it made no difference because I wanted her so much. When this conversation was over, I wanted to pick her up and carry her to bed so I could enjoy her. "Scars are not signs of weakness, but strength. Traumas are not signs of failure, but success. A dark past doesn't mean you lived less, but you lived more. Anyone who judges you for what you've been through is just an asshole who hasn't survived anything themselves. They are the weak ones. And you are the strong one." I couldn't picture her ending up with an average man, living an average life. She needed someone who lived in a different world, had a different perspective on life. Someone who didn't blink an eye over the most gruesome things. "I'm not like other men, baby."

Her eyes softened as she looked at me, her affection growing right in front of my eyes. "Yeah...I see that."

TEN

CATALINA

My ankles were locked around his waist, and he pressed me into the mattress. My hands were deep in the back of his hair as I let him rock me into the sheets. I breathed into his face and moaned, my heels digging into his ass as he continued to give it to me so good. "Heath..." I didn't say much in bed, and despite my experience with my long list of lovers, I'd never said a man's name during sex. But this man was special, the first one who deserved to hear me say it over and over. He sent me to the stars every time we were together, pleased me every single time like it wasn't luck, just pure skill. I brought him closer and bit into his shoulder, moaning through my climax even though I had a reason to be quiet. My teeth sank into his flesh harder than I meant to because I was moaning uncontrollably. God, it was so good. Everything with this man was so good.

He came a minute later, waiting until my teeth released from his skin before he filled the condom inside me. He always shoved his whole dick inside me when he released, making me hiss through my teeth when he came into contact with my cervix, but I never asked him to stop because I knew how much he enjoyed it, how much he liked hurting me with his big dick.

I released a quiet moan as he finished, his thick body still making me sink into the sheets. He breathed against my neck as he drifted down from the clouds. Then he gave me a single hot kiss before he pulled out of me and walked into the bathroom.

I watched him walk away, watched that tight ass contract and relax as he moved. He had sexy legs and an even sexier back. His tattoos were from the waist up, and I'd never really had a chance to examine each one because I preferred to take in the whole picture instead.

That man was mine. All mine. And I didn't have to share.

I didn't have to worry about our relationship going somewhere I didn't want it to because I'd laid the groundwork right away. That allowed me to be with him completely, to drop my guard and treasure every moment.

He returned after he cleaned off, just as sexy from the front as he was from the back. He got into bed beside me, leaving the sheets at his waist.

I rolled onto my side and looked at him, my fingertips sliding lightly up and down his arms. I leaned in close and pressed a kiss to his shoulder, tasting sweat from his exertion, the work he did to make me come.

He wrapped his bear-sized arm around my waist and pulled me close, tugging me against his large frame so we could be close together. I rested my palm against his chest, right over his strong heartbeat. After our serious conversation at the dinner table, we hadn't said much else. In between our sessions of sex, we usually stayed quiet and just enjoyed each other's company.

"What's for dinner?" His strong arm was still around my waist, his fingertips gliding up and down as he touched me. His deep voice was so sexy, so manly. Unfortunately, his perfection ruined all other men for me. How could I move on to some-body else after having this?

"Why are you asking me?"

"Because I've been fucking you for an hour, and I need suste-nance—if you want me to keep going, at least."

"I'm not much of a cook."

"What would you eat if I weren't here?"

I propped myself up on one elbow so I could look down into his face. With my body turned his way, his hand went farther over my back to my shoulder, bringing me closer with a lustful look in his eye, as if he liked my body from this angle. "I don't know. A sandwich? Maybe nothing at all." I was used to men staring at me, wanting me, but no one had ever stared at me the way he did, like he was constantly attracted to me, constantly hypnotized by the way my lips moved when I spoke. This man was pumped with so much testosterone, he always wanted to fuck, even when he'd just finished.

"You would skip dinner?"

"Sometimes."

His hand moved to my ass, and he squeezed my cheeks. "Baby, you need to eat. I love your body, and you need to take care of it."

I noticed he called me baby all the time now, anytime he addressed me. A man had never called me that before because I'd never been in a relationship—not that this was a relation-ship, but it was a first for me. I felt right, and I couldn't imagine him calling me anything else. "I have to keep my weight down for ballet. I told you that."

"I don't think eating dinner is going to sabotage your chances. Imagine how much more energy you would have if you ate properly."

I rolled my eyes. "You aren't my boyfriend, so don't tell me what to do."

His hand stilled on my back, and that aroused expression turned into something sinister. "No, I'm not your boyfriend because that's pussy shit. I'm your man. And I will say whatever the fuck I want to say." He amplified his statement by smacking me on the ass. "You need to eat." He got out of bed and pulled on his boxers.

"What are you doing?"

"Making dinner." He left my bedroom and walked into the kitchen.

I lay there for a while and listened to him move around pots and pans and open cabinets to see what he could throw together. I sighed to myself before I got out of bed and picked up a shirt from the floor. I pulled it over my head and removed my hair from underneath the neckline. I didn't bother putting on a clean pair of underwear because I suspected he would fuck me before we even had dinner.

I went to the kitchen and joined him. "What's on the menu?"

"Chicken Francese and spaghetti." He placed the pot of water on the stove and turned on the heat so it would boil.

I wrapped my arms around his waist and placed my lips against his shoulder blades. "That sounds good. I have all the ingredients for that?"

"Yes. And you have lots of white wine." He moved to the fridge to grab all the ingredients and started to cook in the pan.

I placed myself on the counter with my knees pulled to my chest as I watched him cook.

Sometimes his eyes would wander and look right between my legs.

"Do you mind?" I squeezed my thighs together.

"Not at all." He gave a grin like a smartass and dropped the spaghetti noodles into the water. He moved to me and bent down so he could shove his face between my legs and kissed me. Kissed me hard.

I hadn't expected it, so I grabbed the back of his head and arched my back as I released a loud moan. "Whoa..."

He pulled away and kept cooking like nothing had happened. He flipped the chicken, added more wine for the sauce, and then boiled the pasta in the separate pot.

I eyed the bottle on the counter. "Are you going to use the rest of that wine?"

He smiled and handed it to me.

I grabbed it and drank straight from the bottle. "You can whip this up without a recipe?"

"A recipe is like instructions, and a man doesn't need instructions."

He definitely didn't need instructions on how to kiss me, that was for sure.

He stepped back and leaned against the kitchen island as he waited for everything to cook. With his arms across his chest, he looked at me, from my face to my pussy. "That shirt looks good on you."

"Feels good too." I raised the bottle and took a drink.

He looked at the food to make sure everything was working properly before he turned back to me, his blue eyes watching me like there was nothing more entertaining than seeing me drink from a bottle of wine.

"When are you going to invite me over to your place?"

"I'm surprised you'd want me to."

"Why? I hope there's more than just that basement."

He smiled lightly. "A lot more."

"Then, yeah, I want to see it."

"Come over whenever you want."

"Well, be careful. I might show up on your doorstep every night."

He dropped his smile and checked on the pots and pans again. "You're the only woman in my life, so come and go as you please. My bed is your bed as far as I'm concerned." He turned off all the burners once the food was done and grabbed plates to serve everything.

"You seem comfortable with monogamy. Have you done it before?"

"No. But I don't need the experience to know how it works." He placed the food onto the dishes and grabbed silverware before he handed me a plate. He leaned against the kitchen island and started to eat. "Only fuck one woman. Not that hard to understand."

"But might be hard to implement." I took a few bites and was impressed that he'd thrown this together so easily. "You're probably used to getting ass handed to you all the time..." I'd seen the way women looked at him at the bars, all wanting a chance to sink their claws into him. He was a devastatingly beautiful man, so sexy it was easy to come just thinking about him. He could have anyone he wanted.

"I don't recall that happening with you." He continued to eat, brushing off my compliment like it didn't mean anything to him. He could be a conceited asshole at times, but that seemed to be an act, because other times, he actually seemed humble about his hotness.

"Only because you locked me in a cage in your basement. If that had never happened, I would've hunted you down until I had you. Would've hiked up my dress and fucked you in an alleyway if it came down to it."

He stopped chewing for a second, affected by what I said. "We can still do that."

"I won't be surprised if we do." I ate everything on my plate because it was so good, a gourmet meal right in my kitchen. I tried to control my appetite and not scarf everything down, but that was impossible. I cooked food in the same pots with the same ingredients, and meals never turned out like this. "Damn, that was good." I set the plate aside on the counter.

"Good. You ate everything like a grown-ass woman." He carried his empty plate to the sink and rinsed it off, taking mine next and doing the same. Then he moved to the pots on the stove.

"I'll do it later. You cook, I'll clean."

He released the handle of the pan and turned back to me, the sexiest man to stand in my kitchen. His hair was a little messy because I'd fingered it so many times, and it was obvious that a woman had dug her hands into his hair instead of him being lazy and not taking a shower. He glanced at the time on the microwave then turned back to me. "I should get going."

The disappointment that rushed through me was potent, painful. It was so sudden because I hadn't expected it. Last time he was there, he'd slept over, and I'd just assumed that was what he would always do. But I refused to seem clingy or whiny, so I took the high road and brushed it off. "Okay. Thanks for dinner."

He stared my face, his head slightly tilted to the side as he regarded me. His piercing blue eyes studied me like a pair of binoculars. "If you want me to stay, just tell me that."

My eyes narrowed. "You said you should go, so why would I tell you to stay?" I pulled his shirt over my head and handed it to him, leaving myself completely naked in the kitchen.

He took it but didn't pull it on. "I should go. I have shit to do. But if you want me to stay, I will."

"I'm good." I walked back into my bedroom so I could pull on my little shorts and a top before returning to the front door. Most of the time, I just wanted sex and to have the guy leave afterward. But since this was a different situation, I was a bit frustrated he wanted to go—and even more frustrated that I didn't want him to leave in the first place.

When I turned around, he was in my bedroom, his shirt still in his hand. "Let me tell you how this works." He tossed the shirt onto the bed. "You can tell me anything. You can ask me for anything. I'm at your service."

"You fulfilled your services for the night, so you're dismissed." I'd never needed anybody, and I wasn't gonna start now.

He stayed in front of me, his muscular frame rigid.

"Why are you making this into a bigger deal than it needs to be?"

He stepped closer to me. "Because the longer we're together, the more I can...read you. I can tell there's something you want, but you refuse to ask for it."

I crossed my arms over my chest and did my best to seem indifferent.

He was quiet for a while as he waited for me to come clean on my own, and when I didn't, he stepped closer and placed his hands on my hips, his face close to mine. "Talk to me, baby." He rested his forehead against mine, his powerful hands snaking across my back, protecting me like bars in a cage.

Whenever he was affectionate and authoritative, I wanted to submit. I was usually defiant to the ends of the earth, but I found myself wanting to be the opposite with him. "I just have a hard time sleeping sometimes..."

He stared at me with the same expression, as if he knew exactly what I meant by that, without further explanation. "No one is going to walk through that door except you. You don't need an alarm system—you don't even need a door. No one will touch you. I promise."

"How can you make a promise like that?"

"Because I'm the Skull King. I can make any promises that I want." His hand went to my neck, and his fingers lightly traced the area around my lips. "Would you feel safer if I got you a gun?"

"I don't know how to use a gun."

"I can show you. Would that help?"

Even if I'd had a gun when those guys broke in to my apartment, it wouldn't have helped me. But now I had an alarm system and a tank for a door, so I would have time to react if something like that happened. "Yes."

"Then I'll get you one."

My nightmares were the things that haunted me the most, that forced me to wake up in the middle of the night gasping for air, seeing shadows that looked like adversaries. Having him beside me felt much safer than having a gun in my nightstand, but I refused to ask him for anything. He wasn't my boyfriend, just the man I was sleeping with.

"Anything else?"

I shook my head.

He leaned down and kissed me before he pulled away and got dressed.

I had to fight the urge to ask him to stay, the sleep in this apartment with me so one would come after me. But I managed to hide those feelings away so he wouldn't be able to see them.

After he was dressed, he walked to the front door and said goodbye. "I'll see you later."

"Alright." I rose on my toes and kissed him goodbye.

With both of his hands on my ass, he squeezed hard as he kissed me, giving me his tongue like he'd just walked in the door. He bit my bottom lip gently, telling me how much he'd miss me until the next time he came over. Then he smacked my ass before he walked out the door.

I stayed in the doorway and watched him go, watching his powerful frame shift slightly with his movements as he disappeared down my hallway. I stared at his thick ass, his powerful arms, and those enormous shoulders.

And I already missed him.

❄

WHENEVER I WAS on the stage, my mind was so clear it was like I was meditating. I didn't think about the people in the audience, didn't worry that the other dancer wouldn't catch me after I leaped into the air. It was the closest feeling to peace I'd ever felt.

The bright lights didn't affect me, and it was as if I was in a dream. Asleep so soundly, nothing would pull me from this illusion. I was passionate about dance, to say the least, and when I was on stage, that was when I felt most alive...and dead at the exact same time.

The music stopped, and I held my poise, my toes pointed and my hand raised to the ceiling. My chin tilted to the floor in the form of a bow, holding the position as the orchestra went quiet before the music began to rise, building to a crescendo before I began my spectacular spin.

And that was when I saw him.

Sitting in the same seat as the first time, he was squeezed between two older men, refusing to adopt an appropriate attire for the theatre. The most he did was throw on a sport coat on top of his shirt and black jeans. His blue eyes were focused on mine, and he didn't smile as he looked at me, watching me with the same intensity as when he was on top of me.

The look only lasted a few seconds before the music exploded.

And then I turned away like nothing happened, keeping my professionalism since every eye was on me at that moment.

But I felt my heart race with excitement, felt my body come to life like we were alone in my apartment. He was the only person who could pull me out of the moment, take my focus away from my performance, make me think of anything else but my body.

Only him.

❄

I SAT at my vanity and pulled the pins from my hair, let my strands fall free from the restraints. My scalp immediately felt better once it wasn't being tugged on in that insufferable bun. I felt beautiful while I performed, but with my hair pulled back like that, I never felt sexy.

Until Heath looked at me like that.

I ran my fingers through my hair and knew he would show his face at any moment.

I hadn't even removed my makeup before he appeared in the reflection of my vanity, his stubble a thick shadow because he hardly ever shaved now that we were together…just because I liked it. The sport coat was an article of clothing that didn't reflect his personality at all, but he was still sexy wearing it because of those broad-ass shoulders. He didn't even need the pads that were usually stuffed inside jackets like that.

He came up behind me, his face no longer visible because he was right against me, his stomach and pectoral muscles the only thing in my view. One hand moved to my shoulder, and he gave me a gentle squeeze, his fingers digging into my shirt in a touch packed with ownership.

I closed my eyes for a second because that was all it took to turn me on.

"Get your ass up and kiss me." His hand moved to the hair that fell down my back and gave it a gentle tug.

I left the bench and turned around to face him, finding him just as sexy when his tattoos were masked by his clothes. I kept the chair between us so he couldn't grab me. "Not here." I kept my voice low so the rest of the performers wouldn't be able to hear my words.

His reaction was subtle, but it was potent. His eyes narrowed like I'd slighted him, and now he was about to blow like a volcano full of lava at his core. "What the fuck did you just say to me?" He kept his voice deep and low, but it was full of a threat that was actually terrifying.

My heart raced in dread, and I came closer to him. "Look, my family comes to my performances pretty often, and if the girls know I'm seeing somebody, they might mention it and—"

"Kiss me now." He commanded me like a warlord, treating me like a soldier rather than a person. He laid down the law, drew a line in the sand. "Or I walk away." He wasn't the kind of man to make an idle threat, so he was dead serious. He waited for me to make my move, to piss him off and lose him altogether— or obey.

I wanted to be defiant out of principle, but the last thing I truly wanted to do was lose the best thing that had happened to me recently. Most people probably weren't paying attention, so I might be able to get away with this without being questioned later. I moved into him and rose on my tiptoes, my palms planting against his chest.

His arm circled my waist, and he tugged me into his chest, kissing me hard while his hand dug into my hair. His kiss was totally inappropriate for the setting, and it was completely intentional, just to prove he didn't give a damn what anyone thought, including me. He gave me his tongue and embraced me like we were behind locked doors, in a private setting.

I didn't fight it.

He pulled away, his eyes still angry. "That's what I thought." He released me and stepped back, victorious.

"You're ridiculous, you know that?"

"Oh, I know."

I turned back to my vanity and gathered my things while he stood there, watching me. "You don't own a suit?"

"No."

"You know, there's a dress code for these sorts of things." I looked at his reflection in my vanity.

"Not for me."

I put everything in my purse then turned back around. "What did you think of the show?"

"Boring. But you were fucking beautiful."

Those words tugged at my heartstrings instantly. He wasn't the kind of man to appreciate the ballet, but he still appreciated me. "Thanks..."

His arm hooked around my waist, and he guided me out the back door, walking past the rest of my crew like he wanted them to know I was his, even though all the male dancers were gay. He opened the door for me, and then we walked together down the path in the darkness, the exact path I took the first time I saw him.

Now he was beside me... It was crazy.

His large hand cupped my side while his thumb pressed into my back. His gaze was forward because he knew exactly where my car was as if he'd checked before he came into the theater. "Want to have dinner somewhere?"

"You want to go out with me when I look like this?" My makeup was heavy because I hadn't wiped it away. My eye shadow was exaggerated, and my cheeks were pink with blush. I was in jeans and a shirt because I expected to go home as soon as the performance was over.

He stopped at my car. "Baby, you could be in a burlap sack,

and I wouldn't give a damn. All I care about is what's underneath...unlike you."

I sighed at the insult. "I explained why—"

"You wanna go or not?" He opened the passenger door and prepared to get inside.

"Where's your truck?"

"Home."

"Then how did you get here?"

"Does it matter?" He was still irritated by the whole thing backstage.

I sighed. "Fine." I got into the driver's seat and drove away.

WE WENT to some hole-in-the-wall place that was dead quiet. It had a variety of food, so I ordered a garden salad with strawberries, while he ordered a hamburger and fries. It wasn't a romantic setting, but I liked that he didn't want to take me anywhere nice. It wasn't like he needed to impress me.

We didn't say anything until we got the food. He was clearly pissed at me and wanted the silence to suffocate me. I'd never really been scared of him before, but that cold silence was unnerving. With both his arms on the table, he took a large bite of his hamburger and chewed it while he stared at me.

I put the napkin in my lap and stabbed my fork into the greens.

He suddenly grabbed the extra plate sitting beside him and placed a handful of fries on it before he pushed the dish toward me. Then he kept eating as if nothing happened.

His fries looked good, so I ate a few. "I told you this would be a secret."

"From your brother. Not the world." He took a bite of a fry.

"Well, my friends see my brother sometimes. They might say something."

"Then ask them not to."

"I'm not gonna do that," I said quickly.

"Give me a fake name."

"Or we could just not make out backstage in front of all my coworkers," I snapped.

He stared at me as he kept eating, visibly angered by my words. "Not gonna happen. If I'm your man, then I act like your man. I don't give a shit who's watching." He took another bite of his burger. "What's your plan? To go out with your friends and pretend you don't have a man at home?"

"I don't know...haven't thought that far ahead."

"Well, I'll think for you. Not gonna happen."

"People talk. The last thing I need right now is my brother asking me about this gorgeous tattooed hunk that my friends won't shut up about. And trust me, if they knew we were an item, they would not shut up about it."

"If you think I'm a tattooed hunk, then maybe you should appreciate me."

"I do. I just don't want to be questioned about it."

"Tell your brother to mind his own fucking business. Think of that?"

I sighed and ate a few more fries, ignoring my salad altogether.

"Are you a girl or a woman?" he snapped. "Because the woman I know wouldn't put up with that shit, would tell her brother to fuck off and stop sticking his nose in her business."

"Okay," I said with a sigh. "Stop yelling."

"You think I'm yelling?" His eyebrow rose. "You've heard me yell once before, so no, this isn't fucking yelling."

When he'd yelled at Popov to let me out of the cage, his voice was so powerful, it shook the bars on every cage. "My family comes to my shows sometimes, so if you run into each other, that's going to be incredibly awkward."

"I wouldn't let that happen."

"If he saw you, how would you explain your presence?"

He seemed annoyed by the question. "Let me worry about that."

"Or we can just be careful..."

"It may not seem like it, but I'm always careful."

No, it did not seem like it.

"You aren't going to bars with your friends and pretending to be single. That shit isn't gonna fly."

That probably wasn't realistic.

"Unless you want me to do the exact same fucking thing."

"Then my friends are going to want to meet you."

"Fine with me."

I raised an eyebrow. "You don't seem like the kind of guy that would want to do that."

He shrugged. "It's better than guys buying you drink after drink."

"And what if we run into Damien?"

"Does he go to bars a lot?" he asked incredulously. "If he's settled down, that seems unlikely."

"He meets clients and stuff..."

"How about we deal with this stuff when it comes up instead of spending our time worrying about it?"

I wanted this to be private, to have this relationship behind closed doors, but he seemed adamant about getting what he wanted, so I let it go. "Still mad at me?"

He finished his bite before he answered. "Yes."

I rolled my eyes.

"But I'm sure a good blow job would fix that."

I shook my head slightly. "Oh my god..."

He didn't look apologetic about what he'd said.

I grabbed my fork and worked on my salad again, trying to steer clear of the fries because I'd already had too many. "What have you been doing since I last saw you?"

"Working."

"Is that all you ever do?"

"Pretty much." He grabbed his beer and took a drink.

"And what are you doing at work?"

He looked out the window for a moment before he answered. "I'm working with Petrov's men to turn it into a brothel. It's been bumpy, but we'll get there."

"What happened to the girls?"

"I told you I let them go a week ago."

"But what happened to them?"

He shrugged. "I gave them some clothes and money, and then they left."

They probably returned to their friends and family, people who had been praying for their return every single day. "What else do you do?"

"Collect taxes. Resolve disputes. Shit like that."

"Are you still taking money from my brother?"

He turned back to me and gave a nod. "He doesn't get special treatment because of you."

"Well, if you want to stop this feud, that would probably be a good first step..."

His plate was empty, so he crossed his arms on the table. "I've got you, so why would I care about that anymore?"

True. When I wouldn't be with him, that seemed to be the only solution. But now that I'd given in, there was no incentive for him to treat Damien differently, especially when our relationship was only temporary.

"I got my results back." Now, his gaze intensified as he stared at me, his thoughts moving to the true nature of our relationship.

"And?"

"What do you mean, *and*?" he said coldly. "Would I have brought it up unless my results were good?"

"I'm clean too." I picked the last few good bites from my salad, the strawberries and the cheese, and then set down my fork. I was tired from the long performance, and I was ready to have sex and go to sleep. "So, you've never been in a relationship with anyone?"

He shook his head. "You?"

I shook my head. "The longest I've seen the same guy is...about a week."

"Why is that? You could have anything you want from any man."

And yet, I was in a strange relationship with this criminal. "I'm not settling down until I'm thirty, so I'm just trying to have as much fun as I can now. Whenever I tell people that, they think I'm weird, but when a man says it, it's totally understandable."

"Why thirty?" he asked.

"It's when I've got to start popping out those babies."

"Why can't you be in a relationship with a man until you're ready for kids? Isn't that what people do?" He took a drink of his beer. "They fall in love and enjoy being together until they have to grow their family?"

I had my reasons, and I wouldn't share them. "I guess I'm not looking to fall in love. I'm just looking for the right man to have a family with, a man who will be a good father and provide for us."

He stared at me blankly for a few seconds. "Baby, that doesn't make any sense. You aren't telling me something."

"Why are you asking me all these questions?" I asked defensively. "What's your life like? Are you just hooking up with random women and never calling them back?" Once I asked hard questions, he would back off.

He pulled his beer closer to him. "In a nutshell. Sometimes I meet women and we hook up. But more often than not, I pay for sex." He said it so nonchalantly, like it wasn't a big deal at all.

Both of my eyebrows rose. "What?"

He read the unease on my face. "Whores. Not slaves, if that's what you're thinking."

It was better, but not by much. "Why would a man like you need to pay for sex? Look at you."

"I don't *need* to. I just like to." He drank from his beer.

"Why?"

"What do you mean, why?" he asked. "There's no talking, no bullshit. You just pay for what you want, and you get it. I have a few regulars that I call whenever I'm in the mood."

"Well...if you already have that, what are you doing with me?" I wasn't a woman who would do anything he wanted, who would respond to commands, and I wasn't a professional in pleasure. I was average, probably nothing compared to these women.

He seemed genuinely surprised by the question. "Look at you." He echoed my own words back to me. "I've told you everything about me, so answer my question."

"Whoa, hold on." I raised my hand. "I'm gonna need to see that paperwork."

"My word isn't good enough?" he asked, his eyebrows furrowed.

"Well, this was before I knew you slept with prostitutes."

"Doesn't change what my results say." He grew more irritated. "This isn't going to work unless you trust me. Do you trust me or not?"

"I...I don't know you." I wanted to be with him, but I realized we really didn't know each other that well, and I'd never been in a monogamous relationship before.

It seemed like he might get up and storm out, but he stayed, as if he was controlling his own anger. "I'm not a complicated man. I speak my mind and mean what I say. I'm not with anyone else, and I don't want to be. It's just you and me."

I was still uneasy, but I wasn't sure why.

"Does it bother you that much?"

"I've just never met a man who's slept with a prostitute."

"Yes, you have," he snapped. "Damien and Hades do it. I promise you the men you've been with have too."

"Oh my god, that's disgusting."

He didn't look apologetic. "I'm not gonna pretend I won't go back to it when we're over. I enjoy it and will keep doing it. It's the oldest profession in the world, and these women do it because they want to. I don't see anything wrong with it. Judge me all you want—I don't give a shit."

At least he was upfront about it, I guess.

"I have the balls to say it to your face, not to sugarcoat who I am, which is more than most men can say."

Well, most of my lovers were short term, so there probably wasn't time to mention their pasts.

"But I will say that I prefer you to any other woman I've been with." His temper died down as he stared at me. "It's not just because of the chemistry or how beautiful you are. It's because I respect you, even admire you. You're the fieriest, most fascinating, unpredictable woman I've ever been with...and I really like that."

And just like that, I stopped caring about everything he'd just told me. The prostitutes didn't matter. His criminality didn't matter. Nothing mattered at all.

"I've been completely honest with you. So be completely honest with me." His elbows rested on the table, and his hands came together in front of his chin, his knuckles close to his lips.

"What was your question again?" I quickly got lost in his raw magnetism, his undeniable sex appeal. His curb appeal was astronomical, but he also had a lot of qualities that made him even more attractive, like his bluntness, his honesty, his possessiveness.

"Why do you refuse to fall in love?"

"It's not that I refuse...I just don't want to."

"Why? If you've never been in a relationship, how did you get so heartbroken?"

I'd never been heartbroken. "It's not that. I just know a love like that isn't meant to happen for me. If it did, it wouldn't last, and it wouldn't be right. So, I've chosen to be more pragmatic when it comes to finding a husband, and the only reason I want one at all is because I want to have a family."

He shook his head slightly, as if he was disappointed. "That's a shame. You aren't who I thought you were."

"Excuse me?" What the fuck did he just say to me?

"You're afraid to fall in love...and I thought you weren't afraid of anything."

He didn't understand, and if I told him, he would think I was crazy. "It's not that I'm afraid—"

"You just said you're afraid to fall in love because you think it wouldn't last. That means you're afraid. You're afraid to put your heart out there and get crushed. You're so scared, you won't even try, won't even give it a chance, and the poor guy you do end up with will be madly in love with you and know you don't feel the same way."

"Who said he would be in love with me?"

"Why else would a guy get married and have kids?" he asked incredulously. "We only do that shit because we've found a woman we can't live without, and we have to do it or lose her. Don't play stupid, Catalina."

"I'm not." My voice started to rise. "How dare you sit there and judge me when you don't know me. You told me about your life—"

"And you judged me," he snapped. "You bet your ass I'm going to judge you because you're wrong. How could you possibly think that way? How could you be so fucking scared to do what people do every single day?"

Without any preparation, my eyes started to water, both from sadness and pure frustration. This man didn't understand and he would never understand, and even if I did explain it, it wouldn't make a difference.

When he saw the emotion enter my gaze, he turned quiet, like he knew he'd taken it too far.

"You don't know me." I spoke quietly, slowly, as I got to my feet. "You don't fucking know me. You don't know what I've been through. You don't know what I know. And if you did. you would know I was the bravest bitch you've ever met." I held on to my tears long enough so they wouldn't spill until I turned away.

He got to his feet quickly and grabbed me by the arm.

I twisted out of his grasp with a speed I didn't even know I possessed. "Don't fucking touch me. This is over. Why the hell did I think this would ever be a good idea? So, thank you... thank you for making me realize that you're too much of a fucking asshole for me."

ELEVEN

CATALINA

I couldn't believe I broke down in tears in a public place.

Who was I?

I didn't recognize myself.

Why did I let that man get under my skin like that? I should have just ignored him and kept up my defenses. Or I should have calmly walked out. But I let him conquer me, let him get a hold of my emotions.

And we hadn't even been seeing each other for a week.

I washed all the makeup off my face, had a glass of wine, and then sat on the couch to watch TV. I was too worked up to go to sleep, and I turned off my phone so I wouldn't have to worry about messages from Heath popping up.

Why did I think sleeping with him would be a good idea?

What was wrong with me?

Heavy footsteps approached my door, so I quickly grabbed the remote and hit the mute button so he wouldn't know if I were home.

Then the lock started to turn as if he had a key.

What the hell?

He unlocked each lock then opened the door as if he fucking lived there.

"What the hell are you doing?" I threw the remote down onto the coffee table where it clanked loudly before rolling onto the floor. I was in a baggy shirt with my hair in a loose bun, not expecting company, not wanting company.

He shut the door behind him and locked it, so nonchalant.

"Are you gonna answer me?"

He walked to the couch, his gaze subdued like our last conversation was fresh in his mind. "I gave you a few hours to calm down. But now, I want to talk."

"Cool off?" I scooted back into the couch, sitting up higher because I'd been slouching. "Women like me don't cool off. We burn hotter and hotter until we fucking explode."

"Then it's a good thing I came over here." He sat on the other couch, which was perpendicular to me. His arms rested on his knees as his hands came together, his sleeves and tattoos visible now that he'd ditched the sport coat.

"You can't just walk into my apartment like that. How would you feel if I did that—"

"Wouldn't mind at all." He pulled his key ring out of his pocket, pulled one gold key loose, and then tossed it on my coffee table. He put the rest of the keys back in his pocket.

"Well, I do mind. Give me your key—my key."

He didn't take his key ring out again and stared ahead, not looking at me.

I grabbed the pillow beside me and threw it at his face.

He let it bounce off his cheek and fall to the floor. "You can do better than that."

I snatched the wine bottle off the table and prepared to break it over his head.

"Okay, that's too good." He quickly disarmed me and snatched the bottle out of my hand as he held me back. Then he brought it to his lips before he took a drink and sat down again, placing the bottle on the other side of the table where I couldn't reach it.

I fell into the couch.

"Can you let me talk now?"

I rested my neck against the back of the couch and sighed, knowing he wouldn't disappear until he got what he wanted.

"Baby."

I kept my eyes on the ceiling and flipped him the bird.

He grabbed my wrist and tugged me forward, forcing me to rise and look at him. "Look at me when I talk to you."

I cocked an eyebrow. "Don't boss me around."

He held my gaze for a long time before he moved to kneel on the rug, placing himself between my knees and tugging me forward so we were close together. His hands gripped my hips and he kept us close, so his eyes could pierce into mine. "I'm sorry about what I said." He spoke with sincerity, his pretty eyes locked on to mine so I could see how genuine he was, not just hear it. "I know I got carried away."

"And why did you get carried away?"

That took him a long time to answer, his eyes shifting back and forth as he looked into mine, as if he didn't even know the answer so he had to search for it. "I want more for you. You deserve more. And hearing you say things like that...I don't like it."

Now that he was close to me, his cologne in my nose, his large hands gripping into my hips, my anger was snuffed out like a blown-out birthday candle. "Why do you care, Heath?" We didn't know each other that well, hadn't really talked because our relationship was mostly physical. There was a connection here, but it was built on lust.

He was quiet again, like he had to think his answer through. "For the same reason I got you out of that cage. For the same reason it hurt too much to look at you. For the same reason I chased you and chased you."

"That's not an answer."

He leaned in and kissed the corner of my mouth. "Because you're one hell of a woman."

My breathing was slow, but it became deeper, unsteadier, painful on my lungs. There was something about him that made me go weak, that defused my anger like he had a magic button.

"Tell me why you feel that way."

I couldn't say it out loud, not to anyone. It would make it real, would make me actually believe it, take away all my hope that it was just nonsense. "What does it matter?"

"It matters to me."

I bowed my head, my gaze dropping.

He grabbed my chin and forced me up again. "My eyes are up here."

"I don't want to talk about it, alright?"

"Why?" His hand moved through my hair and cupped the back of my head. "You can tell me anything. Literally anything."

"I just don't want to..."

Disappointment filled his gaze when he realized he couldn't convince me. "Will you reconsider at a later time? Because I'm not going to let this go."

"Why is it so important to you?" I whispered.

"In case it's not obvious to you, I'm not just sleeping with you because you're sexy." He moved his other hand to my chest, right over my heart, and then placed it over his. "Because there's a connection between us. Why else is the sex so good? And you can't have a connection like this unless you care about each other. Unless you're friends. Unless you're more than just two naked people in a bed."

I knew he was right.

"I'm your friend, baby. Whether you like it or not. And I'm a pretty good friend to have." He pulled his hand from my hair and cupped my neck, his thumb resting in the corner of my mouth. "Tell me you'll reconsider someday."

I dropped my gaze again, cornered into an invisible wall.

He forced my face up. "What did I say about looking at me?"

I breathed a deep sigh of irritation. "Yes...I'll reconsider."

When he got what he wanted, his grip on my neck loosened, and the hardness in his expression began to soften. He stared at me for a while, like a conversation was still taking place between us even though neither one of us said anything. "I'm sorry I made you cry. That's not the kind of man I want to be."

"I'm not a crier... I'm not sure why that happened."

"Because I touched a nerve. And that means whatever this is really bothers you."

God, he had no idea.

"I lost my temper because of the way you acted backstage. It doesn't justify my behavior, but I'm just like you...my emotions can get out of control easily. It's like a rampage. Once it starts, it's impossible to slow down."

"I get it."

He placed his forehead against mine and held me there, on his knees in front of me, like an ice pack that cooled my heatstroke. "You still want me to go?"

I wanted to say yes just to be stubborn, but I couldn't. "No..."

"Good." He pulled away so he could look me in the eye. "Because I wasn't going to leave anyway." He gave a slight smile, his playfulness moving into his expression.

"Then I guess you aren't gonna give me my key either."

He scooped his hands under my ass and lifted me from the couch, not struggling at all because he was so damn strong. He carried me in front of him, his face pressed into my chest, my shirt riding up as I locked my ankles around his waist. He carried me to the bed and laid me down on the bed. "No." He pulled my panties over my hips and down my legs until they came free from my ankles.

I propped myself up on my elbows, watching him stand at the edge of my bed and undress. "You're an asshole." Piece by piece, I watched him shed his articles of clothing, watched his perfectly hard body come into view. First, his inked chest was visible, hard lines of muscle mixed with hard lines of ink. A small patch of hair was there, but it was masked by the artwork that covered his canvas. When his bottoms dropped, his strong eight-pack gave way to tight skin with a single vein that led to his big dick, groomed hair around his balls trimmed back so it wouldn't get in the way of a blow job.

"I know. But that's how you like me." He moved onto the bed, his knees dipping into the mattress before the rest of his frame followed. When he was on top of me, he slid his hand under my shirt and pulled it up, getting it off my body because he didn't want anything covering me at all. Then he leaned down and kissed me, his lips starting between my tits.

I closed my eyes and immediately sighed.

He grabbed both of my wrists and pinned them above my head, one of his hands big enough to overpower mine. He squeezed me as he slid his other arm through the arch in my back and lifted me off the bed slightly, pulling my body into his mouth.

He breathed against the valley between my breasts, giving me big, wet, masculine kisses. He sucked my skin harshly then bit the side of my tit, grabbing the flesh between his teeth and giving a gentle bite.

I squeezed my thighs against his hips.

He took his time before he reached my nipple, and when he got it into his mouth, he moaned as he sucked, his tongue swiping over the delicate skin before he moved to the other, giving me a lick with his big mouth before he did the same.

I had no urge to fight him, but my wrists fought against his hold because I wanted to dive my fingers deep into his hair. But he overpowered me easily, pushing my wrists back into the sheets to remind me how weak I was in comparison.

I never enjoyed feeling weak until now.

He moved down my belly button, kissing the skin over my abs until he found my piercing. He swiped his tongue over the cheap jewelry, the fake diamond that glittered in the sunlight when I wore a bikini. He spent most of his time there, like he found that part of my body particularly arousing.

I writhed under his kisses, growing wetter because he knew how to use that mouth like a goddamn professional. I breathed loudly, the sound amplified because all my body could do was focus on the man worshiping me. I rolled my hips and pressed my belly into him, turned on by the way he was so easily turned on by me.

He grabbed my knees and forced them aside, getting my thighs to release his hips. He was such a big man that he could continue to grip my wrists while his mouth moved between my thighs and kissed me.

I immediately bucked my hips at his touch, sucking in a breath between my teeth that came out as a hiss. Men hardly ever kissed me that way, and when they did, they didn't do it the way he did it...like he needed it. "Oh god..."

His hand pinned my wrists down harder as he circled my clit with his tongue. He would cover my entire slit with his mouth and kiss me the way he kissed my mouth, giving me his tongue before he sucked on my flesh completely as if it was my bottom lip.

I started to writhe harder, started to press my body into his lips like I couldn't get enough. My body was no longer under my control, my mind was worthless. He did whatever he wanted to me because I was under his rule. He owned me—and he made sure I didn't forget it.

He gave me a final kiss before he raised himself, looking down at me. "You want to come around my mouth or my dick, baby?"

Jesus, this man. Who had the confidence to ask that question, to know he had the skills to make any fantasy come true? Most of the time, I was lucky to get off, but this guy handed out orgasms like candy on fucking Halloween.

He blew across my opening, making all my nerve endings fire off. "Answer me."

Having a man go down on me was my fantasy, the kind of porn I watched with my vibrator pressed against my clit. But now it was a reality, and my vibrator collected dust at the bottom of my underwear drawer. "Mouth."

His face went back to my opening, resuming everything he'd been doing before, like he already knew I was on the edge of a climax. He could sense my body without being inside me, feel the way I moved against him, feel my emotions just through our connection.

It only took a few seconds before my hips bucked against him involuntarily, for my moans to echo against my ceiling and travel through the cracks to my neighbors through the thin walls. My hands pushed against his hold but didn't get anywhere. I rode out the orgasm with my eyes closed, panting, crying...feeling every emotion all at once. "Heath..." I'd never said a man's name like this, so many times, if at all. He was my king, my god, my everything.

When I finished, he raised himself and moved over me again, looking down into my face just as two tears left the corners of my eyes and dripped to my ears, leaving a track on each side of my face. He didn't give me an arrogant smile at his accomplishment, but instead, he leaned down and kissed my tears away, moving from one cheek to the other.

Now, I really wanted him. Really needed him. "Let me go..." I wanted to hold on to him, grip him tightly, dig my nails deep into his back so he could never leave me.

"You want me?" he whispered against my ear, still kissing the moisture away.

"Yes..."

"How much?"

"So much..."

He moved on top of me and looked me in the eye, even more handsome when his face was slightly tinted in arousal. He finally released my wrists.

My arms immediately hooked around his neck, and I pulled him in for a kiss, wanting those stained lips all over me. I could taste my own climax, taste every inch of my body on that sexy mouth. My legs wrapped around his hips again. "You're the only man I want..." I didn't reject his affection because I was embarrassed or because there was any reason to be ashamed of his tattoos or his hostility. That was the exact opposite of the way I felt, and I wanted him to know that, to see how he drove me crazy.

"I know, baby." He grabbed his dick and positioned it against me, fat, thick, and hard.

"Wait." My fingers halted in his hair. "We didn't—"

"I'm clean. Do you trust my word?" He didn't push inside me, but his cock twitched against me, his cock thick enough to apply noticeable pressure.

I'd wanted to see the paper myself after what I'd learned about his sexual partners, but he was right, I had to trust him. "Yes."

"And you're clean?" he asked, not needing to see the ink on the paper.

"Yes."

Then he gave a gentle shove to get past my opening, to sink into the waterfall of wetness and inch farther and farther, gliding through me in a way he hadn't before, sliding deep inside as our bodies soaked in each other.

"Wow…" My hands cupped his face, and I pressed my forehead to his, moaning because it was the first time I'd ever felt this sensation, ever felt a man inside me bare. I could feel the grooves at the head of his cock, feel the lack of friction as he entered me, felt the heat of our bodies at a greater level.

When he sank as deep as he could go, he stopped to take a breath, to give a gentle moan, like this was the first time he'd felt this too. His forehead rested against mine, and he held his body still, enjoying the connection of our bodies so we could both treasure it, stop and appreciate it. "Be patient with me, baby." He started to rock gently, slowly.

"You're gonna make me come anyway…" I breathed into his face, all the nerves in my body overwhelmed by the way he made me feel, by the way our bodies slid back and forth so perfectly. It didn't matter how big he was once the latex was gone. When we were skin on skin, it was so much smoother, and I swore my body stretched just a little more because of it.

With our faces close together, we breathed, equally overwhelmed by the same sensations. We were both virgins again, enjoying sex for the first time. He gently rocked into me, sinking deep until only a few inches at his base remained outside my body. He never quickened his pace because this was the only speed he could handle.

That was fine with me.

He looked into my eyes as he moved, like he was making love to me rather than fucking me. This seemed to be his favorite position to have me, so he could feel the connection between our minds, bodies, and souls. For a man so hard and cold, he could be so warm, so open.

I closed my eyes once I felt the sensation begin. It was so quick after my climax that had just happened minutes ago, and it swept me away before we even had a chance to start.

"Look at me."

My hand cupped his face under his ear, my fingers digging into his hair. My eyes opened and I looked at him, aroused by the command and the way he issued it so effortlessly. He was a natural leader, natural fighter, and he was the only one who could boss me around with any chance of success.

He moved just a little faster, just a little harder, but not by much. It was the best he could do without exploding himself, without giving in to the desire himself.

My fingers started to dig into his scalp once I felt it, once I felt the explosion deep between my legs, the place where his dick ended and the rest of me began. My moan exploded between my closed lips, and I shivered, electrifying me from head to toe. Then I moaned louder, my lips breaking apart to release my loud screams, more tears erupting from the corners of my eyes. "Heath." I said his name again, clinging to it like a life-line. "Heath..."

His expression hardened, and he closed his eyes for an instant, doing his best to combat the desire to follow me. He'd never struggled before, but now it took all his effort to hold his position, to wait until I finished coming around his slick dick.

My deep breaths replaced my moans, and my hand gripped one of his cheeks. "Come on..." I'd never had a man come inside me, never even wondered what I was missing, but now I was so anxious for him to be the first, to cross the line no man had ever had permission to cross. I wanted him to enjoy it, to feel the same overwhelming ecstasy that brought tears to my eyes—twice. "Give it to me."

His final three pumps sped up quickly before he pushed deep inside, releasing a masculine moan that made his entire body tighten. His triceps locked, his biceps flexed. His ass worked to dig deep inside me. He closed his eyes for an instant because he couldn't control it, but then his eyes were locked on mine as he finally released, groaning in a way I'd never heard before. "Fuck." He was usually quiet during sex, just like men in porn videos, but now he couldn't control his reaction, couldn't stop himself from displaying his deep satisfaction.

We stopped moving, holding each other close as we both breathed, both processed what just happened. My fingers ran down his back, my nails lightly kissing his tough skin. I gave him a gentle kiss on the lips, an embrace of gratitude. He gave me the best sex of my life, showed me that sex could be as good as the books and movies claimed.

Instead of pulling out and rolling off me, he stayed still, his semi-hard dick inflating once again like nothing just happened. He started to rock into me again.

"How are you doing this...?" How could he be ready to please me again? How could he be this hard already? How could this man make me come like this and do it again? And again? How did he have that much testosterone inside his body? This much raw masculinity?

"You." This time, he rocked harder, using his own come as lubricant. "Because of you."

I LAY beside the sexiest man I'd ever known, the sheets bunched around his waist as the blue glow from his phone blanketed his face. He looked through a few text messages, typed quick responses, and then set the phone on the nightstand.

It was sometime in the middle of the night. I didn't know the time because the clock on my nightstand was behind me, and I was too lazy to turn around and look. It didn't matter anyway. Ever since this man had come into my life, time had passed very strangely. "Do you have to leave?" I didn't pry into his conversations over text, but I assumed they were work-related because who else would text him this late at night...unless it was a lady friend.

And I was the only lady friend of his.

"No." He turned his head toward me, his hair pushed up in odd places because of my fingertips. His eyes were a little sleepy, but the look was sexy on him. "I'm all yours."

I loved it when he slept over. The alarm and door made me feel better, but they were no comparison to actually having this man beside me, six foot three of muscles, tattoos, and pure man. I'd seen him get me out of the worst situation with just his words. He could handle anything, protect me from anything.

He must have seen the relief in my eyes because he smiled slightly. "You love having me here."

"Yes." My fingers moved to his chest, and I rested my palm there. It was like resting my hand on a coffee table because he was so hard, so strong.

"Because of me or what I can do for you?"

"Isn't that the same thing?" I turned on my side with the sheets pulled to my chest. It was dark in my bedroom but bright enough with the lights from outside to see his expression.

His smile faded, and he watched me like he forgot what we

were talking about because he got distracted. "If you've never been in a relationship, can I assume that was your first time?"

"I think that's pretty obvious…" My pussy was still stuffed with all his come, but I liked feeling it there, liked feeling his seed inside me. "You?"

He chuckled lightly. "Baby, you already know the answer."

I loved the deep sound of his voice when it came out like that. Even his laugh was sexy. I scooted closer to him across the bed, my head resting in the crook of his shoulder as I hugged his narrow waist.

He hooked his arm around me and pulled me close, his lips resting against my forehead. "I'm not sure how I'm gonna look Damien in the eye next time I see him…"

"Don't be gross."

"Just saying." He kissed my hairline, his fingers digging into my waist.

My fingers traced the line down his sternum, the line between his grooves of muscle. "Can I ask you something?"

"Yes. I have nothing to hide."

I'd never met a man who was so unapologetic about who he was. He reminded me of myself, just a more intense version. "When you're with a prostitute…what do you ask her to do?"

"Why?"

"Just curious." I turned my chin up so I could look at his face.

He shrugged. "Anal. Threesomes. Bondage. Stuff like that."

"So, you're into all those things."

"What guy isn't?" he asked, no remorse in his gaze.

"Well…I won't do any of those things."

"Never asked you to."

"I just mean, doesn't this seem a little tame in comparison?" I thought I was good in bed, but I wasn't that open-minded. I wouldn't share my bed with another woman, wouldn't let him try to shove anything in my ass because that was an exit only.

"Not at all." He pulled me close and placed a kiss on my lips. "Trust me, I'm not going home unsatisfied. I'm not comparing you to someone else and wishing you were different. I'm here with you because there's no other woman in the world I want to be with."

TWELVE

HEATH

IT WAS THE FIRST TIME I'D ACTUALLY DREADED DOING something.

I wasn't afraid. I wasn't anxious. I just simply didn't want to do it because now the situation was complicated.

I stepped inside the production lab and watched the men cast me subtly annoyed expressions, knowing they classified me as the enemy, the asshole who took a huge cut of their profits even though I didn't do a damn thing to earn a single euro.

Steel walked beside me, along with one of my other guys.

When I reached the door, I raised my hand so they would stay back. The door was cracked, so I knew Damien was inside, probably anticipating my arrival. I pushed it open and stepped in, spotting him sitting in the chair behind his desk.

He was straight in his chair, his elbows on the surface with his hands together at his chin. Without turning his head, he flicked his eyes my way and studied me, his expression neutral even though his eyes were filled with fiery hostility.

I spotted the black duffel bags on the floor.

Damien watched me, dead silent.

It was definitely more tense than it'd ever been before, like he couldn't bottle all his anger, all his hatred.

I kicked one bag. "Good month?"

"Just get out," he fired back immediately, furious that we had to breathe the same air.

Catalina had laid down the rock-solid foundation of this relationship, stated her allegiance to her family, so we'd never talked about it again. That meant I didn't have to give her brother special treatment. I could continue to be the antagonizing jackass I'd always been. But now that I actually looked at the guy, my spunk was gone.

I turned to the door and snapped my fingers. "Get in here."

Steel walked inside and pulled out his detector from his satchel. He kneeled down and got to work, tracing the wand over the bag to make sure Damien wasn't trying to pull some cheap stunt, like hiding a bomb in the lining.

Damien was absolutely still, showing no reaction at all.

Then Steel's device beeped.

I turned to Damien, my eyebrow raised.

Steel pulled out the small tracking device. "Looks like he was going to follow us."

I'd expected he would pull something like this soon, that was why I'd decided to start to check his bags. I stared at him for a while, irritated that he'd pulled this shit because I had to respond to it. I couldn't just brush it off like it didn't happen. "Take the bags outside." With my gaze locked on Damien, I nodded to the door.

"Someone's about to get their ass handed to them..." Steel

chuckled and grabbed one bag while Ian grabbed the other. They shut the door behind them and proceeded to carry the bags to the armored truck outside.

I came closer to the desk, both of my hands resting by my sides. "You want to find me? I'm right here." I raised both arms in the air, my pistol stuffed into the back of my jeans. "Do something, asshole."

He dropped his hands from his chin and leaned back in the chair.

It was quiet for a long time, neither one of us wanting to escalate the already intense moment. I stopped until my leg was against the wood of his desk, and I stared down at him. "You're happy, right?"

He watched me, his expression blank.

"You got your woman. You've got your health. Your job." If he were someone else, something very bad would happen. But unfortunately, my relationship with Catalina had already softened me, had already changed my behavior. He would get a crack in his skull from the butt of my gun if he were somebody else, probably worse since this wasn't his first offense. If I didn't put a permanent stop to him, he would just keep coming. "Let it go."

He cocked his head slightly, his raised eyebrows saying everything his lips wouldn't.

"I'm giving you a free pass, Damien. Drop this vendetta and live your fucking life." I gave him a few seconds to respond, and when he didn't, I turned to walk out the door, hoping this incident was enough to settle him.

"No."

I heard his answer loud and clear, felt the breath enter my

lungs before I released it as a sigh. My eyes stayed on the wooden door, wishing I hadn't heard that response. My feelings toward Damien hadn't changed, but as if Catalina were there with me, she grabbed my hand and steadied me, controlled me. I closed my eyes for a second before I turned around to face him.

He raised one finger. "You almost killed my father."

I rolled my eyes.

Two fingers. "You helped Liam break through the glass of my bedroom. I don't know what the fuck you did, but you gave him some kind of micro pulse to shatter the glass. And because of that, Annabella got shot."

I was surprised he'd figured out that, actually.

Three fingers. "You paid off the hospital workers to remove her from her bed, even though she might have died."

They said she was totally stable, but whatever.

Four fingers. "And then you helped Liam take Annabella prisoner."

And I stole your sister...

He dropped his hand. "So, no, I'm not gonna let this go."

With a blank stare, I returned to his desk, unsure how to handle this situation. A man just threatened me straight to my face, and the most logical thing to do was draw my gun and shoot him right in the fucking face.

But I couldn't do that.

If Catalina knew I slaughtered her brother, she would leave in a heartbeat.

So, what the fuck was I supposed to do?

Damien seemed to think he was invincible because he was calm, as if he somehow knew he had the upper hand.

"I don't want to kill you, Damien. But I will."

His eyes stayed the same.

"Consider this your final warning." My voice was quiet so the men wouldn't hear our conversation on the other side of the door. I needed to make Damien back off, but I had no idea how to do that other than issuing a verbal threat. If I took Anna to teach him a lesson, it would just infuriate him more. If I did anything to Hades or his father, the problem would escalate.

Since I couldn't kill him, I had nothing.

Absolutely nothing.

I TURNED the key in the lock and stepped into the apartment. "Baby?"

The TV was off, and there was no sign of life in the apartment. I listened for footsteps in the bedroom, but there was none of that either. I pulled out my phone and texted her. *Where are you?*

Her response was immediate. *What kind of question is that?*

Well, you aren't home.

And how do you know that...?

I smiled as I stared down at the phone, knowing she would figure it out in a few seconds.

Oh my god, get the hell out of my apartment.

Sure. Just tell me where you are.

Her attitude was audible in her text. *You can't just walk into my apartment whenever you feel like it!*

Why? I gave you a key to my place. Man, I loved arguing with her. I could picture her furious green eyes, the way her lips pressed tightly together as she tried to suppress her scream.

But I never gave you a key to mine.

Come on. What if I get horny in the middle of the night?

Then you call—like a normal person.

But isn't this more romantic? I started to pace her apartment as I typed, grinning.

Not at all.

Where are you?

You have a key to my apartment without my consent, so why don't you just track my phone too? Her words were so sarcastic.

Okay. I was about to call one of my guys.

Wait! Don't you dare.

See? I could completely violate your privacy if I wanted to. But I don't.

The three dots appeared, disappeared, appeared, and then disappeared again.

I stopped walking and waited for a response.

She finally sent her message. *I'm out with my friends.*

Where?

I'm not telling you.

Alright. I'll figure it out on my own.

How about I just text you when I get home? Or I guess you can wait there if you really want.

Baby, are you still trying to hide me?

No dots at all.

See you soon.

AFTER A FEW PHONE CALLS, I tracked her down. She was at one of the bars she frequented, wearing a short red dress with her long hair in a slick ponytail. The dress had a sweetheart neckline with sleeves that dropped off her shoulders and hung down her arms. Her ass looked incredible thanks to those black heels, her legs so long and toned. And that ponytail was pretty sexy too, even though I preferred her hair down and all over the place. She stood at one of the high-top tables and talked to her friends, a cocktail in her hand.

I walked up behind her and got the attention of her friends first since they were facing me. They both went quiet when they watched me approach, their eyes focused and their bodies tensed. One was about to sip from her glass, but she just stood there with her lips parted, trying to drink when the glass wasn't even close enough to her lips.

I would have just wrapped my arm around Catalina, but I knew how she might react to an unexpected touch. So, I stopped at the table beside her, turning my gaze on her so her friends would know Catalina was the only woman I was interested in.

Catalina took a few seconds to process it was me, to understand I'd successfully tracked her down.

"Hey, baby." I waited for her to greet me with affection, to see if she would pull the same shit she did last time. She knew there would be dire consequences if she didn't give me what I wanted, if she chose to act like a single woman at the bar when she was far from single.

There was a hint of rage in her eyes because she was clearly pissed off at the stunt I'd just pulled, but she didn't pretend I didn't mean anything to her either. She moved into me and gave me a quick kiss on the mouth, not having to rise onto her tiptoes because her heels were four inches on their own. But her kiss wasn't that affectionate, like she wanted it to be clear she was angry I'd just shown up like this.

Instead of letting her pull away, I circled her waist with my arm and pulled her close, bending my neck so I could kiss her bare shoulder. "I'm gonna get something at the bar. You want anything?"

"I'm covered."

"Alright." I squeezed her waist before I walked to the bar, which was just a few feet away. I leaned against the counter and ordered my drink, and while I waited, I could hear the girls talk, thinking I couldn't overhear them with the music over the speakers.

"Girl, who the fuck is that?" She was the blonde I'd seen at the theater, the one I'd talked to when I'd tried to see Catalina in the past. "Is that the same guy who's come to see you at the shows? Jesus, he is fine. Look at his ass in those snug jeans."

I didn't hide my smile since they couldn't see my expression.

"I didn't know you were seriously seeing anyone," the other girl said.

Catalina finally came clean. "We aren't serious. But we aren't seeing other people."

"Why would you?" the blonde asked. "I mean, look at him. Does he have a brother?"

"Yes," Catalina answered. "But he's married."

"Damn," the blonde said.

"Now I know why you haven't been interested in all the hot guys who have come over to talk to you," the other said. "Something wasn't adding up."

The idea of a good-looking guy trying to make a pass at her, buying her a drink in the hope he could be the one between her legs tonight, irritated me, but then I focused on the point of that statement...that she wasn't interested. She didn't strike me as the unfaithful type, and after everything I gave her, why would she want someone else? I had nothing to worry about. I wasn't the jealous type, and I wasn't going to start now.

The bartender handed me my drink, and I left the cash on the bar before I came back to the table. My arm circled her waist again, and I pulled her close, wanting every motherfucker in there to know she was mine—not theirs.

The girls were immediately quiet, staring at me like they had no idea what to say.

"Baby, aren't you going to introduce me?" I set my drink down.

"Oh...yeah." She cleared her throat. "Tracy, Nina, this is...Heath."

I shook hands with both of them. "Nice to meet you both. I recognize you from the ballet."

Tracy sipped her drink. "So...are you her boyfriend?"

Catalina shot her a glare.

"No." My hand squeezed her side, and I looked down at her. "I'm her man."

HER FRIENDS MINGLED with the guys who bought them drinks, so Catalina and I ended up alone at a table together, seated with our drinks on the table. My arm hung over the back of her chair because I could claim her as mine all I wanted.

Her legs were crossed, and she looked fucking perfect, sitting there with a straight back and her ponytail hanging down her back. She was a petite woman with a big presence. In a crowd, she was mistakable, impossible to glance over.

"Still mad at me?"

She wouldn't look at me, watching her friends talk to their admirers.

I smiled then moved my hand to her bare shoulder, giving her a slight squeeze. "You look beautiful in that dress."

It wasn't clear what caused her to relax, why her irritated gaze faded away, if it was because of the touch or the compliment. Either way, she did, and she turned to me, watching me with less aggressive eyes. "Thank you."

"Red is definitely your color." My fingers lightly touched her ponytail that hung down, admiring the gold hoops hanging from her lobes. My hand drifted down her arm until I pulled it away entirely, letting it rest on my thigh.

It didn't take her long to grow irritated with my behavior, irritated that I'd stopped touching her. I wasn't even sure if she even noticed that it made her mad. But when two girls walked by and noticeably stared at me as they passed, she really grew irritated. Her hand went to my thigh, her fingertips coming close to my crotch. "You don't have to keep your stubble for me." She finally looked at me, stopped giving me the cold shoulder.

"You said you liked it."

"I like you whether you have it or not."

I grabbed the leg of her chair and tugged her closer, bringing us as close as possible.

That was when she hooked her arm through mine and pivoted her body closer, like she wanted my hand on her thigh, wanted me to touch her so everyone would know I was taken.

She changed her attitude quickly. She was definitely the jealous type.

I thought it was hot, so fine with me.

"I usually shave when I know I won't see you for a few days, so it doesn't grow into a beard."

"Beard or no beard, I don't care."

"Really?" I asked. "Because you were awfully picky in the beginning."

She rolled her eyes. "I was just trying to get rid of you..."

"And now you can't get enough of me." I grinned.

She turned to me. "You're the one who barged into my apartment uninvited and then tracked me down."

"Because I can't get enough of you." I squeezed her thigh.

She softened right in front of my eyes even though she tried so hard to resist. "You want to get out of here?"

"We can stay if you want to hang out with your friends."

She watched them for a second, seeing them absorbed in their conversations with their male suitors, before she turned back to me. "I think they're busy."

"You wanna be busy too?" I liked being a smug asshole with

her because it got under her skin, but it also made her want me more.

When she rolled her eyes, it was with a playful nature. She squeezed my thigh then rose from her chair, turning so her perky ass was right in my face. "Let's go."

I gave her a gentle spank before I followed her.

"Could you stop smacking my ass?"

My arm moved around her waist as I walked her outside. "I could...but I know you don't really want me to." We walked out the main doors and headed down the sidewalk.

Her heels tapped against the sidewalk as she walked, her hips shaking from left to right as she moved.

When an alley appeared on our left side, I tugged her hand and pulled her into the dark alleyway.

"What are you doing?"

There was a large dumpster against the wall, so I guided her behind it and pushed her up against the brick wall. "You said if you spotted me in a bar, you'd hunt me down and fuck me in a dark alleyway." I yanked her dress to her hips and undid my jeans.

Instead of swatting me away, she was totally down for it. "Well, this night turned out better than I thought it would..."

I pushed her panties over her ass and pulled them down her legs until I got them off her ankles. I stuffed them into my front pocket and then gripped the back of her knee, raising it up so I could slide inside her with one quick thrust.

Fuck.

Her hands gripped my arms, and she pressed the back of her head into the wall, her ponytail pushed to one side. She tried to suppress the moan so no one would hear us going at it behind the dumpster, but she was unsuccessful.

I pressed my forehead against hers and fucked her against the wall, her heels giving her height that made it easy for me to get my dick inside her perfect cunt. I moved hard and fast, wanting to make this quick rather than a long, drawn-out screw like we did in her bed.

Fuck, it felt so good.

I couldn't last as long as I used to, not once we'd ditched the condoms and it was just her and me. She was the first woman to give me this experience, to give me all of her, utterly and completely, and that simple fact was enough to make me struggle. I was the first man to come inside, and she was the first woman to take my come.

That was romantic to me.

She obviously turned on by the dark alleyway because she moaned more than she usually did, rocked her hips so she could take my dick over and over, squeezed her nails into my arms as she held on. "Heath…"

She said my name all the time, and that was so fucking hot. How many other men's names had she said? Or was I the only one? As I rocked into her, I could feel her cream building up around the base of my dick, feel it sticking to my hair and sliding down to my balls. She was always so wet, always so ready for me. "Baby, this pussy…" It wasn't just her wet tightness that I couldn't get enough of. It was her—all of her. It was her spunk, her fire, her sass.

She pulled me closer and pressed her mouth to mine as she came, masking her noises with my kiss so anybody walking nearby wouldn't know about the free show we were putting on. Her nails clawed deeper, and she bucked against me, coming hard, passionately. She closed her eyes and leaned back, breathing through what she just experienced.

I was ready to come, ready the second I was inside. "Slap me."

She opened her eyes and took a moment to process what I said. Then she did as I asked, slapping her palm across my face.

I turned with the hit, moaning because I loved her small palm against my cheek. "You can do better than that, baby."

She slapped me harder, not holding back.

That time, it made an audible clap, made my cheek burn. I groaned at the hit then came inside her, shoving my fat dick deep inside her so I could fill her entire pussy with my come. My fingers dug into her thigh, and I pressed my face into her neck, breathing hard as I enjoyed one of the best climaxes of my life.

She'd asked why I liked to fuck whores, and now I wasn't sure what the appeal was. Why would I ever want to go back to that when I had this? Paying a woman to be a fantasy was a major step down when compared to having a real fantasy, being with a woman who had infected my body, mind, and soul. She was latched on so tight she could never disappear. At least, I wouldn't let her.

I moved my gaze back to hers and gently pulled my length out of her slit, feeling my come drip out the second I wasn't plugging her up. I pulled up my pants and put my dick back in my boxers, catching a glimpse of all the shiny cream that was plastered onto my length.

She pushed her dress down. "Can I have my underwear?" She extended her hand.

"Why?" I wrapped my arm around her waist. "They're just gonna come off the second we get to your apartment."

HER DRESS WAS on the floor next to my jeans. Her shoes had been kicked across the room, one at the door of her closet, while the other somehow ended up on top of her dresser. Now, she was asleep beside me, the sheets barely covering her chest as her lips remained parted. Her chest rose and fell slowly, and she slept in peaceful bliss.

I watched her for a while, her hair out of the ponytail because I'd yanked it free. There was a noticeable crease in her hair because it'd been in so tight. She had such a pretty face that she looked good when her hair was pulled back, but I still liked it all over the place so I could pull on it like reins.

I wasn't tired because these were my peak hours, so I left the bed and stepped into the shower. The warm water fell around me as I remembered the conversation that took place in this room when I brought her home, bruised and in pain.

I closed my eyes because the memory was unbearable, even now.

I left the shower and wrapped a towel around my waist. Her bathroom was small, a single sink and a small mirror on the wall. I ran my fingers through my hair as I looked at myself. The stubble on my face was getting so thick that a beard would be next, so I grabbed her razor and shaved, cutting myself a few times but indifferent to the sting. She probably shaved her pussy with this same razor, which was exactly why I used it.

I dried my hair then walked out of the bathroom in my boxers, drops of blood on my face from the places where the razor had sliced me. I moved into her kitchen, looking around for something good but only found wine. I grabbed a bottle, disappointed when I saw the kind.

Barsetti Vineyards.

The Barsettis were fucking pricks.

Since there was nothing else, I filled a glass and carried it into the living room. I turned the TV on low and looked through my phone, addressing questions from my guys.

Steel texted me. *Coming in tonight?*

I always had shit to do, but I could tell Catalina preferred it when I stayed here. I had a feeling it had nothing to do with sex, just the fact that I had the muscle and power to make shit happen. I was far better protection than a fucking alarm system. *No.*

Did you handle Damien?

I didn't want to think about that asshole. He was a problem that wouldn't go away, but I couldn't actually do anything about it. *Yes.*

Did you kill him?

If Catalina weren't in my life, I would have. I would have snapped his neck right in his office. *No. But I told him I will if he steps out of line again.*

Good.

"What are you doing?"

I quickly locked the phone so she wouldn't see my conversation. "Drinking." I leaned back into the couch and looked up at her, seeing her wearing my shirt better than I did.

"I thought you left…" She dug both of her hands deep into her hair, gliding right against her scalp as she sighed quietly.

"I'd never leave without saying goodbye."

She dropped her hands and glanced at the wine and the TV. "Why are you awake?"

"I'm a night owl."

She moved to the spot beside me, her knees pressing against my thigh. Her arm hooked through mine, and her head went to my shoulder.

"Go back to bed, baby."

"You are my bed." She kissed my shoulder.

I smiled down at her, loving how attached she got to me. "You were pissed at me just a few hours ago...Look at you now."

"Who said I'm not still pissed?" She raised her head and looked at me, still sleepy.

"You hide it well."

"You just keep making me forget—temporarily."

"Come on, baby." I squeezed her thigh. "You aren't mad, and you know it."

She narrowed her eyes in the cutest way, trying to be mad because she just couldn't force it.

"I knew it." I leaned into her and pressed a kiss to the corner of her mouth.

Now, she didn't even try to seem upset. She melted like butter on the stovetop. Her eyes narrowed on my chin when she noticed that I'd shaved. "You cut yourself?"

"Yeah. You need a better razor."

"You used *my* razor?" she snapped. "I use that on my legs and—"

"Why do you think I used it?" I gave her a slight grin.

She tried to suppress her smile but couldn't. Her fingers

reached out, and she touched my smooth skin lightly. "You look sexy."

"Yeah?"

She brushed her thumb along my bottom lip. "Yeah. I like the way the scruff feels against my skin when you kiss me...down there...but you do look really handsome this way." She dropped her hand.

"That's your thing, isn't it?"

Not understanding my question, she just stared.

"When I kiss you there." She lost her mind whenever I did it, became hooked on my line so firmly. My hand slid between her thighs so my fingers could rub against her panties. I stared at the spot for a few seconds before I looked at her again.

The blush that moved into her cheeks was so subtle, but the rosy tint was enough for me to notice. "So? I'm not ashamed of it."

"No reason to be." My fingers slid underneath her t-shirt so I could feel the silky softness of her legs, the legs she'd probably shaved that morning with the same razor I'd just used. "Just saying, I noticed."

Her eyes turned slightly guarded. "When I watch porn, that's what I usually watch." She made the confession without a hint of apology, like she didn't give a damn what I might say in response.

Both of my eyes widened, and my fingers stilled against her skin. "Let's talk about that some more."

She turned away and chuckled.

I grabbed her chin and turned her back toward me. "I'm serious." I could picture her in bed, the light from the computer screen highlighting her body in the dark, her knees wide open while a vibrator was pressed against her clit.

"I've told you everything."

"But you skipped over the details. So, you like it when a man kisses you there?"

She held my gaze for a while, as if she was considering what she should say next. "I like it when *you* kiss me there."

Now, I stopped breathing altogether.

"Guys don't really do that, especially when it's a short-term fling."

"Have you ever asked?" What man wouldn't want to get between her legs and make her come?

"Yes. They do it, but I can tell they don't want to. Not very sexy."

I did it because I'd fantasized about it before I even kissed her.

"I'm guessing that's one of your things?" she asked. "Something you like to do?"

"Not particularly, no."

She raised an eyebrow. "Then why do you do it with me?"

"Because I want to." I grabbed onto her body and forced her into my lap, her legs straddling my hips as she sat on me. "Why wouldn't I? Look at you." My hands slid under her shirt as I grabbed onto her hips.

Her hands went to my chest, and she watched me with her chin slightly tilted down, her makeup a mess because she hadn't washed her face yet. We'd screwed the second we got home, and then she went straight to sleep. "Want to know a secret?"

"Always." My fingers moved to her chin and forced her to lift her gaze.

She looked into my eyes as she gave her answer. "Yours is the only name I've ever said in bed..." She was slightly embarrassed by the admission but had enough strength to get it out. "I've never done that before, but with you...it just comes out."

That turned me on like crazy, but I didn't say that. I just stared at her, feeling more possessive than before. This sexy woman was mine, and I had her in ways men could only dream about. An unconquerable woman who allowed me to conquer her. "You're the only woman I've ever called baby."

"Yeah?" she whispered.

My fingers stroked down her neck. "Yeah."

Her arms moved around my neck, and she scooted closer to me, her body sitting right on my hard dick. She placed her forehead against mine and closed her eyes, like just being with me was exactly what she wanted. She sacrificed her principles for me because I was the only man she wanted. She was annoyed when I burst into her apartment, showed up at the bar, demanded affection in front of everyone she knew, but she put up with it because I was worth it.

She was worth it.

WE FINISHED our lunch at the table, both tired because we didn't get enough sleep the night before. Sleep came and went, depending on our mood. My sleep cycle had always been all over the place, but I usually went to sleep before sunrise and woke up sometime in the middle of the day. But I wasn't like other men.

I didn't need sleep.

When I was finished with my sandwich and chips, I pulled my phone out of my pocket and looked at the time. "I should go."

She didn't object, probably because it was daylight, and the nighttime was what she feared. "Alright."

I left my dirty dish behind and headed to the door.

She came up behind me, wearing her little pajama shorts and a white t-shirt. She never wore lingerie for me, but she didn't need to. Her little shorts were enough for me, especially when they contrasted against her tanned skin like that.

I turned to her before I walked out the door. "See you later, baby." My arm rested in the deep arch of her back, and I pulled her close to kiss her goodbye.

She never asked when she would see me again. Never texted me and demanded attention. She was either playing it cool, or she really wasn't the kind that got attached. But she did kiss me like she usually did, like she could take me to bed any second. When she pulled away, her hands gripped the fabric of my shirt. "I'm gonna be busy for a while..."

I didn't like that. "Busy doing what?"

"I haven't spent much time with my dad, so I should visit with him. Damien also needs me to help him with something."

"And that's gonna take up all your time?" I asked sarcastically. Fuck, I was the clingy one.

She crossed her arms over her chest. "And I'm the jealous one?"

"I'm not jealous. Just don't want you to blow me off."

"I'm not blowing you off. I have other people in life besides you. I'm sure you do too."

Not really. I had my brother, but the other people in my circle were in the Skull Kings. Not exactly friends, not exactly coworkers either. It was lonely at the top. "I don't see why I can't be the man in your bed when you get home."

She rolled her eyes. "I don't know how late I'll be, and I'm a bit exhausted by our sleeping hours."

"Would you rather me leave instead?" I snapped.

"Okay, you need to chill." She raised her palm. "All I said was I would be busy for the next few days, and you're acting like a lunatic."

Why was I acting like a lunatic?

She rose on her tiptoes and kissed me goodbye. "I'll see you later."

A part of me wanted to argue, but I knew my anger was unfounded. I had shit to do anyway, so it wasn't like I had much time to spare. I squeezed her ass before I walked out.

I SAT at the table in the Underground, Steel across from me. He was on his third beer, but the reason he continued to order was because he enjoyed the attention of the new busty bartender. "Hey, sweetheart." He grabbed his mug and tapped it against the table obnoxiously. "I'm running on empty over here."

She didn't display any attitude, but the look in her eye showed her displeasure. She served him another.

He watched her ass as she walked away.

I wasn't impressed. Both her tits and ass weren't all that great, not when I had a woman who had the whole fucking package.

"Fuck, she's hot." He drank from his glass then looked at me. "Where did you find her?"

"I didn't. She's a friend of one of the girls. Needed a job."

"Good. I'm glad our girls have hot friends." He slouched on the bench, his fingers around his frosted glass. "You don't seem impressed."

"Because I'm not."

"Why is that?" he asked. "Did it work out with your lady friend?"

I didn't talk about my personal life much. "We're seeing each other."

"Glad she came around."

And I was glad she came around my dick all the time. "Anything new I should know about?"

Steel was about to answer when his eyes quickly darted to a different part of the room, somewhere behind me. The look lingered for a few seconds before he turned back to me, choosing to drink his beer instead of answering the question.

I knew something was up.

Then Vox approached, walking slowly with his eyes on Steel. He was a burly guy with midnight-black hair and a noticeable scar over his left eyebrow. He stopped next to Steel and stared down at him, silently commanding him to vacate his seat so he could speak to me in private.

Steel took the hint. "I just remembered I have to do something..." He grabbed his beer and walked away.

Vox watched him go before he lowered himself into the seat, his heavy body making the bench creak slightly because the wood was worn out from our weight over the years. With his arms crossed on the table, he stared at me with two wide eyes, his brown gaze vicious.

I ignored his display of intimidation by drinking from my beer. "Yes?" Vox had been a member of the Skull Kings long before I was. I was relatively new, only initiated when my brother brought me in. But I'd proved my worth in a short amount of time, and I was the only man Balto thought could handle the job in the current climate. Clearly, Vox was still pissed off about it.

"I don't like the changes you're making around here."

"Oh." I took another drink. "That's too bad." My voice remained sarcastic because I refused to care about what he wanted. I took the opinions of my men into consideration for everything that I did, but not this man.

His expression was hard like the face of a cliff, his grimace etched years ago in a permanent setting. "They aren't going to work, and you know it."

"If I knew they weren't going to work, why would I do it?" I asked in a bored voice.

"I don't know." He leaned forward a little farther. "But I'm going to find out." He held my stare, letting heartbeats pass. The rest of the men who were in the hall excused themselves so we could have complete privacy. Vox could be a good leader if he weren't so cruel. He saw the world in black and white, couldn't think about more complicated issues. Maybe that made him a better leader, but he seemed more ignorant to me. "You should work every minute of every day like someone's trying to take your job away from you. Because there is."

THIRTEEN

CATALINA

My father stared at the chessboard, his fingers gliding across his lips as he tried to think of the best move to take me down.

I'd been kicking his ass so much lately that I'd decided to throw the game, so whatever move he made, it didn't matter.

He finally grabbed his piece and made his move.

I forced a concentrated expression before I moved my piece, effectively setting me up for failure.

But he didn't seem to notice and took a different route.

Wait, was he throwing the game on purpose?

"You seem distracted, sweetheart."

"Me?" I asked in surprise. "No. I'm fine."

It was his turn, so he looked at the board as he thought to himself. "So, Damien is gonna ask Anna to marry him."

"Yep. I'm very excited." I'd thought my brother would never settle down, let alone with a cool chick. He was so obnoxious that he seemed like someone who would pick a crazy-ass bitch, but thankfully, he'd fallen for someone I liked. "What do you think about her?"

"Anna?" he asked. "She's lovely."

"Yeah, I like her too." We kept playing.

"What about you?"

"I said I like her."

"No," he said firmly. "Anyone special in your life?"

I kept my eyes on the board so I wouldn't have to hide my reaction. "No."

"You're a beautiful woman, sweetheart. That surprises me."

My dad never asked about my personal life, but since Damien was about to get engaged, he'd probably started to wonder if I was next. "Just taking my time finding the right guy..." I tried not to think about the Heath, the beautiful man in my bed who was definitely not the right guy. He was my dirty secret, the man who gave me what I wanted for the time being. But one day, he would be a good memory.

"There's no rush," he said. "You're beautiful, smart, successful...don't settle unless the guy is perfect."

I gave a slight smile. "Alright, Dad."

"You deserve the best."

My eyes softened, and I tried not to stare at him. It was hard to control my emotions when I looked at him, was forced to look at his deep wrinkles and fading color. Seventy was too young to pass away, but my father seemed to struggle with cognitive problems, simple tasks, and it made me wonder if he wouldn't be around much longer...or at least, his mind wouldn't. I didn't want to get married for five years, and I worried he wouldn't be alive for that.

I wanted him to walk me down the aisle.

"Thanks."

"You want to have children, yes?"

When he phrased it like that, he didn't give me much room to disagree with him. "Yes."

"Good. Damien told me Anna may not be able to have children."

"I wouldn't worry about that. One miscarriage doesn't mean she's infertile. And even if she is, they'll figure out a way. Damien is rich."

"True." Now he moved his pawn to set himself up for failure again.

He was throwing the game.

I narrowed my eyes on his face. "Okay, that's the second time you've done that."

"Done what?" he asked, acting innocent.

"You're throwing the game."

"How would you know unless you were doing the same?" He lifted his gaze, and despite his elderly appearance, he looked me hard in the eye like the leader he used to be, successfully intimidating me. "I may be old, but I'm not stupid, sweetheart. Never let a man win to make him feel good about himself. Never hide your intelligence and your success to make him feel better—that includes your father."

A soft smile came over my lips because I'd underestimated my father. "Alright."

"I mean it." He raised his finger like he was scolding me. "If a

man can't handle your shine, he doesn't deserve your sunlight
at all."

SUMMER WAS FADING.

And I was devastated.

I sat on the patio with Anna and Damien, drinking wine while
sharing a cheese board covered with dried fruits and nuts.
"Ugh, I'm so mad." I grabbed another bottle of my favorite
Barsetti wine and refilled my glass.

"Why?" Anna asked, sitting close to Damien.

"I know," Damien said with a bored look. "Because summer is
almost over."

Anna chuckled.

"My brother knows me so well." I raised my glass then took a
long drink. "That means in two months I won't be able to wear
my sundresses and my shorts..." I hated wearing jeans and
sweaters. I hated being cold. I hated not going outside.

"Two months?" Damien asked with an eyebrow raised. "It'll be
November by then—"

"Shh!" I raised my finger and hushed him.

Damien rolled his eyes.

Anna kissed him on the cheek before she rose from her chair.
"I'm gonna use the bathroom. Don't fight with your sister
while I'm gone."

"That's all we ever do," he said as he watched her walk away.

She moved past the window and disappeared.

Damien grabbed his glass and took a drink.

"So...?" I leaned forward and swirled my glass.

"So...?" he asked sarcastically.

"When are you going to ask her?"

He glanced at the window to make sure she wasn't around. "Can we not talk about that now?"

"She's not a bat that can hear a mile away."

He gave me a glare. "I know my woman is not a bat."

"Come on, tell me. Are you gonna take her out to dinner? Take her on a trip?"

He shrugged. "I have no idea."

"What?" I snapped. "You haven't given it any thought at all?"

"She's already been proposed to—twice."

"So?" I snapped. "Not by you."

"I don't know...I can't see myself getting on one knee in a restaurant."

"Then don't. Do it here."

He shrugged again.

"Can you be romantic for like two seconds?"

"I am romantic," he snapped.

"Then think of something—"

"Shut up, she's coming."

I took a big drink of wine and tried not to act suspicious.

Anna came back to the table and cut into her cheese like she didn't notice anything. "I could eat cheese all day."

"Girl, me too." I cut off a fat slice and dropped it onto my plate along with some honey.

Damien turned back to the window when he saw Hades step inside. Hades looked out the window at us, then gave Damien a slight nod, like he wanted to talk in private. "Excuse me." He left the table and headed inside.

I turned to the window and watched him walk up to Hades, the two of them looking serious like they were having an intense conversation. Hades was still in his suit as if he'd just come from the bank. He crossed his arms over his chest as he listened to Damien talk. "What do you think they're saying?"

She shrugged. "No idea."

"They look mad."

"They always look mad." She kept eating. "It's probably something to do with business."

Maybe I was just paranoid, but I feared they were talking about Heath...and me. But there was no way for Damien to figure that out unless he was trailing Heath...and there didn't seem to be a reason to do that.

"Why are you so worried about it?" Anna must have recognized the unease on my face because she studied me as she smeared her cheese onto her slice of baguette.

I made up an excuse. "You know me... I always worry."

Her expression became confused. "No. You're the exact opposite."

"Well, I'm maturing." I excused myself from the table. "I'm going to go to the bathroom."

"Alright..."

I stepped inside, and the second the men heard the door, they turned quiet, like they were discussing something they didn't want to be overheard. They stood near the dining table, close together like they were plotting.

I pretended like I didn't notice. "Damn, I've got to piss after chugging all that wine." I walked to the bathroom and stepped inside, shutting the door loudly so they would think I was oblivious to them. But I quickly cracked it so I could overhear them if they spoke loudly enough.

They resumed their conversation like they believed my ploy.

"I don't know if it's a good idea, Damien." Hades moved his hands into his pockets, his head slightly bowed as he looked at my brother. "You're lucky he didn't kill you."

"No. He needs to go." He kept his voice low, but the rage was obvious in his tone.

Why did I feel like they were talking about Heath?

"So, what's your plan? It has to be solid because if it backfires, you'll be out of chances."

Damien crossed his arms over his chest, keeping his voice a whisper just in case I could hear him across the room in the bathroom. "We put snipers on the roof. He'll come to get the money on Friday night, and when he walks out with the money, the second he steps foot on the sidewalk, they pull the trigger."

Shit, they were talking about him.

"If you kill him, you're going to anger the rest of the Skull Kings. Then they'll come after you to avenge their leader."

"No. That won't be a problem."

Hades cocked his head slightly, confused by the statement.

"One of his guys came to me and assured me that wouldn't

happen. He's been wanting to get rid of him since he came into power in the first place. He'll take advantage of the situation and take over, get me off the hook. Win-win."

Hades was quiet for a while, like he didn't see any problems with that plan. "Then you have to make sure his men don't see the snipers. And the snipers have to get that shot. Because if they miss and he's in that armored truck, it'll be over."

"I know. I've got four of my best guys."

Hades gave a slight nod and pulled his hands out of his pockets. "Then it should work."

"Fuck yes, it'll work. And that fucking piece of shit will finally get what's coming to him."

I WAS IN SHOCK.

I wished I'd never overheard that conversation.

Now, I was in a predicament I didn't want to be in. I'd told Heath I would never betray my brother's plans if I knew about any of them, but now that I was actually in the position, I didn't know what to do.

If I didn't tell him...he would die.

I sat up in bed, my knees to my chest in the dark. Heath and I hadn't been seeing each other long, and while there was a connection there, it was nothing more than physical. There had been an expiration date from the beginning, and considering his line of work and ongoing feud with my brother, it was no surprise it would end with his death.

So, I had to let it be.

Right?

Heath was guilty of every crime Damien had accused him of. There was no doubt about that. He was getting what he deserved.

That's what I continued to tell myself...over and over.

My phone lit up with a text message on the nightstand. It was two in the morning, so there was only one person who would contact me at this time of night.

As if he knew I'd been thinking about him, he texted me. *I'll be there in two minutes. You better be naked by the time I get there.*

I could hear his voice in my head as I read the words, hear the deep sound of his command ring in my ears. I'd told him I'd be busy for a few days, so I hadn't heard from him in a while, but he obviously grew impatient and took matters into his own hands.

Couldn't happen at a worse time.

My phone lit up with a notification, stating my alarm had been disabled by another user.

He had my alarm app on his phone?

Then I heard the locks start to turn.

I knew if I weren't naked by the time he walked into my bedroom, there would be consequences, so I stripped off all my clothes, finishing just seconds before he stepped into the room, his silhouette clear in the dark.

He pulled his shirt over his head as he walked toward me, his hands moving to his jeans next and getting them undone as he came closer. He stopped and got his bottoms off, his eyes on me, almost looking angry.

When he was in nothing but his skin, he moved the rest of the way and grabbed me hard, gripping me like a prisoner rather than a lover. One hand cupped the back of my head while his fingers were deep in my hair, taking hold of me like he owned me, like I'd been his long before we'd met. His other hand circled my waist, his fingers digging into my flesh as he kissed me hard, kissed me like we hadn't seen each other in weeks rather than days.

That made me forget everything. Everything but this moment.

He turned his head and gave me his tongue, his fingers gliding to my ass and gripping one cheek before he turned his head again and kissed me in a different way, breathing into me, breathing for me. His fingers tugged on my hair, and he sucked my bottom lip, giving me a slight bite before he gave me his tongue again.

I'd never expected a man so hard to kiss so good.

My hand cupped his face as my thumb brushed over the scruff of his jaw, feeling the hair that had grown in since the last time I saw him. I panted against his lips, turning into a dog in heat. I pushed myself into him, feeling my flat stomach touch his hard body, feel my small tits flatten against his sternum. He turned me into a mindless woman who only wanted one thing—this man. Nothing else mattered. Not the world. Not my family. Nothing at all.

His strong arms suddenly picked me up, lifting me from the floor effortlessly so he could bring our faces level and he wouldn't have to crane his neck to kiss me, so I wouldn't have to rise onto my tiptoes to reach his jawline.

His fingers dug into my ass as he held me close to him, our chests pressed to each other and our lips moving together faster, like it was our first time being together, like the lust had built inside our veins to this critical level.

I fell into him...so hard.

"Baby." He spoke against my mouth between kisses, his deep voice so sexy on my ears. He didn't struggle to hold me, as if I was weightless, an extension of his already muscular body. He even slid one hand into my hair and held me with a single arm, like I really did weigh nothing.

Fuck, he was so hot.

He gently rubbed his hard cock against my clit, turning me on more than I already was. He could do everything at once, give me the best kiss of my life, rock against me, and hold me with a single arm.

How did I live so long without this?

He suddenly turned to the bed and gently maneuvered me down until my body landed against the mattress. But his gentleness didn't last long. "On your knees."

I turned to the head of the bed to face the headboard.

He grabbed my arm and forced me to turn around, facing the mirror that leaned against my wall. He got onto the bed behind me, grabbed the back of my neck and pushed me down slightly, my ass rising up. "You're gonna watch me fuck you, baby." He forced my legs apart before he positioned himself behind me. Then he shoved himself hard inside me, giving a big thrust that pushed him inside almost the full way.

I jerked forward and let out a cry, my slick pussy surprised by his enormous size. I gripped the edge of the bed to stop myself from falling forward onto the floor.

He held on to my hips and pounded into me like an animal, giving me his dick so deep, hard, and fast. It was the hardest he had ever fucked me, like he hated me rather than adored me. His eyes looked into the mirror so he could watch me groan through it, watch my tits shake because my body was rocking so fast.

I gripped the comforter and moaned, overwhelmed by everything. I didn't know what else to do other than take it, take that fat dick as it rammed inside me.

One hand gripped my shoulder and forced me up slightly. "Look." He deepened the curve in my back, made my ass rise a little higher.

I stared at him in the mirror, watched his face tighten as he worked hard to fuck me so aggressively. I moaned the entire time, my body and mind working to process what he did to me. Never in my life had I'd been fucked like this, forced to submit like this, been fucked like a whore.

And I liked it.

Even though he hadn't gotten laid in days, he could hold his load remarkably well, especially through the intense stimulation between our bodies. But his determination seemed to override his other feelings, because the only thing that mattered was fucking me so hard that I was sore for days.

It didn't take me long to come.

"Babe..." I closed my eyes as I came around his big dick, moaning uncontrollably because it was so good, so intense.

"Look at me." He grabbed my hair and gave me a hard tug.

I opened my eyes, which brimmed with tears, and watched him watch me come. I screamed so loud my neighbors definitely heard, and tears streaked down my cheeks like waterfalls, diamonds that glittered in the dark. "Oh my god..." I appreciated every second, every minute, every sensation. I rode it all the way to the end, my body convulsing because it was so good.

Just when I finished, he gave his final pumps, slowing down as he filled my pussy with more come than I'd ever taken. He didn't moan or make a single sound, just stared at me like he'd proved a point. He shoved his entire length inside just to hurt me, just to give me every drop before he pulled out again.

The second he was gone, my body went limp, exhausted even though I hadn't done anything except take that monster cock.

He got off the bed and started to dress without even wiping off.

I lay there and caught my breath, ready to sleep hard after what just happened. "What are you doing?" I pushed myself up so I could look at him, naked on the bed with his come spilling onto the sheets I had just washed.

He zipped up his jeans and gave me a cold look. "Leaving." He moved to the door.

"Wait." I turned on the bed so I could continue to look at him. "Don't you want to stay...?" He never fucked me and took off. It was always a few hours packed with kisses, sex, and talking. Now that I had him, I didn't want him to go. It was always hard to watch him walk out, but now it was even harder because I needed more of him.

He stared me down from the doorway. "You said you were too busy, remember?" He left my bedroom and walked out.

I closed my eyes in a grimace, forced to swallow my own words that he'd taken so poorly. I listened to the door open and close, listened to the locks turn, listened to the alarm beep once it was reset. Then I sat there in the dark alone, his come still leaking out of me, wishing that man would stay...and never leave me again.

I TEXTED him the next day.

Come over.

The entire day passed, and he didn't text me back. His responses were always immediate, and now that they weren't, I realized how he used to make me feel—like I was his top priority. Now, he reminded me how insignificant I could be, how he would treat me if I didn't make him my priority.

Lesson learned.

At the end of the night, I texted him again. *Heath?*

This time, his response was immediate. *I'm busy.*

Jesus, he knew how to hold on to a grudge. *I'm sorry, okay?*

Pussy-ass apology.

Then come over here so I can apologize to your face.

Nothing.

Please.

I'll come over whenever I fucking feel like it. And when I do come over, you'd better have learned how to treat a man. Because I'm not gonna waste my time with a woman who doesn't know how to be one.

I WAS home on Friday afternoon, staring at the blank TV as I considered my dilemma. Tonight, the shit was about to hit the fan, and I had to decide if I was going to do anything about it. I had been upfront with Heath and said I would do nothing to avert his demise.

But now, I wasn't so sure.

The locks clicked and the door opened, revealing the hard man who stepped inside my apartment. He shut the door behind him and stared at me on the couch, like that was exactly where he expected me to be.

And he still looked pissed.

Now that he was there, I didn't know what to do. I was paralyzed by his presence, paralyzed by the way he made me feel. I felt dead and alive all at the same time, felt like I couldn't get enough air because he sucked all the oxygen for himself.

"Where's that damn apology?" He came closer to the couch, in jeans and a black shirt, looking sexier than usual when he was angry. His blue eyes were unforgiving, like his stare alone was enough to burn me to the ground.

I left the couch and faced him, weak now that I actually looked at him. How did a man so bad make me feel so good? How did this man strip me down to my bones with just his gaze? It didn't make any sense. "I'm sorry…"

Both of his eyebrows rose. "That's it?"

I had a lot more on my mind than the state of our current relationship. Because it would be dead by tonight if I didn't do something to save it. "I'm sorry that—"

He raised his hand and silenced me with just the simple gesture. "Let me save you some time. This is what I expect from you." He lowered his hand. "If you're my woman, you're the person at the top of my list. When you text, I respond. When you call, I answer on the first ring. I'm never too fucking busy for you. Don't treat me with the same respect, then I'm gone." He stepped closer to me, getting in my face like a drill sergeant. "Do you fucking understand me?"

He was the first man to shut me up without actually telling me that. I nodded.

"Say it."

"Yes...I understand."

"And?" He came a little closer, his eyes wide and wild.

"I'm sorry...and it won't happen again."

"Damn right, it won't happen again." He stepped back, his eyes still unforgiving.

If this was the way he treated his men, then I believed he really did have the power to make people obey, to run an underground organization with unquestionable authority. He was a terrifying adversary.

I wanted him more than ever...and I had no idea why. If another man treated me that way, I'd forget about him and move on. I'd fight tooth and nail. But in this case, it was actually a relief to submit.

With his shoulders tense and his arms flexed, he stared at me coldly. "You just gonna stand there?"

I was mesmerized by those blue eyes, hypnotized by his power. It was the first time I was actually intimidated by him, by the way he carried himself, the way he commanded respect so naturally. I came from a line of powerful men, but I had never experienced anything like this.

He continued to stare at me, waiting.

I slowly stepped into his chest, my hands moving to his stomach as I looked at my fingertips. Just touching him there made me feel a spark of emotion that was inexplicable. We hadn't even been seeing each other a few weeks, but it somehow felt like months, felt like I'd known him all my life... even though I didn't know him at all.

I lifted my gaze and looked into his eyes, feeling that emotion grow once our eyes were connected.

He seemed to feel what I felt, because with every passing second, his hostility lessened. He could read every emotion in my expression and matched it, like he knew I wasn't just sorry, but I was so overwhelmed by these feelings...the way I felt about him.

I wanted to cry...and I had no idea why.

I grabbed the front of his shirt and tugged him down, rising on my tiptoes so I could press my forehead against his. I didn't want a kiss or sex. I just wanted him, to feel this undeniable emotion that always erupted between us, like volcanoes that constantly spewed lava all at the same time.

He closed his eyes once he felt me, like he could feel my heart-beat and match it. His hands finally cupped my face, and he held me like that, just feeling the rush of whatever it was we both felt at the same time. "You're the only man who's ever made me feel this way..."

He opened his eyes and stared at my lips. "What way?"

"I don't know...like this."

He pulled away so he could look into my gaze, his large hands still on my cheeks and neck. "Because you're my woman. And that's how a man is supposed to make a woman feel."

HE LEANED against the pillows with his hands on my ass, his eyes on mine as he watched me move up and down his length. His thumbs reached across my stomach until they touched the sides of my belly button. His breathing was deep and slow, his face slightly tinted because he enjoyed every second of this slow session.

My back was arched dramatically, and I rose and fell down his length, his come slathering his length as it seeped out of my slit. My hands gripped his shoulders, and I kept going, satisfied but determined to continue. I just liked having him inside me, like feeling how hard he was for me no matter how many times he had me.

His hand moved into my hair, and he brought my face to his so he could kiss me, give me soft and hot kisses as I continued to move down his length with snaillike slowness. We'd been doing this all day and into the night, taking each other nice and slow, completely different from the way he took me last time he was here.

My body was exhausted, my pussy sore, but I kept going because I couldn't get enough of this man. My mind was a blank slate because I had no thoughts at all. Sex with him was a form of meditation, when everything else in my life didn't matter at all.

Only this mattered.

I kissed him back before I pulled away, whimpering against his lips because I came again for no real reason. This man just made me collapse with his presence, with his touch, with his powerful soul. I stopped grinding against him and sat on his length, coming around again. I wasn't sure how many orgasms I'd had because I'd lost count after the third one.

He let me finish before his hand started to guide my ass up and down again. Within seconds, he came, pushing his feet against the bed to raise his hips and pump into me as he gave me his seed. A quiet moan escaped his lips as he finished. It didn't even seem like he needed to come, but now he was used to the contact of our bare skin that he couldn't control it the way he used to when we used condoms. When he finished, he left me on his lap so he could look at me.

His hand brushed into my hair and pulled it from my face before he kissed me again, his eyes open.

Was sex always this good for him with other women?

Because it was never this good for me.

I got off him so he could go to the bathroom and clean off. Tired and satisfied, I lay there, my eyes closed as I drifted in a peaceful existence. I didn't fall asleep, but my mind disassociated from reality. I didn't even notice when he returned.

He leaned over the bed and kissed me on the forehead. "I'm sorry, baby. I have to go."

My eyes snapped open, and the dread suddenly hit me like a high-velocity train. I sat up and looked at the time, having no idea how late it was. I'd put my dilemma to the back of my mind because I didn't want to deal with it until I absolutely had to.

Now, I had to.

He studied my worried reaction.

"Can you stay...?" I couldn't betray my brother and tell Heath the truth. I shouldn't have overheard that information in the first place. But I didn't want him to go either.

He grabbed his clothes off the floor and got dressed. "No. I have something to take care of."

No.

"Please." I got out of bed and faced him.

He turned to me and watched me, his eyes narrowing. "Baby, what is it?" He knew me so well that he understood something was wrong.

I kept my mouth shut and breathed through the pain of my silence. My eyes shifted back and forth as I looked at him, anxiety pulling me under. "I just want you to stay..."

He pulled the shirt over his head and accepted my explanation. "I'll see you tomorrow."

No, you won't.

He buttoned his jeans and grabbed his things before he headed to the door.

Oh my god.

I followed him to the door, naked because I didn't care about getting dressed. If I told him, Damien would probably figure out it was me who'd given him the heads-up. And if I did tell Heath, what would he do in retaliation? Would he hurt Damien? Would this war escalate further? Would he die anyway? Or worse, would my brother die?

He turned to me to kiss me goodbye. "I'll see you soon." He pulled me in close for a deep kiss before he turned to the door.

I grabbed his arm and yanked him into me again, gripping him hard as I buried my face in his neck, holding on to him so tight I wasn't sure if I would let him go.

He stilled at my touch, his arms by his sides, but then he returned the embrace, his powerful arms wrapping around my back with one hand going to the back of my neck. He held me that way for a while, his breathing steady and even. He had no idea what he was about to walk into, what was about to happen.

I breathed hard against him, keeping my tears at bay because he couldn't see them fall. How could I let this man go? But how could I intervene? It was the toughest decision of my life, and no matter what I did...I lost.

He kissed my temple before he pulled away.

I felt the life drain from my body as he moved, felt my heart break into several pieces.

He gave me one final look before he turned away and walked out.

I felt my body in scream in pain, felt the tears flood my eyes once he couldn't see my face. I stood in the doorway and watched him walk away, that muscular man moving down the hallway and disappearing from my life forever.

But there was nothing I could do...nothing at all.

FOURTEEN

HEATH

THE ARMORED TRUCK PULLED UP TO THE BUILDING, AND I stepped out with Steel and Ian in tow.

"You think he'll try anything?" Steel had his backpack over one shoulder.

"No." I took the lead, dreading the upcoming interaction. Catalina had complicated my life in ways I didn't want to admit. Her hold on me was so strong that I couldn't see clearly, especially when it came to Damien. "He knows I'll kill him."

The guards let me inside, and I descended to the production lab, seeing the men work like bees in a hive, ignoring my presence even though they knew I was there. I headed to the office, where the door was wide open like he was waiting for me.

I stepped inside and spotted the two bags of money on the floor. "Let's try this again, shall we?"

Damien sat behind his desk, his expression just as cold as last time. Wordless, he just sat there, looking at me like he wanted nothing more than to slit my throat and watch me bleed all over his rug.

"Check it." I faced him with my arms by my sides, listening to Steel and Ian move to the bags on the floor and check all that cash.

Damien's hands lay in his lap, his elbows resting on the armrests on either side of his chair. He refused to speak to me, as if it was an act of defiance.

I held his stare with the same intensity, unafraid of his silent protest. The guys worked behind me, using all their tools to make sure Damien hadn't slipped a tracking device inside or planted a bomb.

Steel zipped up the bag. "Mine is clean." He picked up the bag and rose to his feet.

"Mine too." Ian did the same.

My expression didn't change. "Good job, Damien. You followed directions. You get a gold star."

His skin flushed red like his anger had been provoked, but he still chose to stay silent, refused to speak to me.

"I'll bring you a treat next time." I walked out the doors first, my men following behind me. We made the long walk out of the production lab, up the several flights of stairs, and to the main entryway. The armored vehicle was visible at the curb through the glass doors.

Then my phone rang.

I pulled it out of my pocket and saw Catalina's name on the screen. I almost didn't answer it because I was in the middle of something, but after everything I'd said about making her my priority, I knew I had to take it. "Baby, I'm busy right now."

She was crying.

I halted and raised my hand to Steel and Ian, telling them to stop. "What's wrong?" I'd only see her cry once before, and that was after she was rescued from hell. She had a strong backbone and wouldn't crumple like this unless she had real reason.

She spoke through her tears. "Damien has four snipers outside his building...they're gonna shoot you once you leave."

My heart started to beat hard once the imminent danger was evident. It was just the three of us and a few guys in the van, so we were outnumbered, like fish in a barrel. Damien had set me up—set me up good. But instead of worrying about that, I addressed what she'd said. "You said you wouldn't tell me this." She'd broken her promise, broken her own rules, to save my life.

She breathed hard into the phone, searching for a response to what I just said. She was quiet for twenty seconds. "Please don't kill my brother..."

I stared out the main doors, the street deserted at this time of night. Steel stared at me as he realized something was wrong, that this hiccup in our plan was unusual. Now her behavior earlier that evening made sense, why she'd hugged me so hard on the doorstep. She'd known when I was inside her, known when we kissed and touched each other. She'd decided not to intervene...but then changed her mind.

"I saved your life. You owe me..."

If I were going to kill her brother, I would have done it already. "I have to go." I hung up and slipped the phone into my pocket. I didn't have the time to deal with her right now. Her message was received. Now I had to decide what to do.

Steel stared at me. "What?"

I kept my gaze out the doors. "We've been set up. There're four snipers outside."

Steel immediately pulled out his gun from his jeans, even though that wouldn't do shit.

Ian dropped the bag of money. "What do we do?"

Our guns wouldn't do anything, and I could call for backup but that would take too long. "Stay here." I turned around and returned the way I came. I took the stairs two at a time, descended back into the lab, and spotted Damien speaking to his men, grinning like he'd already won the war.

I reached the floor and marched toward him.

When he realized I was there, he read the look on my face and immediately figured out his plan had backfired. He drew his gun.

I punched his wrist so it fell out of his hand. Then I pulled my gun and pushed the barrel against his skull, my fingers clicking off the safety and cocking the gun. My arm hooked around his neck and squeezed hard so there was no escape. "Shoot, and he dies." I kept my eyes on Damien but addressed his men.

Damien fought against me, but he stopped when I pushed the metal barrel farther into his scalp.

"Come on." I dragged him across the floor, forcing him to move with me. "You fucking piece of shit, I give you mercy, and this is what you do."

He choked against my hold, dragging his feet.

I slammed the gun into his head and kept dragging. "Move, asshole."

Blood dripped down his skull to his shoulder, but he obeyed, struggling to breathe.

I pulled him up the stairs and to the main floor where Steel and Ian waited for me. "Get the money. Let's go." I kicked the front doors opened and pushed Damien first, using him as my bulletproof vest. I yelled to the top of the next building, where I could see the shadows move as they aimed their guns. "Shoot, and he dies." I kept him on the sidewalk, the space between the entrance and the armored vehicle. I kept him right in front of me so they couldn't sneak a shot. "Tell your men to stand down."

Damien stayed quiet.

I slammed the gun into his scalp again.

He grunted in pain then obeyed. He raised his hand, signaling to his men to drop their weapons.

Steel and Ian carried the bags to the truck and threw them into the back.

I pushed Damien to his knees, like I was going to execute him.

He stayed on one knee, blood dripping down onto his shirt. He looked up at me, breathing hard in both and rage.

My other men hopped out of the truck, their guns raised and aimed on Damien.

I felt the gun shake in my hand because I was tempted to pull the trigger, to snuff out his life forever. I'd given him the chance to put this behind us, and the motherfucker still resisted, pulled this stunt and almost got me.

He held my gaze, refusing to show fear even though he would only survive this because of a miracle.

A miracle called Catalina.

I hit the safety on my gun and stuffed it into the back of my jeans.

Damien couldn't hide his surprise.

I kneeled down in front of him, bringing us to eye level. "I'm disappointed in you, Damien. Nothing will ever be the same now."

Blood dripped down his temple and made tracks down his cheek.

"So, this is what we're going to do. For the next three months, I'm taking all of your profits, every single euro. You'll have to dip into your savings to pay your crew, so hopefully you're prepared."

He pressed his lips tightly together in anger, but he didn't argue, probably because he was shocked he got to live.

"Understand?"

Silence.

"And I'm going to check, Damien. My fingers are gonna be up your ass looking for change."

He still refused.

"Say yes."

His nostrils flared.

"Say yes, asshole. Or I'll do it." I pulled out my gun.

He breathed hard, hating himself for what he had to do. But he knew this was his last chance, and he had to sacrifice his pride if he wanted to go home to his woman. "Yes..."

I smiled. "Good boy." I patted him on the head like a dog and rose to my feet.

"That's it?" James asked. He raised his pistol and aimed. "We need to kill this motherfucker."

"It's fine." I turned away from Damien. "Get into the truck."

James wouldn't drop the gun. "Why does this asshole get so many—"

"Get. In. The. Fucking. Truck." I stared at James, needing unflinching obedience right now.

James stared at me and lowered the gun.

"Get in." I turned to the rest of the men.

But out of the corner of my eye, I saw James raise his gun again, his finger moving over the trigger.

I operated instinctively, not thinking about my actions until it was done. I raised my gun and pulled the trigger.

James staggered back, dropping his gun and gripping his arm where he'd been shot. "Fuck!"

I shot my own man and felt sick doing it. But I did it...for her. "When I give an order, you obey it. Get your fucking ass in the truck, and let's go." I watched the men obey this time, not even looking back at Damien.

I was the last one to go, but I stopped to turn back to Damien, to see him still on his knees on the sidewalk. It took all my strength not to do what James had been about to do, not to execute this motherfucker who had been a pain in my ass for nearly a year now.

Damien held my gaze, breathing hard like he was afraid I might change my mind.

But I finally shoved my gun into the back of my jeans and got in the truck.

And drove away.

ALSO BY PENELOPE SKY

Order Now

Printed in Great Britain
by Amazon

29856583R00158